Malevolent Magic

A BRYLIE SCOTT PARACOZY MYSTERY

MILLIE THORNE

To all of those willing to face their anger

EBook: 978-1-954702-56-1
Paperback: 978-1-954702-57-8
Hardcover: 978-1-954702-58-5
Large Print Hardcover: 978-1-954702-59-2

Edited by Lisa Hollett, Silently Correcting Your Grammar, LLC
Cover by Jacqueline Sweet
For inquiries, contact authormilliethorne@gmail.com

Welcome to Reverie Springs...

DON'T MIND THE HEXES

millie
THORNE

Chapter One

I'd only ever been in two physical fights in my life, both at funerals. Both moments of heightened emotion overflowing into a physical event I neither regretted nor felt proud of. The citizens of Reverie Springs seemed to be on a mission to instigate fight number three...sans mourning.

"It's against the law." Joan Turlington, enemy of my great-aunt Gwendolyn and someone who took day drinking to a level that seemed more than a little unhealthy, stood in my newly opened hardware store, throwing a tantrum most toddlers would have been impressed with.

My patience for the woman had been wearing thin for days, but the determination to get through to her held strong within me. "Joan, as has been explained to you every day this week, it is not illegal for my dog to be in—"

"It's illegal. I'm calling the police."

I nodded, clinging to what little patience I had left, even as my wrist burned with an itchiness I could hardly ignore. The woman was lying about the law—she knew it, I knew it, my wrist itching all but confirmed it, but she refused to back down. Just like with the fights at the funerals, no one would have blamed me for losing my temper, but I really didn't want to.

"I'm fine with you calling them," I said, scratching at my wrist and wishing she would just...go away. "But I'm going to need you to stop disrupting the other customers and move away from the registers. People have things to buy and places to be."

She didn't move. Not that I'd expected her to. It seemed as if the woman had never really been challenged on her bad behavior, which had only emboldened her actions and made her think yelling and complaining and disrupting the daily lives of others was her right and responsibility. I, on the other hand, thought she needed to be knocked down a few pegs and called out every single time she tried to control something she had no right to be involved in. Like the operations of my store.

"I am so sorry," I said to the customer at the counter, reaching for the two packs of lightbulbs he had placed to be scanned. "Did you find everything you needed today?"

"Of course. Lightbulbs are usually pretty easy." He pulled out his credit card and shot me a smile, the move making him look like some sort of stereotypical Hollywood star—tall, blond, and handsome.

I didn't swoon, but I could see how other ladies in town might when pinned under that blue gaze. "The switch to LED felt a little rocky, but I think we've all gotten the hang of it at this point."

"Definitely. Warm white all the way." His smile fell, and he glanced to the side, seemingly keeping a wary eye on Joan as he lowered his voice. "Are you going to be okay if I leave? I can wait for the sheriff with you."

"Oh, I'm fine." I moved to bag the bulbs as he finished his

transaction on the card reader. "She's like a toothless Doberman—all bark, no bite."

"Well, then I'll head back to the office." He sent me another Hollywood smile, turning up the brightness, it seemed. "I'm Dr. Don. I run the clinic out on Route 45."

"Ah, so the town does have a doctor. I wondered."

"We sure do. Come see me once you're all settled, and my assistant will get you set up as a patient. Never know when you'll need to be on our roster."

I nodded as politely as possible, slightly creeped out by the idea of being on his *roster*. What doctor called their patient list a roster?

"I'll have to do that, Doctor. You have a great day now."

He gave me another too-bright smile before heading for the door, giving Joan a wide berth by passing behind my display of leaf rakes. That was just what I needed—the townspeople being afraid to come into the hardware store I had only just opened because some lady with an overabundance of self-importance had decided to harass me. And tell lies about my dog, apparently.

"There are aggressive animals in this store. It's obscene!"

The itchiness...it grew. I was going to need to take an antihistamine if she didn't hush soon. I had no idea what animal she felt the need to call aggressive—my Basset hound Elmer lay curled up under the counter, snoring like it was his job. She couldn't be afraid of him.

It took about ten minutes and two more obviously uncomfortable but understanding customers coming through my business for Joan to get what she wanted. Sort of.

"Good afternoon, ladies." A man in a uniform like the sheriff's, but not the sheriff, strolled in, reflective sunglasses in place and hand on his hip as if ready to pull his weapon at any moment. A bit overkill, in my opinion—Joan may have been annoying, but she didn't seem violent. Still, I felt better that he had come. Annoyed he was needed, but better.

"There you are." Joan tapped her phone to end the call to whomever she'd been ranting to and hurried toward the sheriff. "There's a dog in this business."

The man nodded, those sunglasses not giving anything away. "I do believe Miss Scott here has the right to keep her dog with her as it's a private business."

Joan huffed. "Where's the sheriff? He won't let this stand."

"Ma'am, the sheriff and I have had a number of conversations about your issues with this dog. We have reviewed the state, county, and town laws regarding animal access to businesses. There is no legal precedent for refusing Miss Scott to keep her dog in this hardware store."

Joan looked livid. Meanwhile, I had to fight to hold back my smile. No sense goading her, after all.

"I don't think that dog should be allowed to run wild on the streets of Reverie Springs," Joan said, obviously doubling down.

I laughed. I couldn't help myself.

The man pinned me with a stare, one I could feel even from behind those mirrored lenses. "Something you'd like to add, Miss Scott?"

"Not really," I said with a shrug. "I just find it comical that anyone would think my Basset hound is running in any way, wild or not."

"Meaning?"

I held up a finger, allowing the store to quiet. Well, quiet as much as it could, seeing as how Elmer still lay nearby...snoring. Once I knew the officer had heard the loud rumbles coming from under the counter, I shrugged again.

"That's my dog. He's the laziest thing on four legs. He's not running at all and especially not wildly."

The man stepped closer, leaning to get a look at Elmer's under-counter bed area. "He just stays there?"

"Most of the time. He follows me around if I'm stocking or cleaning or something, but that's his preferred spot."

"Is he—" he leaned closer, ducking to get a better look "—snoring?"

"Yes."

"Huh." He leaned over farther, getting a good look at my upside-down hound. "What's his name?"

"Elmer."

"As in Fudd?"

"No."

"Deputy Carmichael," Joan snapped, demanding our attention.

The man—Deputy, not Sheriff—turned slowly in her direction, no longer smiling. Looking much more in charge of the situation than before. "Mrs. Turlington?"

"You should be writing her a citation."

He leaned against the counter, moving slowly and deliberately. Looking very much like a predator about to strike. "For what, exactly? I don't see any laws being broken."

"Reverie Springs has a leash law—that dog is unleashed."

"I may be new to Reverie Springs, but I'm fully aware of the laws here. That dog is asleep in a bed in a secure location inside a private business. He's not a danger to society, and there's no need to write her a citation. Now, if Miss Scott would like to discuss the possibility of writing you one—"

Joan gasped. "I beg your pardon! For what?"

"—or perhaps she would like to file for an order of protection to stop you from harassing her."

No way was I stirring up *that* hornet's nest, but I did like the fact that the man seemed to understand the situation without my having to explain myself. That was a nice change, as was dealing with someone who might actually be willing to do the paperwork for such a thing. I had serious doubts the sheriff would want to bother with all that.

"Miss Scott?"

I looked up, surprised to have gotten so lost in my thoughts that I had completely zoned out of the conversation. "Yeah?"

"Would you like to file a complaint for harassment or trespassing? I assume you asked Mrs. Turlington to leave and she refused."

"Oh, yeah. I mean, yes, I asked her to leave, but she refused. I don't think—"

The front door opened at that moment, and Ander Mendoza walked in. Big, bearded, and with a default mood of grumpy, the man intimidated from the jump. Add into that the fact that he looked about ten shades of pissed off in that moment, and I had a feeling no one would want to mess with him. Well, no one except me.

"Hey, Chef." I smiled his way, happy to see him even in his extra-grumpy state. "What brings you in?"

Ander crossed the floor in a handful of steps and moved to stand in a spot that put him slightly between Joan and me. Subtle protectiveness, but noticeable to me.

"I figured I might be missing some sort of show, considering there's a cop car sitting outside your business." He tilted his head toward me, keeping his eyes on Joan as he lowered his voice to ask, "You okay?"

I nodded and gave him a better smile. "I'm fine. Deputy Carmichael was just helping me out with Joan."

"Leash laws again?"

"Yeah."

"You're such a criminal."

"What can I say—I like to break rules and cause trouble."

Ander grinned for just a moment before bringing back his grumpy frown and aiming it at the troublemaker, crossing his arms over his chest in the process. "We doing this again, Joan?"

Joan took a step back, looking defeated. "I guess if no one will take the laws seriously, then I will be on my way."

Deputy Carmichael pushed off the counter to rise to his full height once more. "That might be best, ma'am. And I would suggest you find another store for your hardware needs if something as trivial as a dog sleeping under a counter bothers you this much. Miss Scott doesn't need her business being interrupted by your antics."

Joan looked ready to spit nails, but she kept her mouth shut. Instead, she gave him a curt nod then stormed out the door, probably wishing she could slam it as she left. Thank goodness for hydraulic door closers to keep that from happening.

I waited until she had disappeared past the front windows to unclench my jaw and relax my shoulders. "Thank you, Deputy Carmichael. I appreciate your understanding."

"It's no problem, Miss Scott."

"Call me Brylie."

"Brylie." He smiled down at me, moving a tad too close for my comfort. "That's a beautiful name."

I would not have called myself an expert on any sort of courtship shenanigans, but I got the vibe that the man was flirting...with me. Right in front of Ander, whom I would have allowed into my personal space without issue. Deputy Carmichael was not as welcome.

I took a step back and pasted on a flat smile. "Yes, well—my mom picked it from some book. You know Ander from the restaurant next door, right?"

Ander inserted himself between the deputy and me, looking even angrier than when he'd walked in but still offering his hand. "Nice to meet you, Deputy. I understand you're new to the sheriff's office."

The two shook hands, both puffed up like roosters ready to fight. I had no idea what to do other than show my allegiance, so I placed a hand on Ander's arm—just below his elbow—and stayed slightly behind him. The deputy obviously noticed, though it didn't seem to deter him.

"Yes, new to town and new to the department. I've heard great things about your restaurant, though. I can't wait to try it."

"Pop in any time we're open—if you're on duty, I can even make you something to go."

"That's appreciated." He looked my way once more. "I guess I'll get back to patrolling the mean streets of Reverie Springs. Call if you need anything, Brylie."

The way he said my name made a shiver roll up my spine, and not in a good way. "Yeah, thanks."

I waited until he had left and the door had closed behind him to speak. "Well, that was a fun afternoon."

Ander turned my way, rubbing his hands up both my arms as if to warm me up. "You okay?"

I nodded and leaned into him, resting my forehead against his chest. "Yeah, though I think I need some cortisone cream for my wrist after all those lies she told. Thanks for coming to check on me."

"You don't need to thank me for that. Anything I can do to help?"

I was about to say no, but considering the man was a

trained chef with a stocked kitchen, I decided to take advantage a little. "Got anything sweet at the restaurant today? I could use a dessert break."

Without a word, he grabbed my hand, headed for the door, and tugged me behind him, only pausing long enough to whistle for Elmer. The hound rose slowly, stretching his long body and yawning in a ridiculously loud way before plodding along after us. I turned the sign on the door to Closed and locked up behind me, following Ander to the restaurant. He was between the lunch and dinner rush, so there wasn't a single customer inside yet, which left us all alone. Oddly so.

"No waitstaff?"

"I've got three coming in tonight for the dinner crowd, along with my new busser. It's pretty dead between lunch and dinner, though, so there's no need to have anyone staff the front before four-thirty. Now, sit. I've got something I want you to try."

I did as I'd been told, sitting at an empty table close to the kitchen. Elmer curled up underneath and lay on my feet as usual, his snore cutting through the soft music playing. Ander returned in under a minute with a plate in his hand. On top sat the most perfect-looking slice of a dark berry pie with some sort of sauce artfully circled underneath it and a little ball of something that could have been ice cream or whipped cream. Either way, he had caught my attention.

"That's beautiful."

"Thanks. I'm trying out a few new bakers for my desserts, and this is my first pie from one. It's a blackberry pie with hints of juniper, so I made a gin-flavored whipped cream to go with it. Tell me what you think."

He didn't need to tell me twice. I loaded my fork with a small bite of the pie and snagged a little of the whipped cream as well. When that bite passed my lips and the flavors exploded on my tongue, I moaned loud enough to wake my dog.

"Oh my goodness," I said, already reaching for another bite. "This is amazing."

"Yeah, I thought so too. She makes great stuff, and it's all gluten free, which gives me solid options for the few people who come in with celiac."

"I know you've hired out your desserts all summer, but I can't believe you're *this* excited about serving something the great Ander Mendoza didn't make from scratch."

He chuckled and sat back. "I know my limits. Pie crust is a hard limit."

"Well, this baker makes an amazing one. This is really flaky."

We sat and chatted as I finished my pie, both of us laughing and enjoying the other's company. I liked Ander—a lot—and he seemed to like me as well. Enough to be willing to help me on the repairs needed at Willow Manor, the house I had inherited that seemed to have a mind of its own.

"I'll be at the restaurant all day tomorrow," Ander said as he walked me to the door after I had finished my pie. "But I can come by first thing Monday morning to work on the kitchen with you."

"You don't have to."

"You say that every time, and my answer never changes. I know I don't have to, but I like to. It lets us spend more time together and keeps me busy when the restaurant is closed."

"You could just relax, you know."

He huffed. "I'll relax when I'm dead. For now, I like to be of service to my favorite fellow business owner."

I grinned, unable not to, and rose onto the balls of my feet to kiss his cheek. "That's super sweet. It's also why I close my store the same day you're closed."

"Like my company, Miss Scott?"

Ander's dark eyes met mine, and that familiar, warm feeling of being swept away wrapped around me. Ander's energy and mine liked to dance together, to ride the wind of the summer storm of attraction that brewed whenever we spent time alone together.

My grin widened. "I just might, Mr. Mendoza."

And with that, I left him to handle his Saturday dinner service, taking Elmer with me. Sans leash. A few more hours at the store to clean up and then I could go home to the manor and Great-Aunt Gwendolyn, the witch who had gifted me this incredible new life.

Reverie Springs and I were getting along just fine.

Chapter Two

So maybe thinking Reverie Springs and I could get along had been a bit premature. Or perhaps I was living through the Mondayest Sunday in the history of my life.

"Afternoon, Brylie." Mary—Ander's day waitress and someone I had begun to grow a true friendship with—waved from across the restaurant. She had another customer to deal with, a man I had never seen before, so I strolled to a table in the back with Elmer on my heels. As soon as I sat down, Elmer plopped onto my feet and promptly fell asleep, his snore more vibration than sound. His exhaustion a bit concerning.

"Sorry about that." Mary hurried over, coffeepot in hand and a smile on her pretty face. "You're late today."

I sighed. "Yeah, it's been a day."

"It's barely past lunch."

"It's been a day since six this morning when Thomas Lee decided to run some sort of tractor thing back and forth in the fields behind the manor and wake us all up."

"Eek," she said, grimacing as she poured me a cup of hot, dark bliss. "Yeah, that's early. Especially for a Sunday. I wonder what he was working on. He didn't mention any harvests when I saw him earlier."

That woke me up. "You saw him today?"

"Just a couple of hours ago. He came in to have breakfast with the Turlingtons."

The Turlingtons. Joan—hater of leashless dogs—and obviously someone else I had yet to meet.

"You said Turlingtons—plural. Is Joan married?"

"She is, but Clyde never comes in here. She brought her daughter."

Surprise hit me hard. My great-aunt Gwendolyn had never mentioned that Joan had a daughter, though considering how much Joan had kept her sister Rose and Gwendolyn at arm's length, it shouldn't have shocked me. It did, though. It really did.

"I had no idea she had children." I frowned, reaching for the filled coffee cup as soon as she finished pouring, ready to doctor it up to my liking as I got used to this new twist to the Turlington saga. "Are they dog haters, too?"

Mary chuckled. "Not that I'm aware of. How is my favorite hound this morning?"

We both glanced under the table. Elmer didn't even budge, just kept snoring away.

"He seems more tired than usual," I said, frowning. "Though I'm sure it's just from the early wake-up."

"Probably. Though, keep an eye on him. Sometimes as a parent, you have to go with your gut."

Parent. Pet parent. Mary was an actual parent with a little one at home. One who had come to call me Aunt Brylie and never tugged on Elmer's ears, which made us both happy.

"How is Louise? I haven't seen much of her lately."

"She's fine. Loving preschool and making a lot of new

friends. Every time her dad picks her up, she's got about an hour of downloading to do for him—what toys she played with, how recess went, what the teachers taught her. I almost feel bad for the guy."

"Almost?"

She shrugged. "Sometimes, I like thinking he's getting what he deserves. But that's a story for another time. Preferably when whiskey is involved."

"I'll make sure to have some on hand."

She laughed again, but the bell over the door chiming as two people walked in brought her attention back to work. "I need to get moving. Have an idea of what you want, or do I need to grab you a menu?"

"Pretty sure I'm past the menu phase. I have the thing memorized at this point. Let me get the mushroom burger and sweet potato fries, please."

"The Brylie special. Got it." She shot me a wink before hurrying across the restaurant, calling my order to Ander then rushing to greet the new guests. I sat back and watched the interaction, seeking calm after a morning of noise, dirt, and not nearly enough coffee. I took a sip from my cup, groaning in pleasure. That was what I had needed.

"Hey there, beautiful." Ander set my plate in front of me, giving my shoulder a squeeze before moving to stand across the table form me. "Everything okay?"

I nearly cried over how delicious the burger looked. The man knew how to feed me well. "Everything's perfect now. This morning was rough."

"I saw your text about the tractor. Know what he was doing in those fields?"

"No clue."

He grunted, frowning. "Be careful with Elmer out there.

Thomas may not have put anything down that could hurt him, but if he turned soil, there might be something to worry about."

Because it hadn't been that long ago we'd almost lost Elmer to fertilizer poisoning. Not on purpose—no one had tried to make him sick. He'd just happened to get into something he shouldn't have. Living on property with a fully functioning farm right behind you came with risks, apparently. I had not been prepared for that when I'd moved to Reverie Springs.

I still wasn't always prepared, hence the disruption this morning.

"Yeah, I'll keep him out front when he goes outside. Just in case. Hopefully that will be enough."

Ander nodded, then glanced across the restaurant at the other table. The couple seemed to be giving Mary their orders, which meant he needed to get back to work.

"Give me ten, and I'll bring Elmer some chicken and rice, okay?"

"Sure. Thanks. I appreciate it."

"No problem. I gotta work extra hard to keep that boy healthy for you."

And he did. Every single day, every single meal. The man kept my dog spoiled and happy, which was a gift I hadn't realized would be so meaningful to me.

I was halfway through my burger when the chime over the door sounded again. I glanced up, more out of habit than anything, and froze for an extended moment. Joan Turlington had just walked in with real estate agent Corbin Lamb at her side and a younger woman behind her. A daughter, perhaps? The other woman didn't look much like Joan—darker hair, smaller body frame, softer features—but they obviously knew each other.

And all three apparently wanted to talk to Ander.

I continued eating as I watched the trio approach the chef. Corbin stayed back at the end, allowing the two women to interact with Ander alone. The chef greeted the women with what I had to assume was a smile—his beard hid a lot of his facial expressions, but the corners of his eyes crinkled, so that usually meant a smile. Both women began talking to Ander, though with different demeanors. Joan seemed aggressive and harsh—not at all surprising, to be honest. The other woman, though, appeared to be speaking softer, kindlier. She also kept laying her hand on Joan's arm as if to stop the woman from saying or doing something she didn't like. It worked—eventually, Joan huffed and walked back to where Corbin waited, leaving the younger woman to continue speaking with Ander in a more relaxed way. She also handed him a basket filled with items wrapped in what looked like cellophane. I wanted to get a better look—curiosity nearly overriding my better judgment—but Joan distracted me.

"A dog in a restaurant," she said, obviously talking to Corbin, but raising her voice enough so everyone could hear her. "Other guests shouldn't have to be afraid for their safety while eating. Those things bite."

The other customers glanced up, the lady's expression more curious than irritated. The woman leaned forward a little and must have spotted Elmer beneath my table. She didn't look disgusted, though—she instead smiled wider and tapped her companion's arm. They both moved and twisted, obviously taking a look at my sleeping sentinel.

"He won't bother you," I said, speaking just loudly enough so they could hear me. "He's really not into moving any more than he absolutely has to, so he'll stay right here until I leave."

"He's adorable. I'm not worried," the woman said, which made Joan frown even harder.

"Leave it alone, Joan," Corbin said, sending me one of his smarmy smiles. The real estate agent and I hadn't gotten off on the right foot—his calling me Riley and refusing to apologize for it, just one example of why—but he would have sold his eyeteeth to be the listing agent for Willow Manor. No way would he risk ending up on my bad side just in case I chose to sell, which I never would.

Joan huffed but stayed in her space as Ander and the other woman continued chatting, Joan's eyes locked on the two. I dug into my lunch, watching the same scene play out. When Mary came back to my table to refresh my coffee and drop off a cookie, I saw my opportunity to appease my curiosity.

I kept my voice low as I murmured, "So...who's the chatty one with Ander?"

Mary shot a furtive glance their way, the tenseness in her face overriding her small smile. "That's Heather Turlington— Joan's younger daughter."

Before I could respond, Elmer woke up, rose to his feet, and yawned. A sure sign his restaurant nap had gone on long enough and he was ready to go back to the hardware store for his afternoon nap.

"Looks like it's time for me to go." I smiled up at Mary. "You'll put this on my card, yeah?"

"Of course. You two have a great rest of your Sunday and a good day off tomorrow."

"You too." I dropped cash on the table for her tip, grabbed the cookie—something new and not anything I would ever turn down—and headed out the door, trying my hardest not to stare at the woman still talking to Ander. I bit into the cookie before I made it to the door, loving the hint of almond that gave the treat a uniqueness. I would need to tell Ander how much I liked the treat. I tucked it away, though, looking forward to finishing it with a cup of tea later in the day.

Though, as things tended to go in Reverie Springs, I didn't even make it halfway to the hardware store before I bumped into someone I knew. Not literally—I at least saw the man coming.

"Thomas." I slowed and smiled, trying my hardest to stay positive with the man who had instigated my horrible morning. "You were up early today."

"Yes, ma'am, I was. Had to get as much work done as I could before breakfast."

Yup. Long before breakfast. "Understandable. How are you doing today?"

"I'm good, Miss Brylie. Real good. I was actually looking for you."

"For me?"

"Yes. Well, sort of—I was coming to the hardware store to see if you've got any garden sprayers. Mine is beyond repair at this point."

"Oh, sure. Come with me."

I got him set up with what he needed, his purchase resetting the sour mood I had woken up with, and walked him to the front door. As he headed toward the restaurant, I stood outside, enjoying the sun and keeping an eye on Main Street for a few minutes. A car rolled by as I lallygagged, the driver honking and yelling my name in a friendly sort of way. The attention caused me to wave and smile automatically. Once I got a look at the driver, my smile became a bit more forced. Corbin Lamb, real estate agent and obviously a friend of the Turlington family. He must have left Joan and Heather to their day, as his passenger seats sat empty. That was at least one good sign. Still, his presence—as fleeting as it may have been—had me retreating inside once more. No sense inviting an argument on such a pretty day.

I made it halfway across the store—on my way to make signs at the sign counter—when the door chimed again. I turned to find Heather Turlington standing in my store. The very store her dead aunt had owned. The one her mother had not been too happy to see reopened after Aunt Gwendolyn had given it to me. This did not bode well, but I pasted on my best smile and tugged hard on all of my customer service training.

"Hey there. What can I help you find today?"

"Oh my gosh, the store looks amazing!" She grinned and turned in a circle, checking out everything from ceiling to floor. "Aunt Rose would be so happy to see it open and know someone else was serving the community the way she had done."

I grinned, completely calm and not sensing any lies being told. "Well...thank you."

"Oh! My manners." She hurried over with her hand outstretched. "I'm Heather Turlington. My aunt Rose owned this place before she died. You're Brylie, right? Miss Gwen's niece?"

The energy radiating from her felt warm and bright, almost cozy in a way. This woman had heart and good intentions. I could have liked her except for the fact that her mother...well, her mother was Joan.

Still, I shook her hand, my smile relaxing into something more real. "Great-niece, but yes. It's nice to meet you."

"Nice to meet you as well. I'm just so excited to see someone come in here and take over for Aunt Rose. That woman loved this store."

And my aunt. She had loved my aunt deeply, but I had no

idea how much Heather knew about her aunt, so I skipped pointing that out.

"So, is there something you're looking for today, or are you up for wandering the aisles?"

"I plan to wander. I've missed this place." She dropped her hand onto my arm and gave it a squeeze much like I had seen her do to her mother at the restaurant. Her energy spread from the point of contact, sending tingles along my bones. Positive tingles. Heather was nothing like her mother. "It is so good to finally meet you."

With that, she headed deeper into the store, swiveling her head back and forth as she came to the aisles until she found something to investigate. Within minutes, she reappeared in the main aisle, beelining it for the counter with gardening gloves and a watering can in her hands.

"These are just too cute. I couldn't pass them up."

"They are—I really lucked out with this collection." I rang up her order and bagged her items, listening as she rambled on about her new gardens and how she was learning to grow her own food. All normal casual conversation topics. The woman seemed friendly and good-natured, nothing like her mother. I wondered what Aunt Gwendolyn thought of her because my intuition told me they would have been friends.

We were just about done—Heather in the middle of a story about Rose and Aunt Gwendolyn teaching her to drive—when the door chimed again. A sense of static flew through the air, though whether from Heather or the new customer, I had no idea. But I suddenly felt uncomfortable in my own store.

"Hello there, Deputy," Heather called, throwing the man in uniform who had just strolled in a smile. "Hope you're having a calm Sunday."

"So far, so good, Miss Turlington. I hope you're having the

same."

"Always." She grinned, directing her attention my way. "It was nice meeting you, Brylie. I'm sure I'll see you again. And I'll see you in class, Deputy."

With that, she hurried out the door, passing the deputy. I no longer felt the static, but my instincts had been pinged by something. I could only guess it was him.

Time to paste that smile back on my face and play the part of friendly store owner. "Class?"

"I believe that learning never ends."

"Doesn't everyone? So, is there something I can help you with today?"

"No, ma'am. I just wanted to stop in and see how Reverie Springs' most popular resident was doing today."

"I'm the most popular resident?"

"With the single men in town, absolutely." He smiled my way. "So...a hardware store."

My back stiffened, years of being a woman working in a place with a majority of male customers putting me on edge. "Yup. Was there something you need help with or..."

His smile twisted into a slight smirk. "You think you can help me?"

"I know she can." Aunt Gwendolyn appeared at my side, her gray dress defying gravity as normal, a jewel-toned scarf tied in a jaunty way around her neck. "The girl might as well have been born in a hardware store. Isn't that right, Brylie?"

The tightness in my shoulders eased, my jaw unclenching. Old lady to the rescue. "That's right. Whatever the issue, I can probably help you out."

"Good to know. How are you doing today, Miss Gwen?"

Aunt Gwendolyn shot me a wink, her smile wide and bright. "I'm doing just fine, Deputy Carmichael. I see you've met my great-niece. Were you coming by just to say hello, or did you have a project to work on today?"

Those reflective lenses pointed my way. "I was just coming by to say hello."

I should have been flattered. I was not.

"How nice," Aunt Gwendolyn said, her tone flat and fake. Her words making my wrist itch. "I was just coming to see her myself. I thought it might be a good time for a cup of tea. Would you like to join us?"

"Oh, no thank you, ma'am. I appreciate the offer, but I do need to get back to work." He nodded my way. "I'm sure I'll see you again, Miss Brylie."

"Probably." Though hopefully not.

I waited until the man left to let the full-body shiver crawling up my spine out. "Is it just me, or is there something wrong with that man?"

"It's not just you, dear—he sets my teeth on edge. He seems to be popular with the single ladies in town, though."

"Not this single lady."

She shot me a wicked smirk. "Are you single anymore? I think Ander might have something to say about that."

I didn't have a response to her statement, though my face and neck felt surprisingly hot. "Did you say something about tea?"

Thankfully, Aunt Gwendolyn didn't just know when to step in and help me with a creepy customer; she knew when to let a subject go.

Two cups of tea and a lot of laughs later, I told Aunt Gwendolyn to give me a few minutes to make signs before we locked up and went home. Unfortunately, when I made it to the sign desk at the back of the store, my favorite sign marker appeared to be missing.

"What the..." I picked up all the sign stock on the top but to no avail. The one marker I used for every sign was gone. "I know I saw that marker earlier today."

Frustrated, I headed to the back of the store, thinking maybe I had picked it up before my tea date with Aunt Gwendolyn. Sadly, it didn't turn up, though I did find the cookie I'd brought back from the restaurant on my desk. Or at least, I assumed it was the one I brought back—I couldn't remember setting it on my desk, but no one else used the space so I had to have at some point. I unwrapped it and took a bite, assuming my brain had simply stopped working—missing markers and multiplying cookies had to be signs of stress or something.

I walked the store one more time, looking for the fat black marker I loved so much. Eventually, I gave up and headed for the front of the store in defeat. I would just have to make my signs with an inferior marker tomorrow. No way could I concentrate enough tonight not to get irritated by the change.

I had my hand on the door handle when I realized I had left the rest of my cookie somewhere in the store. No way was I going back for it—my patience had already been destroyed by the hunt for the marker. Cursing under my breath, I tugged the front door open and walked through, pulling it closed behind me with enough force to make it slam. Shutting all the negativity I felt swirling around me inside the store. I was done for the day.

"There she is. See, Elmer, I told you she'd be out in a second." Aunt Gwendolyn smiled at me from beside my minivan. Elmer sat next to her, ready to go home. Both patiently waiting for me.

I needed to take a deep breath and stop stressing over the

little things—a lost marker and an unfinished cookie were such little things.

"I'm here. I just need to lock up." I turned to lock the door, something dark on the window to the side of the door catching my attention. Someone had written on my window. The symbol wasn't big or anything to be worried about—an almost perfect, solid heart—but that certainly hadn't been there earlier. Or had it? If I had somehow misplaced my marker and forgotten my cookie, could I have walked past that heart and never noticed it?

I felt very off-balance all of a sudden, a fog in my head unlike anything I had experienced before, my internal temperature rising and making my stomach turn a bit.

"Everything okay?" Aunt Gwendolyn appeared at my side, laying her hand on my arm just below my elbow. "Brylie?"

"Yeah, sorry. I just...found this heart."

Aunt Gwendolyn followed my nod, humming when she noticed the little symbol. "Perhaps someone is trying to tell you something."

"Or perhaps one of the twenty people who walked through these doors today decided to vandalize my entrance."

Aunt Gwendolyn tsked and looped her arm through mine, tugging me away from the store.

"Let's look on the bright side. That heart's cute—and you need some love in your life."

"I have love in my life."

I also had friends, a man I liked spending time with, a growing business, and a house that I enjoyed working on. I didn't need love—I needed people not to mess up the things I cared about.

And to figure out why my brain had suddenly stopped working correctly.

Chapter Three

Waking up feeling hungover after an evening of nothing more than tea and a couple bites of a cookie made me wonder exactly how much spending ninety percent of my time with an octogenarian had been affecting me. From the sighing and snorting coming from the end of my bed, Elmer had no such thoughts—he simply wanted me to wake up and let him outside.

"Okay, okay." I stretched and rose, both my head and stomach turning as I did so. "I'm not feeling well, and you have to be so demanding."

He barked. My hound rarely barked, which meant the boy needed to go out pronto. Unless I wanted a mess on my floor, there was no time for sickness.

"Let's go, boy." I rushed us downstairs and through the back door, following Elmer outside to keep an eye on him. As I watched Elmer waddle to his preferred spot, movement out of the nearest pasture caught my attention. Thomas Lee—farmer, neighbor, and customer of the hardware store—walked toward the house, waving. Smiling, even. Which meant I needed to be social.

"Good morning, Miss Brylie."

"Good morning. You're up early...again." If he got on that tractor this morning, I was going to—well, do nothing. But I wouldn't be happy about it.

He nodded, glancing over at the blueberry bushes he cared for that sat between what I considered my backyard and the fields he leased. "Have to be up early to beat the sun. I try to finish my outdoor chores by lunch."

"That seems like a good plan. How are the fields doing for you this year?"

"Good, good. I've got some beautiful brussels sprouts coming in, and my grapevines are finally taking off."

"You planted grapevines?"

"Yeah, closer to my house. Thought it might be fun to try wine making at some point."

Something about him planting vines like that—ones that took years to mature and often became permanent fixtures on a landscape—rubbed me the wrong way, but I brushed that feeling off. He had been working the land for a number of years—of course some things would appear to me to be more permanent than not. Perhaps he could just...dig up the plants and move them if he stopped leasing the fields. What did I know about growing grapes, after all?

"That all sounds exciting," I said, fighting to keep my smile in place. "I'll have to come buy some of those brussels sprouts from you—I love them."

"I'll bring you some once they're ready. They're not the most popular product at my stand." His smile fell, his eyes tracking Elmer for a moment before they returned to meet mine. "I need to put down some fertilizer tomorrow."

My heart sank, something like dread almost strangling me. "Does it contain phosphorus?"

Because that's what had almost killed my dog, the one who picked that exact moment to stroll back across the yard and lumber his way up the stairs to pass out at my feet.

Thomas was already shaking his head when I looked back up at him. "No, ma'am. That said, I don't really feel comfortable putting it down and not letting you know after what happened to Elmer. It shouldn't end up close to your house since I'm putting it on the west fields, but it is a dry fertilizer. The wind may take it farther this way before the rain hits in the afternoon."

I didn't itch; I didn't feel any static coming from him either. The man wasn't being dishonest or sneaky, which meant he truly worried about Elmer. I could appreciate that.

"Thanks for telling me. I'll make sure to let him out through the front tomorrow, just to be on the safe side."

"Good. That's good." He leaned down to pat Elmer's head before rising once more and giving me a polite head nod. "Guess I should get back to work. You have a nice day, Miss Brylie."

"You too, Thomas."

With that, he headed back into the fields, while I turned to lead Elmer into the house, where he promptly fell over and conked out. I tried to keep my thoughts positive, but an unfamiliar crankiness had taken hold inside me. The irritation of having to change my daily routine scraped against my bones, and worry for my dog burned hot and bright. And yet, I had no good reason for feeling that way—Thomas had warned me, which was what I had asked him to do after Elmer's brush with death. How could I be mad that he had done what I wanted?

I had obviously woken up on the wrong side of the bed.

"I need a hot shower and some caffeine. Elmer...guard the house."

Considering how his snores practically echoed through the foyer, I doubted he would be guarding much of anything. Typical Elmer.

A hot shower, a good twenty minutes untangling and smoothing out my hair, and some serious pep talks to keep me from simply returning to my bed later, and I was ready for the day. Mostly. I still needed caffeine. Thankfully, a familiar truck pulled up just as I made it to the first floor. Ander hopped out and headed for the porch, giving me a grin when I opened the door for him. One I returned when I saw what he had in his hands.

"You are my savior today."

He cocked his head as he took the stairs in one jump. "Needing some coffee?"

"Definitely."

I led the man into the manor, sipping on the travel cup he had brought me. I felt spoiled—Ander brewed amazing coffee and always made sure to bring some for me. The basket of pastries in his arms was new, though.

"You trying to fatten me up?" I nodded toward the basket. "You don't usually bring me cookies and Danishes and...oooh!" I lunged, snagging a treat. "Scones. My favorite!"

"Yeah?"

"Absolutely. My dad used to make them for me." I took a bite and moaned. "Cranberry orange. My ultimate favorite."

"Eat them all. I brought them for you and Miss Gwen. Speaking of which, where is my second favorite witch?"

"She's not here. One of her friends picked her up before I even woke up to take her to some rock place."

"Rock place? Like, for landscaping?"

"No, like for witchy stuff. Crystals. I don't know—she'd asked me if I wanted to go, but I really wanted to spend the day working on the kitchen."

"Your aunt surprises me on an almost daily basis."

I laughed, unable not to. "Yeah, well, try living with her. The other day, I found her ringing a bell as she walked through the house. Said she was sound cleansing because she felt negative energy in the house."

Ander looked around, his expression intense. "I don't feel any negativity, so it must have worked."

I choked out a laugh. "Must have. Now, what's on the agenda for today, Chef? How are you going to throw off my plans with your demands for how a kitchen should be set up?"

He huffed and pushed me away with a gentle shove. "Let's just get to work."

"Fine." I rolled my eyes and smiled, grabbing another bite of the scone before heading for the back door. "I'm going to check out the workshop, see if I can find any wood for the pantry shelves."

"Don't need wood. Metal's better."

"I'm not arguing this again. I want wood shelves." And with that, I walked outside, shutting the door behind me before Elmer could follow. He'd be safe with Ander.

The workshop was in fact an unattached garage set back from the main house. Miss Rose—Aunt Gwendolyn's life partner who had passed in an accident five years before I showed up—had built it so Aunt Gwendolyn could brew her stinky hexing potions outside of their home. I couldn't say that I blamed her—I had been present for five brewings since I had moved to Reverie Springs. That smell was something one never forgot.

The workshop felt cool as I walked in, the shadows inside

deep and dark. Thankfully, Rose had installed electricity, so I turned on the overhead lights. So much of the space had been eaten up by the materials I'd needed for fixing up the manor. Rose had obviously used the space for the same reason—I'd found boxes and boxes of the wood flooring she'd installed throughout the first floor of the house there just as I'd needed it. The poor house's grief over Rose's passing and being left abandoned had manifested in leaky pipes and unexplainable puddles. Thankfully, she seemed past that phase, and I had been walking on only dry floors for over a month.

"It's the little things," I murmured to the great, open space of the workshop. I picked my way through the construction materials, setting aside items I thought might be salvageable or that I could find a place for.

I was just about to leave to head back to the house—a few pieces of wood in hand to attempt to build some pantry shelves —when a sound caught my attention. It wasn't a squeak or a squeal per se, but it did hit a high-pitched frequency that made me think of an animal in trouble. I inched toward where I through the sound was coming from, cautiously making my way deeper into the workshop.

"If it's a bat or a mouse or something that bites me, I'm going to be so pissed."

When I finally reached the source of the noise, I stood absolutely dumbfounded. The originator was neither a bat nor a mouse. In fact, it wasn't alive. The sound came from a door that had been leaned up against the far wall of the space. A door that looked exactly like the ones inside that Aunt Gwendolyn had told me Rose had refinished by hand. A door that had gone missing when Carl—a neighbor and former friend of Aunt Gwendolyn and Rose—had begun breaking in to the house to steal what he could sell.

A door that looked really close to the size needed to replace the one for the pantry that had been stolen.

"You have got to be kidding me."

The lever handle dropped a tiny bit, releasing a squeak. Attracting attention. As if the door had somehow become sentient. I really didn't care if the door was alive or not. The fact that someone Aunt Gwendolyn had considered a friend had been breaking in to the manor and stealing from her had gutted her. I knew walking over to that pantry every day to grab her tea and not having a door on it reminded her of that indignity. This door could help repair some of what the thief had done to the house.

I couldn't leave it behind.

"Come on, old girl. Let's see if we can bring you back to your glory." I hefted the slab of wood and picked my way across the workshop, excited to show Ander. I didn't have to wait long—the man was standing on the deck when I made it outside. He came running as soon as he saw me.

"You should have yelled for me," he said as he took the wood from my arms and hefted the weight himself. "You don't need to carry stuff like this."

"I can, though."

"I said need. You don't *need* to. Not that you can't."

"Good. Just so you know." I bumped him with my shoulder, smiling his way. "I found a door."

"I see that. Any plan on where to use it?"

I jumped ahead to open the French doors that would take us back into the house, holding one wide so he could walk through. "I thought it might be workable for a pantry door. If it's wide enough."

"Let's check." Ander lugged the door into the kitchen and set it down beside the pantry. He then carefully lifted it once more and lined it up with the doorjamb. "It needs a little trimming, but I think it'll work."

"Aunt Gwendolyn needs this. I already found the herbalism print that used to hang on it—the one Rose bought her as a gift. We can restore her pantry for her." I grabbed his arm, almost jumping up and down with excitement. "She will be so happy to see this finished."

"Yeah, I think she'd like that. I can trim it and sand it today, but I wouldn't stain it quite yet. It's supposed to rain pretty hard tomorrow, and it might turn the stain sticky until the humidity drops."

"Right. Oh!" I spun, checking on Elmer, who lay snoring under the island overhang. "Thomas said he's putting something down in the fields tomorrow because of the rain. I need to write myself a little sign and stick it to the French doors so I remember to take Elmer out the front."

"He could just stay with me."

"What?"

Ander shrugged. "He can stay at my house for the night. That way, you don't have to worry about him being around whatever chemicals Thomas is using at all." He looked away, fiddling with the door. "You could stay too. If you'd like."

Uncomfortable, thy name is Brylie.

The world grew warm, the very air against my skin irritating me. Pressure unlike any I had ever experienced turned me into a flushed, sweaty mess in a matter of seconds, and words absolutely failed me. I had no idea what to say, what to do, how to react. I had no—

"Relax," Ander said, giving me a gentle smile. "I know we're not there yet. I would happily sleep on the couch to give you your space. Or you can just forget I offered and send Elmer on his own. Guys' night at my place."

I took a deep breath and tried to resettle my nervous system, stepping closer to give him a soft kiss on his cheek. "You're a good man, Ander Mendoza."

He tugged me against him, wrapping me up in a one-armed hug that should have been comforting but somehow wasn't. "You might have mentioned that a time or two. Now, let's talk about these pantry shelves."

I took a deep breath, fighting to relax. Pushing the uncomfortable warmth running under my skin as far down as I could. "I want wood ones."

"Wood will bend under the weight, and they don't allow airflow. You're better off with metal. Like the ones I have at the restaurant."

"But I don't like the look of that metal. It doesn't fit the aesthetic of the house."

"Brylie—" He froze, head up and frown deep. I listened as well, hearing the same thing he likely did. A car coming up the driveway.

"Expecting company?" he asked, already moving toward the front of the house. His demeanor relaxed once he was able to see out the windows, though. "It's Miss Gwen. Someone must be dropping her off. Let me see if she needs some help carrying her rocks."

I nodded and watched him as he walked outside, still overly hot and uncomfortable. Suddenly feeling a little nauseated as well. I slipped back into the kitchen and grabbed the scone I'd been nibbling on, taking another bite. Hoping it would settle my stomach. I strolled—scone in hand—into the conservatory, breathing deep in the dappled sunlight that poured in through all the windows. Finding a little peace among the flowers and plants Aunt Gwendolyn had been bringing back to life since she'd moved in.

A cabinet in the corner called to me, practically pulling me across the floor toward it. I went with open eyes and an open heart, allowing my intuition to guide me. Stones and sticks lay on the top of the table, and books sat precariously on the shelves above. One drawer sat half opened, a true jumble of candles and fabric and who knew what else spilling out. We hadn't made it to this cabinet yet, hadn't given it the attention it needed after being abandoned for five long years.

I suddenly wanted to clean it out and put everything back to rights in it.

"Everything okay?"

I turned, still letting my fingers rest against a cool green stone. Aunt Gwendolyn smiled my way from the entrance, flitting her gaze to my hand and back. Obviously catching me touching her stuff.

"Yeah. This cabinet still needs cleaning and organizing."

She stepped closer, her skirt dancing right along with her every step. "It certainly does. Did you feel drawn to it?"

"I did. I started feeling a little sick in the kitchen, so I came in here to get some air, and this caught my attention."

She hummed, reaching past me to pick up the stone I had been touching. She held it out toward me, letting the small stone sit perfectly in her palm for me to see. "Green jasper. It's used for protection mostly, though it's also referred to as the rain-bringer."

"Fitting, considering it's going to rain tomorrow."

"Indeed. You said you felt sick? Not...nervous?"

"Not nervous. Sick to my stomach."

She sighed and looked around, worrying that stone in her hand. "The house needs another cleanse, I think. And you need this."

I took the stone as she handed it to me, holding it almost awkwardly. "What do I do with it?"

"Tuck it inside your bra. It'll help keep you safe." She moved past me, digging into the drawers of the cabinet until she found a bundle of something dry but slightly green. She had smoke cleansed the house once before, so I knew what that was—cedar and kitchen sage.

"Safe from the smoke?" I asked, unable to put the pieces of her actions together.

"No, silly. Safe from whatever your intuition told you to be worried about enough to guide you to this cabinet and that stone. Go on now. Tuck it in there."

I did as I was told, tucking the rock into my bra on the right side. It warmed quickly enough that I barely noticed it after a few seconds. Except for, you know, the feeling of a rock. In my bra.

And I'd thought people in my home state of California had done weird stuff at times. Nothing beat Reverie Springs on the weirdness scale.

"Come," Aunt Gwendolyn said. "Let's smoke cleanse together, then I want to tell you all about the crystals I bought. I'm so excited to charge them and put them out."

I followed her into the kitchen, where she headed straight for the stove. A couple of clicks and the whoosh of a burner starting, and she had a flaming bundle of dried plant matter. She blew out the flames over the sink, letting the bundle smolder until it released a thick, light-colored smoke.

Ander chose that moment to walk into the room. He appeared to have been Aunt Gwendolyn's chosen pack mule as he carried three big boxes with him. He gave Aunt Gwendolyn a concerned look then glanced my way, eyebrow raised. I shrugged in response. Thankfully, Ander was a smart man. He kept his mouth shut, put the boxes on the counter, and walked over to where he had set the old door from the workshop. Within seconds, he had sawhorses set up and the door laid out, ready to sand. Aunt Gwendolyn, meanwhile, had apparently reached the level of smoke she liked because she began to walk through the room, waving the bundle around and muttering under her breath.

"Thank you for bringing in my packages, Ander," she said as she moved past him.

He nodded and kept sanding. "Any time, Miss Gwen."

And with that, the old woman left the room and took off to cleanse the rest of the house, leaving behind the almost comforting scent of burning cedar and sage. As she turned the corner, I caught sight of her shoes. Her blue shoes were the color of a bright, sunny sky. For a woman who had been in mourning for five years and had only worn black or gray when I had met her, that shot of blue was a shock. I loved it, though.

I also loved following her through the house, getting lost in the smell of the smoke, and noticing how silent the house went when Aunt Gwendolyn was around. No creaks, no settling, no squeaky floors. The manor mirroring her happiness, her level of comfort.

I had a feeling that my home and my great-aunt were slowly coming out of mourning. And I couldn't wait to watch that unfold.

Chapter Four

My morning bedroom being silent, with no snoring Basset hound to wrangle and take care of, felt weird. Maybe the fact that Elmer had gone home with Ander the night before and, therefore, I had slept all by myself for the first time since I'd rescued the beast had led to my horrible night's sleep. I woke with a headache, I did not feel rested, and my stomach hurt. Again.

"What a way to start the day," I murmured to the empty room. With a sigh, I rolled out of bed far earlier than I had any business doing. The sun hadn't even begun to rise, but I knew more sleep wasn't an option. I wanted my best friend back, which meant showing up at Ander's place before he headed into town to start working for the breakfast rush. Hopefully he'd have coffee.

I really needed coffee.

A quick shower later, and I hopped into my minivan, wet hair and all. I had a deep need to find my dog. An intuitive desire to make sure he was okay. I had no doubt that Ander could care for Elmer just fine, but there was nothing like setting my own eyes on him. So I pulled out of the driveway with my headlights still on and headed for Ander's place across town.

"You should have just stayed there," I said to myself as I drove down the highway. "A platonic sleepover—Ander's slept at the manor. You could have slept on his couch like he's slept on yours."

Even as I spoke the words and chided myself, I knew I wouldn't have felt comfortable there. Staying at his house felt far more intimate than him staying at mine. Why, I had no idea. But being in his space felt like more. More of what I couldn't pinpoint, but the very idea of *more* overwhelmed me. I had enough on my plate with the hardware store, the home repairs, and learning how to deal with my family's witchy ways. More would just have to wait.

I turned into Ander's drive and breathed a sigh of relief. The little single-story house practically glowed against a rapidly brightening sky. Ander was awake, so I wouldn't be bothering him. Which was good—if I ever was ready for *more*, he would be the man I would want it from. Eventually. No need to ruin my chances and all that.

"You are a mess," I said to myself as I threw the van into park and opened my door. Ander must have heard me pull in because he appeared on the porch, no shoes on, coffee in hand, and Elmer by his side. Both looked happy to see me. Something in Ander's expression, in his eyes as they followed me, soothed the craziness in my head. He had never once pushed me to agree to whatever constituted more in my head. He had simply shown up, supported me, and kissed away my stress. How could I not want more of that?

Silly me getting all tangled up in labels.

"Good morning, beautiful." He leaned down to pet Elmer on the head as he said, "You were missed last night. By both of us."

"I missed you two as well." I stepped onto the porch and walked right into his embrace, offering a quick kiss to his cheek as I whispered, "I missed both of you."

He chuckled and tugged me in for a tighter hug before letting me go and handing me the mug he had been holding. "Have some coffee and come inside."

"Do you have time for—"

"I always have time for you."

He led the way into his little home, the golden glow of his lamps settling my mind even more than the sight of him had. Ander's house wasn't big or grand like the manor, but it felt homey. Comfortable. The man didn't like clutter, so the place stayed very clean and organized but not at all stark. Much like the restaurant, he had a style that warmed the space. I liked it.

"What's on your agenda for the day?" he asked as he poured another cup of coffee. He took back the one I had barely taken a sip from and gave me the fresh one, always taking care of me first.

"Run the store as usual. I might have a delivery today, but otherwise, nothing special. You?"

"I have the cleaners coming by to deep clean my kitchen area and vent hood, so I'll be working a bit later than usual to keep an eye on them. I'll come over as soon as they're done."

"You don't have to—"

Without warning, he practically collided with me, herding me backward until I bumped into the counter. Until I stood trapped by the man in his own kitchen. With fiery eyes and a gravelly voice, he leaned in to whisper to me.

"I know I don't have to. I never have to. I always want to."

I couldn't resist. I rose onto the balls of my feet and kissed him hard and deep, sighing as his hands moved to grip my hips. As he pulled us even closer together. The man never failed to make me feel special and cared for. He made me feel like *more* was inevitable and something to look forward to even when I forgot that fact.

He made me *feel* after a long time of not.

"Fine," I said when we finally broke apart. I kept my hands on his biceps, kept us connected. Kept leaning into him to stay close. His warmth relaxed me. I was greedy for it. "But I'm cooking for you tonight."

"You won't hear me argue that one." One last quick kiss, then he took a step back. "We had better get this show on the road. The rain's supposed to start soon."

"Right. Work."

"Don't sound so excited."

I sighed, looking out the window at the darkness that remained outside. "I'd rather stay here and cuddle on the couch while we watch the rain."

His eyes darkened, and he positively loomed over me. "Work, schmork. I can put my PJs back on."

I laughed and shoved him, loving the way he fell right into the joke with me. "No laziness today, Mr. Chef. You have hungry people to feed."

"And you have customers with broken toilets to help fix."

"Absolutely. But hey..." I gave him a smile and raised my eyebrows. "Next time it rains on a Monday, I say we make it a pajama day."

"You're on."

With that, we moved into work mode. Ander hurried through the house to turn off the lights as I enticed Elmer to walk outside with me. Within minutes, I had my dog belted into his seat and Ander had the house locked up. Time to go to town.

I spent the drive smiling and singing along with the radio, my mood brighter after hanging with Ander even for just those few minutes. I headed straight down Main Street once we reached town, ready to start my day at the hardware store. Something caught my eye as I rolled past the restaurant, though. Something that filled me with a sense of dread. It must have caught Ander's attention as well because he pulled to a stop in front of the restaurant instead of parking along the side street where we usually did. I parked in my normal spot and helped Elmer out before rushing toward the restaurant. I found Ander kneeling beside his iron tables and chairs, bent over the thing that had caught my attention in the first place.

A chair lay on its side, two legs missing. Just...missing.

"Think something fell on it?" I asked.

"Nope. I think someone beat it with a hammer."

"Why do you say that?"

He pulled the chair closer, letting me see the marks along the bottom and back. The many, many dents laid into the metal. Someone had taken a hammer to the chair, and by the looks of it, it hadn't been a heavy one. They'd really had to work to get those legs off.

A fact that made no sense to me. "Why would anyone try to mess with your chairs?"

Ander sighed and rose to his feet, keeping hold of the broken chair. "It was probably some bored kids in town. I'll just...have to replace it."

The uncomfortable sensation of guilt rose within me. He would need to spend money to replace the chair. He had only added the outdoor dining options because I'd asked him to, and now he would be spending more money. For me.

That didn't sit well with me.

"I can see if the warehouse has anything available like this. I get it at wholesale."

He nodded, looking far grumpier than he had been at his house. "Take a look and let me know. Might be cheaper for me to dig around for something used, but I'm open for anything." He reached for me, tugging me close. "So long as it keeps you eating at my restaurant."

I leaned into his hold, hugging him. "Nothing could keep me away."

"Good. Now, let's get you to work."

Ander walked me to the hardware store then headed back to the restaurant. I had a few hours before I opened, but that didn't matter. Elmer and I could keep ourselves busy. We managed to do just that, reorganizing the back room and prepping for the upcoming season change, all the way until it was time to open the doors. And as had become the norm, my first customer was Aunt Gwendolyn.

"How'd you get here?" I asked as she strolled in. The woman didn't drive—hadn't sat behind the wheel once since I'd moved to town. I didn't even know if she *could* drive.

She must have known exactly where my mind had gone. "I do have friends in this town, you know."

"Friends willing to pick you up and drive you around this early?"

"If they don't want to cause me vexation, yes."

The guffaw I let out had Elmer jumping awake. Vexation. Because when people vexed her, she hexed them. And I had no doubt that smelly potion she brewed every month was one people only risked once.

Mystery solved, at least to me. "Well, now that you're here, what are you doing today?"

"I thought I'd help you here in the store. There has to be something this old lady can do for you."

"I was planning to finish resetting my long-handle tools to be ready for winter. Want to replace some price labels for me?"

"Sounds perfect."

We headed to the garden department, the one that took the most work to keep seasonally accurate. I had already removed most of my garden tools and added more snow removal supplies. I'd need to get a couple pallets of salt and a display of thermal gloves, but otherwise, the department looked close to ready for snow. We just needed to make it through fall first.

"Did you go to Ander's this morning?" Aunt Gwendolyn asked, sounding almost sneaky. As if she were digging for information.

I had no trouble admitting what I'd been up to. "Of course. I had to pick up Elmer. They had a manly sleepover."

"I bet he was happy to see you."

Whether she meant Elmer or Ander, I had no idea. Didn't matter, though. "Absolutely. Though the morning took a bit of a negative turn once we got to town."

"Why's that?"

"Someone damaged one of his outdoor chairs. It was left lying without two of its legs."

She frowned. "Where did you find the legs?"

"We didn't."

Aunt Gwendolyn got really quiet, her face growing pale. Without a word, she disappeared into the back of the store in a swirl of light-gray fabric. I stood and stared, unable to make sense of what had upset her so much. Waiting for her return.

I didn't have to wait too long.

"Where did you go?" I asked.

She shook her head. "Upstairs. Thank goodness I still have so much of my stuff up there."

She handed me a rock. A black one this time. I stared down at it, confused.

"What's this?"

"Tuck it in your bra."

"What?"

"Bra. Now. Tuck it."

"But I already have the jasper—"

"Now."

I did as I was told, almost cowering under her aggressive orders. "What's this for?"

"It's a protection stone."

"You already have me with the green jasper in my bra."

"This one's stronger and protects against different things. You need them both."

"Two rocks in my bra?"

The woman reached into her dress, pulling out a handful of stones in various colors. "You'll learn, Brylie. These are a necessity to witches like us."

No static, no itchiness. No lies detected. I couldn't say I had ever heard of putting rocks in your bra, but I certainly wasn't going to argue with her.

"So, what will this one do, exactly?"

She reached inside her dress again, returning her rocks to... wherever she kept them. "It'll help keep you safe."

"What do I need to remain safe from in Reverie Springs?"

"You never know, Brylie. Just...keep it in there. The other one I gave you, too."

So, because someone had broken off the legs of one of Ander's chairs, I had to fill my bra with rocks. That didn't make sense. Of course, I wasn't one to go up against a witch the likes of Aunt Gwendolyn. She wanted rocks in my bra? She would get rocks in my bra.

And I would need to start wearing thicker shirts to hide the fact that they were there.

Chapter Five

The good thing about a day of rain was the fact that I had the opportunity to sell a lot of tarps and pumps. The bad thing was the weather brought up horrible memories of my first month in Reverie Springs. Excess water, Willow Manor, and I did not need to go together anymore.

My shoulders tensed and my jaw began to ache as I pulled into the driveway, grateful the lights were still on and the house looked okay. Not that I would know for sure if anything had gone wrong until I walked inside. Willow Manor sometimes copped an attitude with me. Last month, that attitude had been communicated via water; this month...it could have been anything. Including even more water.

"We're going to get wet, Elmer. Don't give me any grief about it."

The hound huffed his unhappiness with the situation but still readied himself to leave the van. I removed his seat belt and then slid out, rushing around to his side. The rain soaked me before I could even open his door, but there was nothing I could do about it. We had no attached garage or portico to protect us from the elements. I would have thought to build one, but the slope of the roof and the architecture of the house didn't lend itself to such things. I would deal with the rain to keep the old girl looking gorgeous. So long as she didn't throw water all over the floors. Again.

Elmer and I made it to the porch without slipping or falling in the mud, a feat in and of itself, considering. I let him in first, giving him a quick sit command just inside the door. There I found a stack of old towels, my cozy pajamas, and a large rug laid over the wood floors that didn't normally sit there. Aunt Gwendolyn had obviously prepared the hall for our return. I loved that old woman.

"Let's dry you off, buddy." I toweled him down, paying special attention to his long ears, before using a clean towel to soak up the worst from me. Once I knew I wouldn't leave a trail of water behind me, I stripped right there in the foyer and dove into my flannel pajamas. It felt almost decadent to be walking through the house in such comfortable clothes since it wasn't late enough for bed, and I loved it.

I tossed the wet clothes and towels into the laundry room then slipped into the kitchen. Elmer followed, likely looking for his food or a treat. I wanted tea.

But when I made it to the pantry—still doorless since we had yet to stain the replacement slab—I froze. Ander had installed the shelves. Metal ones. Like at the restaurant. Not wood.

"Oh." I stood and stared at the bright, industrial metal beneath my wood-lidded glass containers and tea caddy. Silver against warm browns and creams. I suddenly felt uncomfortably warm in my flannel. A little too on edge for the softness against my skin. A feeling that only made me mad at myself.

"You are too darn picky, Brylie Scott."

And I was. The shelves sat tucked away in a closet where visitors would never see them. They were strong and sturdy and would last a lifetime. I had no reason to be annoyed with something as trivial as a shelving unit.

But I was. Very much so.

"It's way too hot in here." I turned away from the pantry and headed to the hallway instead. The thermostat read a comfortable sixty-nine degrees, so why I felt as if I were cooking, I had no idea. "If I'm going into menopause this early, I'm going to throw a fit, Elmer."

The dog didn't answer me. Rude.

When I returned to the kitchen, I found Aunt Gwendolyn there, likely having snuck in from the conservatory. She stood staring at the pantry door that sat on sawhorses, running her fingers up and down the dark wood. I had been about to say hello when I noticed the sadness in the room. The mugginess that practically floated around the woman. That pantry had been set up by her and Rose, and that door had been stolen after Rose's death. Seeing it damaged but in the house, knowing that soon the same art print that Aunt Gwendolyn had given to Rose as a present would be mounted on its surface, had to instill a little melancholy. Aunt Gwendolyn likely didn't care that the shelves were metal—she cared that someone had loved her enough to put her life back together.

I was being far too picky.

I crept up behind the old woman and wrapped my arms around her, giving her a hug. "Are we getting it right?"

"You very much are." She patted my arm before sniffling slightly. "This—returning something so meaningful back to what it was—makes me happy."

Accomplishment achieved. "Good. I was about to make a cup of tea. Would you like one?"

"Absolutely."

I grabbed a sweet mint tea from the closet—caffeine-free, of course—and took it to the island. Within minutes, I had water boiling in the kettle and two mugs placed on the counter with a honey jar nearby. We were ready.

"Thanks for leaving out the pajamas and towels," I said once the tea had been steeped and sweetened. "That made coming home much easier and more comfortable."

"Of course, dear. I figured you and Elmer would get soaked out there on the drive." She took a sip of tea, staring into the cup afterward for a long moment. "I always left out towels and comfy clothes for Rose when it rained. She hated getting those floors wet."

I choked on my tea, fighting to keep breathing through the heat of it burning the top of my mouth as I laughed. "She would have been enraged at this place when I first showed up, then. All I saw was water on those floors."

"And you had to replace them."

"Most of them, yeah. The water did a number on them."

"So she was right to worry about it." She took a sip of tea, smiling at me. "And you fixed it so her floors could shine once more."

"I did. I should probably grab a fresh towel for Ander."

"Is he coming over tonight? It's getting a bit late."

I tapped my phone to see the time, frowning when the numbers popped up. "He said he was coming, but you're right. It's late. I wonder what's taking him so long."

"Maybe he got caught up at the restaurant."

Memories from that morning danced through my mind. "Hood cleaning. That's what he said this morning—something about cleaners coming to clean the exhaust hood at the restaurant."

"Ah, well, that makes sense, then." At that moment, the sound of an approaching vehicle caught both of our attention, and Aunt Gwendolyn smiled. "Perhaps that hood is finally clean."

I hopped up and strode toward the front of the house, not rushing but oddly excited. Still, I ran my hands along the walls and kept my eyes on the floor just in case all the rain had decided to make its way inside. Not a drop sat on the dark, hand-scraped flooring. I said a silent thank-you to the house, knowing she could have the place flooded again if she wanted to. Thankfully, she didn't seem to want to. A fact I very much appreciated.

The front door burst open, and a damp Ander practically exploded into view. "It's still coming down out there."

With a smile, I grabbed a clean towel and handed it to him. He whispered a thanks before attacking his hair and face with the towel. Once done, he slipped out of his shoes—setting them neatly to the side of the door—and grabbed my hand to pull me along behind him. "I'm starving. What's for dinner?"

I froze, something close to dread making my stomach go hard and rancid. "I was supposed to make dinner."

Ander turned slowly, looking confused. "Right. You were supposed to make dinner. Did you..."

"I forgot. I absolutely, totally forgot until you just said that." I tugged at my shirt, nearly sweating in the oppressive heat that seemed to have come up out of nowhere. "I'm a jerk."

"You're not a jerk," Ander said, pulling me after him once more. "You were busy. Come on—let's whip up something together."

And with that, he dragged me into the kitchen, where Aunt Gwendolyn sat waiting for us with a smile on her face.

"My favorite chef has arrived. How are you, dear?"

Ander beelined it to her and kissed her cheek. "I'm good. And you? I didn't see you at the restaurant today."

"I've been busy. As have you—how did the hood cleaning go?"

With that, Ander began cooking in my kitchen, as he tended to do. Aunt Gwendolyn chatted with him the entire time, her ease with him highlighting their friendship. I made my way to the pantry door that lay on sawhorses. A bag of hardware rested on the table, and a toolbox sat on the floor. It still needed staining, but it looked good. In fact, it looked ready to install.

"What are you doing?" Ander said as he hurried my way once I had the door upright. "It still needs staining."

"I know, but I want to see it in place."

"Let me help you."

The house grew warm again, my skin certainly flushing. I yanked on the door a little too hard and kept moving. "I can do it myself, Ander Mendoza."

He held up his hands and took a step back. "Understood. I'm here if you need help."

I nodded once before refocusing on the empty hole where this door belonged. The desire to cover it grew more intense, the absolute need to hang this door becoming my obsession. I paid no attention to the conversation across the room or the smells coming from my stove. All I cared about was the hunk of wood and the hinges.

It took me a few minutes—most of the time spent balancing the door while I started some screws, but eventually, I had a pantry door once more. It looked good. I especially liked the way it covered the bright metal from view.

I wiped my forehead and stood back, smiling. "It fits well."

Aunt Gwendolyn wandered over, looking at the door with a soft smile on her face. "Just about back to rights."

The heat grew, and I rushed to throw open the windows. "I have the herbalism print in the storage space. I'll hang that up once we stain it, but I needed to see it in place. Ander did a good job trimming it to fit."

"Thanks," he said, sliding up behind me. "It's going to look perfect once it's stained and that picture is back on it. Then we can move on to one of the other 583 projects left to do around here."

I blew out a breath and moved closer to the open window, needing the air. Aunt Gwendolyn opened the pantry door, cocking her head when she saw inside.

"You added shelves."

I swear, my neck stiffened in that moment, and the temperature rose another ten degrees. "Ander did."

Ander, already on his way back to cook, grunted. "Good ones. Those will hold everything you need, and you'll never have to worry about water damage or too much weight."

A thousand degrees. The kitchen felt as if it were a thousand degrees. I may as well have been standing on the sun for how hot it seemed.

"Why is it so hot in here?" I asked. Aunt Gwendolyn turned to look my way, frowning.

"It's not hot, Brylie. Especially not with the windows open."

I glanced around the kitchen, noting a perfectly comfortable-looking Ander—who happened to be staring at me with a concerned sort of furrow to his brow—and a sleeping Elmer. No one else looked as hot as I felt. Which only made the heat seem more oppressive.

"Great. So now I'm stuck in my own personal summer. Just what I need."

With that, I stomped outside, preferring to get a little wet than stay in the abysmal heat.

That no one else felt.

Chapter Six

Wednesday dawned bright and sunny, which would have been great had I not woken up with what felt like a hangover. Again.

"Why do I feel like I spent the night drinking Jaeger bombs and making decisions I'll regret? My night was nowhere near as wild."

Elmer huffed from where he sat at the end of the bed, looking at me as if he expected me to jump up and take care of him. Which really was what I needed to do, even if the idea of leaving my warm, comfy bed made me want to throw a tantrum. Could you get a hangover from drinking tea? If you could, I had. My dirty leaf water had betrayed me.

Elmer growled, making his dissatisfaction with the way his morning was going known.

"I'm up," I finally said, earning an excited sort of huff as I crawled out from under my blankets. "Let's go."

Elmer led the way downstairs and out the front door, taking a good deal of time sniffing around the yard before finding the perfect spot to do his business. I kept an eye on him, forever worried he would run off into the backyard or get into something that Thomas had fertilized. Not that the dog ran most days. Or investigated much. He was more the "outside, business, inside, nap" sort of creature.

Once Elmer had finished his morning routine, we headed inside so I could complete my far more exhaustive one. After a shower, a blow-dry, a quick makeup session, and a ransack of my closet, we were ready for our day working at the store. I had hundreds of packs of leaf bags on order, having completely underestimated how many would be needed. I had expected most of the people around Reverie Springs to burn their fallen leaves, but apparently a few of the farms liked to collect them for their garden beds and compost piles. I had been focusing on snow when leaves had become a huge boon to my bank account. I would plan better next year.

Next year. Because I was staying in Reverie Springs. A thought that still made butterflies flutter through my stomach.

We arrived on Main Street with plenty of time to stop for a coffee and see Ander. The night before had been a bit rocky, and I wanted to apologize and thank him properly for the pantry shelves. Even if I wasn't thrilled with the aesthetic of the metal, he had gone out of his way to install shelves that were needed. Ones that would last.

Ones that would still be holding my tea and boxes of cereal a year from now.

"So much planning," I said to Elmer as I helped him out of the car.

My mood sank the second I walked into the diner. The energy inside felt dark and heavy, even though the dining room sat mostly empty. The culprit turned out to be Ander himself. The man was on the phone. The landline. The one he kept only for his sister and takeout ordering. He paced back and forth into the kitchen, looking like a man ready to explode as he spoke in a hushed voice into the receiver.

Today was not the day to loiter.

"Morning, Brylie," Mary said, looking stressed and uncomfortable. "Uh...Ander's—"

"Busy. I see that. Can I just get a cup of coffee to go?"

She looked relieved. "Yeah, I can grab that for you."

With that, she hurried off to the waitress station near the kitchen, giving Ander a wide berth as she passed him. He didn't seem to notice her, something that stood out as odd. Ander was nothing if not polite to his favorite waitress. It seemed yelling into the phone—because with each pass of his pacing, his voice grew louder—seemed more important to him in that moment. His conversation was obviously not a good one.

As I stood there waiting for Mary to bring me a coffee, an uncomfortable, itchy sensation began on my right arm. I tried to ignore it, to make myself believe it was a normal itch, that a hair had fallen from my head to tickle me or I had dry skin in that one spot, but after about twenty seconds, I had to stop making excuses. Ander was lying on that call. Whether they were white lies or big lies didn't matter; he had chosen not to be truthful, likely to the sister he had once said I wouldn't even want to meet.

Apparently, at least to Ander, I didn't want to meet her, and he didn't want to tell her the truth. About what, I had no idea. And I wouldn't be asking him.

"Here you go," Mary said as she strode toward me with a to-go cup in hand. "I'll make sure Ander brings over some baked goods or something once he's cooled off."

"Oh, he doesn't have to do that. I don't want to give him more to do."

"I'm sure he's mad that he didn't get to see you."

I peeked over her shoulder, watching as Ander slammed his hand down on a counter and his voice grew louder. "I think he's just mad. If it gets too loud over here, you can come hang with me at the hardware store."

Mary grimaced as a cuss word in Ander's deep voice floated across the air. "I might take you up on that."

With a quick and shallow smile, I took off for the store. No one needed to hang around and listen to whatever personal discussion Ander was having, especially not me. Elmer padded along behind me, his nails clicking on the sidewalk. I had been watching him instead of where I was walking, which was why I almost smacked right into someone.

Someone I knew.

"Oh," I said as I came to an abrupt stop. "Heather. Hi."

"Hi, Brylie." Heather—daughter of the awful Joan—gave me a smile, even taking a moment to glance down at Elmer. I braced myself to be yelled at about not having him on a leash, but Heather just glanced back up at me and widened her smile, her energy calm and warm. "On your way to work?"

"Yup. Just had to stop for a little go-go juice." I wiggled my cup for her attention. "I'm too busy in the mornings to make my own, and Ander's coffee tastes better anyway."

"A perk of dating the chef," she said with a conspiratorial grin.

My mouth opened of its own accord, words tumbling out that I hadn't meant to say.

"We're not dating."

Something about those three words in that order made my stomach hurt. Were we dating? We had gone on dates, and the man tended to hang out with me at the manor most evenings.

But was that dating? And why had my instinctual response been to say we weren't?

Heather's smile dimmed, and her brow furrowed a bit. "Oh. I guess I just assumed."

The space between us became uncomfortable, the conversation halted. I had ruined the good energy she'd brought, which meant it was time to extricate myself from the situation.

"Well, I should get to work," I said, trying my hardest to bring a little enthusiasm back to my voice. "It was good to run into you."

"You too. Have a great day." With that, Heather strode past me while I...well, I slowly started walking toward my destination, sipping on my coffee as my brain practically short-circuited.

Once inside the store, I took a deep breath and frowned down at my bestie.

"Why did I say Ander and I weren't dating? Of course we're dating. Aren't we?"

Elmer stared up at me for about three seconds then yawned, moaning loudly at the end of it as if to make a point that he was not interested in this conversation. Which was about what I should have expected.

"Okay, lazy dog. Go to bed. I have work to do."

About an hour later, I flipped the Closed sign over and opened the front doors, wanting to let in as much of the cool breeze blowing through Reverie Springs as I could. It was a perfect fall day—cool but not cold, bright, and breezy. People would be needing those leaf bags, and I had them and a stand of both metal and plastic rakes set just inside the door. All hail good weather.

"Good morning, Miss Scott."

I turned, halfway back to the register, and smiled as Deputy Carmichael came walking in. "It's a little early for the whole Miss Scott thing. Brylie's fine."

He grinned, assumably eyeing me from behind those reflective sunglasses he always wore. "Brylie, then. How's your day going?"

"So far, so good. And you? Solving any big cases in the RS?"

"Not yet." He sauntered closer—and truly, sauntering was the only way to describe the exaggeratedly slow walk the man took—before leaning against the counter and giving me a smile that made me more than a little uncomfortable. "So, tell me, Brylie Scott. How did a woman who looks like you end up work—"

Elmer growled. Not a low, snoring-type growl. No—my faithful companion crawled out of his bed under the counter, turned his sleepy-eyed glare on the deputy, and growled at him.

My dog was not in the mood for the deputy's flirting.

The deputy jumped to his full height and took a large step backward, moving away from Elmer. "I thought you said he's a quiet, lazy dog."

"He is." I shrugged. "Guess he doesn't like you standing so close."

At that moment, Ander came striding into the store with a plate of cookies and another cup of coffee. My big, mean-looking chef likely coming to apologize for not being able to talk earlier. I still felt a little weird about knowing he had been lying on the phone, but that didn't stop me from being glad to see him.

"Morning, Chef."

"Hey. Sorry for earlier." He slipped behind the counter

with me, standing much closer than the deputy had been, and handed me the coffee. "It's been a brutal morning."

"Seemed like it."

That was the moment Ander looked up at the deputy. His smile fell, his easygoing demeanor shifting. "Deputy Carmichael. Some sort of problem on Main Street today?"

"Not at all." He glanced from Ander to Elmer. "How come he doesn't growl at Ander?"

"Ander feeds him." I snagged a cookie from the plate, taking a big bite. "Might want to bring treats next time."

"Who's bringing treats?" Aunt Gwendolyn asked as she swept in from the back of the store. "Good morning, Brylie dear. And Ander, you're looking as handsome as ever. I swear, we just said goodbye to you a few hours ago." She turned her attention to the deputy, who stood near the rake rack, much farther away from the counter than before. "Deputy Carmichael. Keeping the store safe this morning?"

"Doing my best, though that dog sure seems to be unhappy with me being here."

By the look on Ander's face, Elmer wasn't the only one. Not that I had any plans to say that out loud.

"Ander doesn't look too thrilled either," Aunt Gwendolyn said, obviously having no filter that day. "Are we going to have a fight over Brylie? I don't think we've seen a good love triangle in this town since that baseball player tried to steal Joan from Clyde."

"Aunt Gwendolyn," I hissed, my face and neck going awfully hot.

"What?" She gave the deputy an innocent sort of smile. "Can't an old woman call it like she sees it?"

"I'm done here," Ander said suddenly, looking angrier than

he had while on the phone that morning. "Did you feed that dog yet?"

I had never wanted to hit a man like I did Ander in that moment. "Of course I did."

Ander huffed. "He needs more than that bagged garbage you give him. Come on, Elmer. Let's go make you a decent breakfast."

Stunned. I stood absolutely stunned. Ander had never spoken to me like that, had never been so mean. He knew I bought the best dog food available for Elmer. It wasn't like I fed him Ol' Roy and hoped for the best.

"You don't need to take your bad mood out on me," I finally said, keeping my voice low and controlled. "I didn't do anything."

Aunt Gwendolyn placed a hand on my arm, looking at Ander in concern. "Brylie, why don't we—"

"I think the lady wants you to leave," Deputy Carmichael interjected, not helping the situation.

"No. I—" But Ander had already begun walking out, with Elmer on his heels. He didn't even look back. A sour feeling settled in my stomach, and I suddenly wanted to cry. "I think I need to take a break."

"That sounds like a good idea." Aunt Gwendolyn patted my arm before heading for the deputy. "Let me walk you out, Deputy Carmichael."

I leaned over the counter, taking deep breaths as I tried to settle the chaos working its way through my brain and body. What had just happened? How had I become the focus of Ander's anger? I had no idea, but I didn't like it. Not one bit.

"Brylie." Aunt Gwendolyn slipped in next to me and wrapped an arm around my shoulders. "What just happened?"

"I don't know. I just..." I swallowed hard, a familiar sick feeling making my throat grow tight. "Is it hot in here?"

Aunt Gwendolyn paused. "No, dear. Not at all."

My stomach twisted. I pushed past her and rushed toward the back, fighting hard to hold in what really wanted to come out. I made it to the bathroom just in time, falling to my knees and emptying my stomach into the bowl. Aunt Gwendolyn stayed with me, holding back my hair and whispering some sort of chant over me.

When I finished and felt confident that I had nothing else in me to throw up, I rose to my feet and headed to the sink to rinse out my mouth.

"I should keep toothpaste here apparently," I said, wiping my mouth on a paper hand towel before tossing it in the trash.

"I have some upstairs still, dear. I'll get it for you."

"Thanks." I leaned over the sink, still feeling hot, as she took off up the back stairs. I felt as if there were an octopus trying to break out of my belly, but at least the heaving had settled. Something slammed behind me, the noise startling but not enough to turn and look. My head felt too heavy, my body weak. Whatever that banging turned out to be would just have to wait.

"Got it," Aunt Gwendolyn said as she slipped in behind me.

"Did you slam a door or something?"

"No. Why?"

"I heard a loud banging noise."

She stayed silent for a long moment. "I didn't hear anything."

"Huh." I rose to my feet, slowly for sure, and reached for the toothpaste. She had also brought me a toothbrush, new in the package. Just looking at the two, knowing how minty the one would be and that I would need to stick the other in my mouth, made my stomach lurch. "Oh, maybe not."

"Brylie—"

"Nope." I leaned over the bowl, trying to stop the sick from rising this time. "This is horrible. I must have eaten something bad."

"Perhaps. How about I drive you home? I think you need a day of rest."

The offer seemed both really nice and almost scary at the same time. "I didn't know you still drove."

"I don't. Not since Rose—she always drove me around. When she died... Well, I'm not very comfortable behind the wheel these days. But you need to go home, and I'm all you've got, so I'll take you."

She *was* all I had—and after my fight with Ander, I felt that more than ever.

I sent a quick text to Mary, letting her know we were closing the store and Aunt Gwendolyn would be by to pick up Elmer. No sense in facing Ander after all the mess earlier. We locked up the store and turned off the lights, heading out the back. A strange buzzing met my ears as we opened the door onto the alley, and Aunt Gwendolyn jumped.

"What on earth?"

I peered around her shoulder into a cloud of...I couldn't even tell what. At least, not at first.

"Are those bees?" I looked closer, focusing on the dumpster they seemed to be swarming around. "Wait...is that...honey?"

And then I threw up again, all over my shoes.

Chapter Seven

Two days. I ended up sick and virtually useless for two solid days. I had shut myself into my room on Wednesday. By Friday, when I finally rolled over and looked at my phone screen to see the time, I felt better but had no idea what was happening around me. Home? Could be flooded again or just fine. Store? Could have sunk into Main Street. Elmer? No clue. Though since the dog wasn't jumping at me and trying to get me to let him out, I had to assume someone had stepped in on that front.

"Thank you, whoever took Elmer for me," I said into the emptiness. I may have been all alone in the room, but I was sure the person would appreciate the intent and understand my inability to climb out of bed just yet.

I stretched long and deep, rolling onto my stomach and hugging my pillow when done, trying hard to remember the last two days. I got nothing. All I knew was that I still felt pretty under the weather and had no recollection of much more than sleeping and hurting and my stomach being ripped apart from the inside by aliens. Not literally, but it had sure seemed that way.

The house felt too warm, and that uncomfortable heat finally drove me from my bed. I threw off the blankets and sat up, giving myself a good ten seconds before attempting to rise to my feet. My head hurt and I felt weak, but I wasn't dizzy or sick to my stomach anymore, so I headed for the door.

I made it all the way to the kitchen before it hit me—Elmer seemed to be gone. No way would he have let me walk that far without seeking me out, which meant he was not in Willow Manor. That saddened me more than I would have expected.

"Brylie?" Aunt Gwendolyn appeared from the conservatory, looking a little more tired and pale than usual. "Oh, dear girl. How are you feeling?"

"Okay, I think." I settled at the counter, needing to rest for a minute. "What are you doing?"

"I was just mixing up a tea blend for you. I've been manifesting that you'd wake up and feel better today."

Of course she had been. "What's in the blend?"

"All good things. Herbs and plants for protection and health. You sit—I'll put the kettle on."

I laid my head on the counter. "Fine. Make me your dirty leaf water."

She laughed as I knew she would. Aunt Gwendolyn had always been a lover of tea. I had only recently come into an appreciation for it, mostly because of her insistence that it was good for me. It didn't hurt that she always blended her teas with flavors I liked.

I closed my eyes as the kitchen filled with the sounds of Aunt Gwendolyn and her tea making—the whoosh of the burner igniting, the rustle of the leaves being shaken together, Aunt Gwendolyn's soft humming. The house sat quiet and yet filled with the sounds of life. The world around me soft and accepting...happy. I felt safe there.

But something was missing.

"Where's Elmer?" I asked once Aunt Gwendolyn had her boiling water ready to pour.

"Ander took him. He's keeping him for a few days for me. I had enough to worry about with taking care of you. Ander took over caring for your child."

I snorted a laugh, sitting up when Aunt Gwendolyn poured the water over the leaves. This had quickly become my favorite part—watching the woman work her kitchen magic. See, Aunt Gwendolyn didn't just *brew tea*. She brewed tea with intention. While the water extracted all the good flavors and nutrients from the leaves, Aunt Gwendolyn chanted over the cup, adding a bit of spice—cinnamon, by the looks of it—and stirring clockwise or counter, depending on whether she felt the need to attract or repel. Her words added music to her magic, her actions a practiced dance she had long ago mastered. Aunt Gwendolyn making tea was an experience.

At the end, once the tea had steeped to her liking and she had finished her whispered prayer, she added a little bit of honey and then slipped the cup across the counter.

"You remember why I add the things I do?" she asked, as if she hadn't been going over her process every day with me.

I nodded. "Cinnamon for luck and abundance, stir clockwise to invite the energy inside, speak with intention, add honey to attract sweetness."

"Good girl."

"Speaking of honey..." I took a sip of the tea, nearly moaning as the delicious spices and hint of sweetness touched my tongue, sighing softly as I swallowed and set down my cup. "What ever happened to the bees?"

"The ones on the dumpster?"

"I'm not aware of any other ones." I yawned, unable not to. Still so tired, even though I had apparently slept for two days.

Aunt Gwendolyn tsked and flew into motion, coming around the counter to grab my arm and help me to my feet.

"Ander can fill you in on all that once you're better. Come. Let's get you back to bed. Leave your tea."

I wasn't in a place to argue with her. I had gone from awake and okay to sleepy and drained in an instant. Thankfully, I *could* go back to bed. Aunt Gwendolyn had stayed with me; Ander had Elmer covered. Nothing more than the store seemed pressing. People would just have to wait to buy leaf bags and window sealing kits.

Aunt Gwendolyn walked me all the way upstairs, disappearing once I crawled into bed but returning in seconds with a bottle of water. Where she'd been stashing that, I had no idea, but I took it gratefully. I crawled under my blankets and whispered a quiet thank you as the woman tucked me in and turned off the lights. My head hit the pillow easily, the quiet of the room surrounding me. The energy of the house settled once more into something gentle and comforting, warm and decidedly feminine. As if the structure itself had stepped in, another woman taking care of me when I needed it. I appreciated the feeling.

Before I could fall asleep, though, my phone lit up. I grabbed it more out of habit than anything. Smiling when I saw the alert from Ander on the screen.

Are you awake?

I tapped to make a call instead of texting back, laughing as he answered. "Did you really just send me a *You up* text?"

His own deep chuckle felt like flannel against my senses,

warm and soothing and just...nice. "I guess I did. How are you feeling?"

"Tired. Still. But Aunt Gwendolyn made me some tea and forced me to go back to bed, so I'm resting."

"She's been very worried about you. We all have."

I couldn't hold back my smile. "I know. I'm okay. How's Elmer?"

"He's fine. Eating me out of house and home and taking over my life, but I don't mind."

The warm feeling both around and inside me kicked up a notch, comfort and home filling me with ease that still wasn't quite enough.

"When do I get him back?"

"If you're up for taking care of him, I can bring him back tonight after the restaurant closes."

I blinked, totally lost for a second. "What time is it?"

"Coming up on eight. I'll be closed within thirty minutes, but then I need to clean up."

"Okay. Yeah. It just...feels later." Because with the curtains drawn and the lights out, my room sat in total darkness. It could have been two in the morning for all I knew. "I might be asleep when you get here."

"I'll call Miss Gwen before I head out, make sure someone is there to take receipt of this beast."

"Perfect." I yawned and stretched, my eyes growing heavier by the second. "Thanks, Ander. I owe you one."

"You owe me nothing, beautiful. Get some rest. I'll get your dog back to you tonight."

I thought I might have hummed a response, though I wasn't sure. I also had no idea if I ever pressed the screen to end the call. All I knew was warmth and comfort and rest. At least, until my bed shook sometime later.

"What's happening?" I turned over just as Elmer came waddling up the mattress. His wet nose bumped into my cheek, and he groaned a happy little sound as he settled against my side. His weight, his warmth, comforted me even more. Everything back to normal.

Well, everything except the fact that Ander stood in my bedroom.

"Hey," I said, giving him a smile.

Backlit as he was by the hallway light streaming in through my open door, I couldn't see his response, but his voice sounded happy as he said, "Hey yourself. How you feeling?"

I nodded and snuggled closer to Elmer. "Better now. Thank you so much for taking care of him."

"It's no problem. He's a good dog, and you needed someone to let you rest. I'm just glad I could help." He looked down for a moment, the energy shifting slightly. "I've missed you."

I had never thought three little words could bring about so much emotion within me, but those ones did. "I'm sure if I had been awake at all, I would have missed you too."

He laughed and set his big hand on my leg, connecting us, before taking a seat at the end of the mattress. "Well, I'd rather you sleep than not. I want you better."

"Once I get past this food poisoning, I'm sure things will get back to normal."

He froze, his entire presence shifting a bit. "You didn't have food poisoning."

Which...made no sense. "Of course I did. What else could make me so sick to my stomach for days?"

"I don't know, but you can't have had food poisoning."

"Why not?"

"You only ever eat my food, and I'm careful. Plus, other

people would have been just as sick since so many of us eat the same things. Food poisoning doesn't make sense."

Which…made sense. "So, what else could it be? A stomach bug?"

"Those are usually super contagious, and no one else is sick."

I knew he was right—that norovirus could shut down whole cruise ships—but it had seemed logical for a moment. Maybe no longer. "Weird."

"Yeah, it is." He squeezed my leg. "I'm going to let you rest now. If there's anything you need, just send me a message. I'm always here for you."

"Thank you. I really do appre—hey!" I pushed myself up to rest on my elbow. "What ever happened with the bees?"

"The ones on the dumpster?"

Seriously, the fact that both he and Aunt Gwendolyn had felt the need to ask me that, to require clarification when they had no connection to any other bees, grated at my nerves. "Yes, those ones."

"I called Old Ben. He used to rent out his hives to help pollinate the local fall crops, so I assumed they were his. He came and collected them so he could take them back in the hives on his farm. Mike came by with his power washer to help us clean the dumpster afterward, so hopefully we won't get any additional insect or critter activity in the alley."

"You did all that?"

"Of course. Bees are integral to food production—I didn't want to see them destroyed just because their presence was inconvenient."

"And strange. Where did the honey come from?" Because they wouldn't have made that if they'd just been swarming or looking for a new place to build a hive.

"No clue." He rose to his feet, coming to place a soft kiss on my forehead. "Let's not worry about bees and honey anymore tonight. We can solve that mystery after you're back on your feet."

I lay down, snuggling Elmer once more. "Fine. Thanks for bringing this one back to me."

"No problem." He headed for the door, stopping just before he slipped out into the hall. "Get better, Brylie. I really have missed you."

With that, he closed the door behind him, plunging me back into the warmth and darkness of my bedroom. Elmer's soft breathing became the only sound around me, his weight pulling me toward sleep faster than anything else could have. Thank goodness whatever had made me sick hadn't affected anyone else.

But what on earth could have sent me to bed for two solid days?

Chapter Eight

Saturday ended up being a busy day at the store—whether from the gorgeous fall weather we had or the fact that I had left the place closed for two solid days. My cheeks hurt from smiling at the end of the day, and my throat itched a bit from all the talking, but my mood remained high. I loved a busy day with the townspeople.

"Ready?" Aunt Gwendolyn asked as she sashayed her way across the floor. She had pink on tonight—not a lot of it, but a few details over her usual gray that brightened her up. I loved seeing it.

"Absolutely. I'm starving."

"You didn't eat for two days while you slept. You need to catch up."

She wasn't wrong. I turned off the lights and headed for the door. It was time to close up shop, but we weren't going home. I had no interest in cooking anything, and a frozen dinner in the microwave sounded near torturous. I wanted a late dinner at the restaurant, and luckily, Aunt Gwendolyn had jumped at the chance to join me.

Elmer followed us out of the store, sitting on the concrete as I locked the doors behind me. The darn dog couldn't even stay on his feet for an extra thirty seconds.

I could only shake my head at his Elmer-ness. "Maybe Elmer needs two days of sleeping."

Aunt Gwendolyn laughed. "Oh, honey. That dog needs two months of rest, and he still wouldn't be much more energetic than he is right now."

She wasn't wrong.

We walked into the restaurant, still smiling and laughing about my ridiculous hound. Mary met us at the door, but not in her usual waitress clothes and with a bag in her hands.

"Oh," she said, looking surprised but smiling. "What are you two doing here so late?"

"I could ask you the same question—are you working tonight?"

"No, no. Louise is with her dad tonight and I got stood up by my date, so I popped in to grab a salad from Ander. I didn't want to cook my own dinner or resort to eating some frozen thing with 8,237 chemicals in it."

"Same...except for the being stood up part. I'm sorry." I frowned but then nearly jumped in place. "Oh! We're about to sit down and have a late dinner. Why don't you join us?"

Aunt Gwendolyn grinned. "Absolutely, you should. I need to know about this date—hexing day is coming up, after all."

Mary looked slightly hesitant but excited at the same time. "Are you sure? I would hate to intrude."

I looped my arm through hers and tugged her with me as I headed toward my usual spot in the restaurant. "There's no intruding here. Besides, you got a night without Louise and obviously dressed up—you need to be out."

The three of us settled at a table, Elmer immediately plopping on my feet below. A nice woman I hadn't yet met came over to greet us and grab our drink order before rushing off to assist the last few customers in the place.

"So," Mary said once we each had a beverage. "How are you feeling after a long day at the store?"

"I'm good. A little tired, but that's not unexpected."

"Any idea what made you so sick?"

I took a sip of my soda and shook my head. "No clue. I would have thought it was food poisoning—"

"No way," she interrupted with a shake of her head. "Not with you eating 95% Ander food. The man is vehement about food safety."

"That's pretty much what he said when I mentioned it. If not that, then a bug. But those are contagious, and Aunt Gwendolyn didn't even catch it."

"Nope," she said with a smile. "I'm fit as a fiddle."

Mary shook her head. "That's so weird."

And it was, but at that moment, a certain grumpy chef caught my attention as he left his lair and stalked my way, looking far less grumpy than usual.

"I didn't expect to see you ladies here tonight." He grabbed the bag from in front of Mary. "You want to order something else now that you're sticking around, or is this salad still your preference?"

She paused for a minute, looking almost guilty. "It's fine. I'll eat the—"

"Salads are for lunch," Aunt Gwendolyn interrupted with a kind voice and a mischievous glint in her eyes. "Ander dear, can I get your strip steak with the Parmesan crust, medium, and the potatoes Diane on the side. Brylie?"

"I'll have the same."

"Me too," Mary said, seeming to relax. "I'll take my salad home for tomorrow."

"Perfect," Ander said, giving the bag a little shake. "I'll put this in the walk-in to keep it cold. Grab it before you go."

With that, he disappeared into the kitchen, leaving the three of us to chatter among ourselves. And chatter we did. Aunt Gwendolyn got Mary to admit who her date had been with—"That man should know better. I'll hex him for you"—while they both went in on me about Ander—"I'm just saying, the man lights up whenever someone even mentions your name. I call it his Brylie face." The energy at the table remained bright and fun, the conversation flowing and filled with laughter. It was girls' night out, and I loved every second of it.

I especially loved the look on Ander's face when he came back to the table with the server. The man carried one plate and stepped around the table to place it in front of me before grabbing a chair and settling in on my left.

"So...what's been the topic of discussion tonight? All that laughing I heard in the kitchen has me curious."

The chatter came back, Aunt Gwendolyn leading the charge of poking fun in her gentle way, but my attention split. I couldn't help it, really, because Ander had his hand on my leg. Not too high up, not presumptuous, just one of those simple sorts of touches you share with *your* person. An easy, casual connection through affection. I liked it.

Of course, I also liked my steak. And the potatoes. I could have eaten those for the rest of my life without a single complaint.

Eventually, the waitress brought over a plate of small desserts—personal pies and cookies, brownies, and slices of cake. A perfect assortment of treats to nibble on as we finished our meal. I immediately reached for one of the little pies. It oozed a dark red liquid, so I guessed raspberry or strawberry and was downright excited to figure out which.

"Mmmmm, raspberry," I moaned after taking a bite. "This is delicious."

"You didn't finish your dinner yet," Ander said with a laugh.

I shrugged. "I don't always like to wait for what I want."

He raised an eyebrow, his dark eyes locked on mine. I grinned, enjoying the light, flirty air between us. The way his usual stormy energy seemed calmer and brighter.

"Brylie, do you do any canning?" Mary asked, stealing my attention from the man by my side. The one who gave my leg a squeeze before we moved on to discussing food preservation and fall harvests of the area.

And so the evening went, us eating, laughing, and joking while Ander sat with us. I knew he had things to do in the back —the man cleaned that kitchen from top to bottom every night—but he never left us. Never went off to do the work waiting for him. It was fun to get to spend so much time with him and see how the four of us fit together.

"Feeling better?" he eventually asked, leaning in and keeping his voice down as Mary and Aunt Gwendolyn chatted about the farmers market coming up the next weekend.

"Much. Thank you again for taking care of Elmer for me."

He squeezed my leg once more, his beard shifting as he smiled my way. "I'd do anything for you, beautiful."

I couldn't breathe. Couldn't focus on anything other than the look in his eyes and the energy between us. The storm that blew through whenever we moved into that *more* space. I had lost my footing in reality and been shoved into the realm of possibility. Of future maybes and why nots. At least until Aunt Gwendolyn cursed.

"You okay?" I asked, my gaze already locked on her. My body turning in her direction almost on instinct. "What's wrong?"

"I'm fine, dear." Aunt Gwendolyn gave me a confused look. "Are you okay?"

I stuttered, trying to find words. To make sense of what had just happened. "I'm fine, but what made you curse? You don't usually cuss like that."

Her eyes went wide, and she glanced over my shoulder at Ander. "Brylie, dear. I didn't curse."

"I heard you."

"I didn't curse."

Mary, brow furrowed but eyes clear, reiterated, "She didn't curse."

"Huh." I sat back, suddenly feeling a little off. "I could have sworn..."

"Ander," Mary said, taking on the awkward attention that had fallen on me. "Who's making these amazing desserts?"

Ander had his eyes locked on me, his face frozen in concern. I patted his hand—the one still on my knee—and nodded. He took my hint and shot a look at Mary.

"I've still got a couple of people I'm buying from to see what works. These are from three different vendors, so let me know your thoughts."

"The pie is great, though I already told you that." I took another bite, still a little distracted by the fact that I would have bet my life Aunt Gwendolyn had said something she apparently never had.

"This cake is amazing. Very moist." Mary laughed when I made a face. "Not a fan of the word moist?"

"Usually, no, but I accept it in terms of cake."

Everyone at the table laughed, and the conversation went back to farmers markets and baked goods.

Eventually, the evening wrapped up. Ander walked the three of us to our cars, even going so far as to buckle Elmer into his seat belt harness in the back for me.

"Bye, ladies," Mary said as she slid into her car, salad at her side. "Thanks for keeping me company. I'll see you in the morning, Ander."

With that, she drove away, leaving Ander, Aunt Gwendolyn, and me standing on the side street by the hardware store.

"Whoo, I'm tired," Aunt Gwendolyn said, giving an exaggerated yawn. "I'm just going to hop inside the van and lay my head down. I'll likely fall asleep in under a minute. Won't have any idea what's happening around me. Good night, Ander. Take your time, Brylie."

She hopped into the passenger seat and shut her door loudly. Leaving us alone on the darkened street.

"That woman is not subtle in the least," Ander said with a laugh. Still, he tugged me closer, wrapping his arms around my waist. "Thanks for coming to the restaurant."

"Thank you for an amazing meal, as always."

"Any time." He leaned in slowly, dropping a soft, sweet kiss on my lips. "I'd like to take you on a real date."

"You would?"

"Yeah. Not that I don't love your aunt's company..."

"That would be nice."

He sighed and dropped his forehead against mine. "Okay.

I'll plan something—maybe next Sunday? I know it's not a traditional date night—"

"Sunday would be perfect." I grinned up at him. "I know your weekends are taken up by the restaurant."

"I appreciate your understanding that."

"I'm a business owner, too. Weekends are just…"

"Yeah. They're *just*." He gave me one more sweet kiss and squeezed me closer before taking a step back. "Get on home, Brylie Scott. I have a restaurant to clean."

"Be careful."

"You too."

I slipped into the driver's seat, waving to him as I pulled away.

"He's a good man," Aunt Gwendolyn said.

"I thought you were falling right asleep?"

"Elmer snores too loud for that. Besides, I'm an old woman —I like to witness a little love now and again."

I rolled my eyes, turning onto the highway that would lead to the manor. "You're getting ahead of yourself."

"Perhaps." She glanced down into the console area, obviously distracted by something. "Brylie…why aren't these in your bra?"

I glanced over, unable to get a good look because I needed to keep driving. "What?"

"The crystals I gave you. They belong in your bra."

They belonged in the display case at home, but I wasn't about to tell her I thought that. "I forgot all about them."

She hummed. "I'll recharge them tonight, and you can start carrying them again tomorrow."

Rocks in my bra didn't seem the most effective protection against anything, but I had a feeling that was not a fight I would win.

We made it home without incident, the three of us strolling into the house together. The second I walked inside, though, the oppressive heat hit me in the face.

"Oh no. Why is it so hot?"

Aunt Gwendolyn shot me a funny look before walking toward the kitchen. "It's not hot in here, Brylie."

I swallowed down the growing unease within me, already sweating as I followed her. "It's got to be in the nineties in here. How are you not hot?"

I took a quick glance at the thermostat on my way past it. Nope—not hot. And yet the air felt absolutely sweltering.

"Come," Aunt Gwendolyn said. "I'll make you some iced bedtime tea. Maybe that will settle your system."

I tried to follow her, I really did, but the mess in my kitchen caught my attention, and I froze just inside the doorway. Tools, building supplies, drawings...all left behind and taking up space. The room had been this way since we'd started the project, but tonight, I couldn't handle it. Between the heat and the mess, my temper had no option but to snap.

"I don't know why Ander can't clean up after himself." I reached for a hammer left on the counter, tossing it angrily into the canvas tool bucket on the floor. "How are we supposed to live in this mess?"

Aunt Gwendolyn frowned at me. "Honey, are you okay?"

"What? Of course I'm okay. I'm just..."

But I wasn't okay. Suddenly, without warning, I definitely felt not okay. I spun and ran back down the hall, sliding into the bathroom just in time to empty my stomach into the toilet.

"Brylie!"

Aunt Gwendolyn once again held my hair back, rubbing my neck and stretching to grab a towel. She ran cold water over the fabric as I was sick again, eventually placing it on the back of my neck. Cooling me down.

"What on earth is happening with you?" she asked.

I leaned my head on the seat, the coolness of the tile beneath me and the towel on my neck the only comfort I could find.

And I failed to find an answer to her question.

Chapter Nine

I did not go down for two full days that time. In fact, I woke up the next morning after being sick for half the night and started my day like normal. Perfectly normal. Yup.

"You look hungover," Aunt Gwendolyn said the second she walked into the kitchen where I had sat down and been unable to get back up.

So maybe normal was a stretch.

"I wish that were it." I sipped my tea, trying my hardest to push back how horrible I felt. "This being sick without reason thing is for the birds."

Aunt Gwendolyn mumbled something that sounded like an agreement as she moved toward the stove where the kettle sat. "Would you like another cup of tea?"

I grunted my answer, adding in a headshake when she turned to look my way. "No, thank you."

She went about her morning, humming softly to herself as she made a cup of tea. The house sat quiet and still, a soft sort of energy running through it. A warmth that comforted. It almost felt as if the room were hugging me, and I needed that.

"You know," Aunt Gwendolyn started as she appeared on the opposite side of the counter from me, teacup in hand. "With the pantry about done, I think the kitchen is almost back to rights. What do you think you'll work on next?"

That comfortable heat exploded around me, growing hotter in an instant. Making me sweat without any sort of warning. I hated that heat.

"The pantry isn't done, and Ander will never be done with this kitchen. It's like he thinks it's his or something."

The room went silent, Aunt Gwendolyn freezing into place like a deer on the side of the road that you shone your headlights at. The heat receded, the anger inside me diminishing. I sat up, my face pulling tight as I tried to reconcile what had just happened. As the reality of my snapping at Aunt Gwendolyn like that hit me.

Shame burned hotter than the heat of anger ever could.

"I'm sorry. I don't know what came over me." I coughed, hanging my head. "I don't know why I got so mad like that."

"Because your soul is exhausted." Aunt Gwendolyn set down her teacup and swept around the counter. "Come, child. Mother Earth is calling us. It's time to get our hands dirty."

She pulled me off the stool, literally dragging me into the conservatory. The air in the glass room felt warm and heavy, thick with humidity and filled with the scents of things that were alive. Things that called to me to look and smell, to touch. The room seemed filled with a magic that was impossible to ignore.

"Where do we begin?" I asked as I ran my fingers along the soft, heart-shaped petals of some sort of hanging plant. Aunt Gwendolyn had been busy out there apparently because the living plants far outnumbered the dead. The first time I had walked into the space, dirt and empty pots had filled the space. Now, it almost looked like a plant store.

"Let's get to work on our kitchen herbs. A lot of them have properties that bring magic into our everyday life."

"Really?"

"Yes, Brylie. Take rosemary." She hoisted a larger pot onto the workbench, spinning it so I could see the script writing on the side that did, indeed, spell out rosemary. "You can obviously use this in your cooking and even teas, but it's also a wonderful plant to use in protection spells or to bring good energy to a new relationship. It can drain negativity from around you and bring about happiness and fortune. I like to keep it near the door to the conservatory to welcome the luck."

I stood back as she dug her fingers deep in the dirt, watching the way she worked with so much love and grace. The woman knew her plants, that was for sure. She also knew when to stop talking and let me be, when to simply give me space to find my own words.

Her silence was better than any question ever asked.

"I think I'm sick again," I said, my voice low and rough. Aunt Gwendolyn hummed and waved me closer, grabbing my hand and placing it on the dirt beside hers. Showing me how she wanted me to dig a little deeper. So I did.

"I can't figure it out. I'm not as bad as last time, but still sick. And sometimes, the air around me gets really hot. It doesn't make sense because none of you are hot, but I suddenly feel as if it's a thousand degrees. Like..."

I huffed, frustrated. Unable to find more words to explain. Thankfully, I didn't need to.

"Like you're having your own personal summer." Aunt Gwendolyn removed our hands from the dirt, spinning the pot slowly. Running her fingers over the word on the lip as if it was special to her. As if it held deeper meaning than the simply herb type. "It sounds very much like menopause, but you're still a bit too young for that. Have you ever had trouble with your hormone levels?"

I sighed. "No, never."

"Perhaps we should get them checked—just to be sure."

"Perhaps." Though I didn't want to. Not at all. I wanted everything to just go away and get back to normal. I never wanted to feel that oppressive personal heat again. I wanted to be able to rest and relax without worrying about...well, anything. But that wasn't life. "So what do we do with the pot now? Is it not going to grow?"

Aunt Gwendolyn laughed. "Patience, child. Rosemary is a perennial plant, an evergreen. This poor love took a very long nap while I was gone. She'll need a few days to wake up properly and begin her journey back to her former glory."

She ran her fingers over the word rosemary again, her eyes soft and her smile gentle. I knew that look—recognized the energy of both love and grief coming from her. I didn't need any magical sensibilities to understand the moment.

"Did Rose make you that pot?"

She nodded. "It was an old one Carl had left in his barn from when his wife had been alive. He gave it to Rose, and she painted it for me, for us. For the rosemary plant I wanted by the door. She always liked to make the mundane pretty for me."

"I wish I could have met her."

"I wish you could have, too. She would have adored you." She took a deep breath, and her smile grew larger, the sadness lightening until it had almost disappeared. "Let's get this lovely lady a drink. She could also use a little more compost added to her sandy soil. Just a bit to give her a boost."

"I'll bring some home from the store."

"Excellent."

And so it went, Aunt Gwendolyn leading me from planter to planter while I listened and absorbed her wisdom. Rosemary, chives, mint, dill, sage—all normal kitchen herbs infused with her magic and attention. She cleaned their pots and watered their roots, setting them in a neat row where they could get a good amount of sunlight. I mostly watched as she worked, soothed by the earthy smell of the conservatory. Calmed by the kiss of humidity in the sun-dappled air.

This was what I had come to think of as home—time with Aunt Gwendolyn and magic in the air. These were the moments I had missed out on throughout my life, the feelings that had been denied to me. Why my mother had turned her back on this life, I would never know, but I always ended up feeling a little sad, thinking how she and I could have spent time in the conservatory with Aunt Gwendolyn. We could have met Rose. We could have...

Could haves that became couldn'ts because of accidents that got in the way. Life could be amazing, but it could also be painful and grief-filled. I really needed to focus on not taking a single second of my time with the amazing woman beside me for granted.

"I'm so glad you found me," I said, focusing hard on a pot that had sage painted on the side of it. "Truly, I am."

Aunt Gwendolyn didn't turn, didn't stop working her magic, but her smile grew and her voice sounded a bit strained as she answered. "I'm thankful to have found you, too. You were meant to come home."

I threw an arm around her shoulder and gave her a quick, sideways hug.

Before either of us could grow too sappy, the front door

slammed, and Elmer barked before running off through the kitchen.

"Expecting someone?"

I laughed. "That's a happy bark. It must be Ander."

The man walked into the kitchen just as we exited the conservatory, looking all big and broad and taking up so much space in my kitchen. He also looked tired and carried a grocery bag.

"Hey," I said, giving him a smile. "Rough day?"

He huffed a laugh. "Rough week. But it's over, and I'm here to spend some time with my favorite ladies. I brought all the stuff to make pizzas—I hope that's okay."

"Pizza sounds amazing," Aunt Gwendolyn said. "I have a little more work to do in the conservatory, so I'll leave you two alone. Good to see you, Ander."

"You too, Miss Gwen." He turned my way, those dark eyes steeling me in place. The look in them so familiar. So warm and caring. This man showed up when most wouldn't, and I liked that. A lot.

I hurried across the floor, feeling so much love and peace in this home. So much comfort. I hadn't been this happy in a lot of years, and the gratefulness of this new life had just seemed to hit me.

"Of course it's okay," I said just as I reached him. I wrapped my arms around the chef and hugged him close, leaning in as he bent to nuzzle into my neck and sighed.

"I needed this," he whispered.

"Me too."

"You feeling okay?"

That question reminded me of the night before, of freaking out over him being in my space. Of the feeling of being overwhelmed. Of being sick.

"Yeah, though I had a rough night."

We broke apart, Ander frowning as he looked down at me. I moved to settle into a seat at the counter and watched as he washed his hands before returning to the island to begin pulling out the pizza supplies. His frown never lessened.

"You haven't felt well a lot lately."

"I know, and it's weird." I grabbed a slice of pepperoni from the stack, stopping when I noticed the dirt still on my hands from working in the conservatory. I hurried over to the sink to wash, not wanting to make myself any sicker than I already had been.

"What makes it weird?"

"Well, I haven't been this sick in years, and it's so out of the blue." I dried my clean hands on a towel then returned to the counter, retaking my seat. "I can't figure it out."

"You used to be sick like this a lot?"

"Back in California, yeah. Never could figure out what was causing it, but I would have days of feeling so sick to my stomach. It was awful."

"Sounds a lot like what's happening now."

"Yeah, it does."

He ladled sauce onto a round of dough, taking it almost all the way to the edges before reaching for a ball of fresh mozzarella already cut into slices. He was fully immersed in placing the cheese and toppings, completely ignoring me—or so I thought—when he asked, "Think maybe it's time to see a doctor?"

My stomach sank, a buzz of something like anxiety making my head start to hurt. But the house stayed calm, the energy in the kitchen warm and comforting just as it had been in the conservatory. I had nothing to fear, nothing to run away from. Just a handsome man who cared about me, an old lady who loved me enough to share her time and wisdom with me working away in the room behind me, and a life I had never thought possible playing out before my eyes. A simple doctor visit seemed easy.

"Yeah, I think I should."

Chapter Ten

Monday dawned bright and sunny, a perfect day to stay home, open all the windows, and make things beautiful once more. I started in the kitchen, scrubbing trim and wiping down cabinets to get rid of the worst of the construction dust. There would be more, of course—we weren't quite finished yet—but it made me feel better, knowing the worst was gone. Aunt Gwendolyn joined me for a bit but then moved into the conservatory, the plants inside calling to her. Or so she said. Personally, I assumed she didn't want to deal with all the cleaning in the kitchen. Elmer even followed her, the traitor. Both leaving me alone to deal with the worst of the mess.

Ander showed up around an hour before lunch, strolling into the house after a quick knock on the door.

"Brylie?"

"In the kitchen." I rinsed out my rag and hurried to the hall, smiling the second I saw him. "Hey there, Chef."

"Hey there, hardware store owner." He leaned down for a

quick kiss as he passed me, shifting the two bags he carried to make enough room. "Come on. I've got a present for you."

"Present?" I skipped after him, the idea of presents making me giddy. "Is it food?"

"Nope." He set the bags on the counter, smiling as he reached inside. "But they'll help you make food."

I frowned. "Who wants to make food?"

The laugh Ander choked out had me grinning. With a headshake, he finally retrieved the item from the first bag, laying out a dark leather roll filled with black-handled knives of all sizes. A lovely set, for sure, and likely expensive.

"Oh," I said as I reached for them. "These are pretty."

"They're really good quality. I have a similar set at home. I even got you the magnetic bar."

He placed a long, black strip on the counter, following it up with some hardware that must have been needed to install it. I knew what that bar was, of course. Ander kept his knives on something like it at the restaurant—a magnetic strip that let the knives stick to the wall instead of being tucked away. I understood it for the restaurant, but this was a home. *My* home.

"No knife block?"

"The strip is so much more convenient." Ander shot me a grin then moved to the sink to wash the knives.

I stared at the strip of black against my old, stone counter, digging deep to stay grateful. Knives were expensive, and as a chef, of course he would be particular about what kind he used. I had no problem with that. But installing a magnetic track—having knives just hanging on the wall as if they were art—did not play into my charming kitchen decor. Like the metal shelves, he had made a decision for my house that didn't appeal to me. I wanted to be grateful, I really did—but I also wanted a knife block.

"Don't you think that black and metal will be...too much for this kitchen?"

He looked up, brow furrowed. "Huh?"

But before I could voice my concerns, his phone went off. He cursed softly under his breath and reached for a towel, rushing through drying his hands so he could pull the device from his pocket and tap it to life. "Ander here."

He continued to dry his hands, the energy in the room growing darker as he stood there listening. Aunt Gwendolyn even came out from the conservatory, eyebrows furrowed and a long piece of white stone shaped like a knife in her hand. Fitting, sort of.

"What's happening?" she asked in a whispered tone. I was about to whisper back that I had no idea when Ander turned for the door.

"I'm on my way. Thanks for calling."

I was up and following him without missing a beat. "What's going on?"

"The door to the restaurant is open." He paused to slip his shoes on at the door. "I know I locked it."

"I'll come with you." I turned to Aunt Gwendolyn, who didn't even need a reminder.

"I'll take care of Elmer."

"Thanks." With that, Ander and I ran outside, hurrying toward his truck. I waited until we were settled and he had backed out of his spot before asking, "Who called?"

"Deputy Carmichael. He said he was patrolling the area and noticed it open. He stopped to check, assuming I was inside cleaning or something, and called when he realized I wasn't there."

"Good thing he checked."

"Yeah, I guess the guy's good for something." His words carried a cutting edge to them, his tone harsher than I would have expected. I didn't pry into that, though. Ander was driving like his life depended on making it to town in the shortest amount of time. He didn't need me distracting him.

We pulled up outside the restaurant in a matter of minutes, Ander parking the car behind the sheriff's department cruiser and hurrying out of the truck. I followed, worry sitting deep in my stomach.

Deputy Carmichael met us at the door. "Ander. Miss Brylie. Glad to see you both." He turned and led the way inside. "I performed a perfunctory search once I realized you weren't here. I didn't notice anything amiss, but obviously, you would be able to spot anything out of sorts better than I can."

"Thanks." Ander looked around the room, an angry sort of scowl on his face. "Let me check over the kitchen."

Deputy Carmichael waited until Ander had disappeared before turning his attention to me. "Busy Monday?"

"It really wasn't until your call." I gave him what felt like a tired smile, too distracted by worry that someone had stolen from Ander to put more effort into it. "Thanks for checking on the restaurant. I know Ander appreciates it."

He huffed. "Somehow I doubt Ander appreciates anything I do."

Before I could question him on that, Ander appeared from the kitchen, no longer scowling. "Nothing. Not a single thing moved or stolen that I can tell."

Deputy Carmichael shrugged. "Perhaps you simply forgot to lock the door, then."

Ander gave the deputy a glower. "I never forget to lock the door."

"Then maybe we have a door-unlocking magician in this town. I noticed the back door to the hardware store was also unlocked when I went to check."

"Wait," I said, holding up my hands and tilting my head as his words ping-ponged through my brain. "The hardware store was unlocked, too?"

"Yep. Back door. I looked inside, but everything seemed okay. I was going to wait to take you over there to check until after we got done here."

"You checked inside the store for me?"

"Of course." His smile grew, his expression turning much friendlier than I was comfortable with. His energy growing into something that felt almost invasive. "I pay attention to the pretty women in this town."

As much as the man made my skin crawl—and he did in a weird, harmless-yet-creepy sort of way—I had to admit he knew how to flirt. And I didn't hate it. I didn't like it either, and the man had no shot at catching my interest, but the attention wasn't all bad. Though I took a step away from him, the energy he gave off a little too much for me. The rage coming from my chef letting me know I needed to defuse the situation if at all possible.

That move wasn't nearly enough apparently, because Ander looked ready to spit nails.

"I thought you were here to deal with a possible crime, not hit on Brylie."

Deputy Carmichael zeroed in on Ander, his expression sly and cutting. Which should have prepared me for his words.

"I guess I misread Brylie's own words. I thought when she told people she wasn't dating anyone that it meant...well, that she wasn't dating anyone." He glanced my way. "Perhaps I heard wrong."

I sighed, not really wanting to deal with any of this, but knowing I needed to. First up, Ander, which meant getting rid of the deputy. "Thanks for calling about the restaurant and checking on the store. It doesn't look like we need your help anymore today."

Deputy Carmichael stood and stared at me for a long minute, tension growing between us, before he finally broke and turned away. "Glad I could help. Call dispatch if you need anything."

And with that, the man turned and walked out the door. The relief I felt at his exit lasted only a matter of seconds because Ander looked...well, he looked hurt more than mad. Something I hadn't been prepared for.

"Ander, I—"

"Did he lie?"

I froze, trying to keep up. Understanding far too late he meant about the doors being open. "No. He didn't lie."

Ander nodded, staring at the ceiling for a long moment before pinning me with his dark gaze once more. "You look pale. Come. Sit at the counter with me. I'll make us a quick snack since we're here."

He turned and walked away, leaving me standing in the dining room with nothing but a feeling of impending doom. I took a deep breath then did what he had said, stopping at the soda machine along the way to grab us each something to drink. Once I sat down, I took a sip of my beverage. Ready to wade into this particular minefield.

Ander beat me to it. "Want to tell me what that whole you're telling people you're not dating anyone thing is about?"

He never looked up from the flat top where he appeared to be making a couple of sliders, but his shoulders were tense, his back straight. He looked like a man stressed about something. That something being me.

I sighed. "I mentioned it to Heather the other day when she questioned me about you. I regretted saying it immediately, but I also never felt it was a lie."

He finally shot a glance my way. "Why not?"

"Because we've never discussed what we are or where we're going. We date, but saying we're dating implies something we haven't really decided upon. And to be honest, I don't want to have those sorts of discussions. I like what we have together and don't feel the need to label it."

He tossed the burgers on buns and set each one on a plate, accompanied by some chips and a cookie. Once ready, he moved to the counter, setting the plates down and standing right in front of me. Not taking the seat at my side. I grabbed the cookie and took a bite, unable to sit under his dark stare without doing something.

Finally, he grunted what sounded like approval. "Are you seeing anyone else?"

Cookie...dropped. "No! I would never do that to you."

"Do you *want* to see other people?"

I twisted my napkin, my insides twisting along with the paper. "No. And it may be selfish of me, but I don't want you to see other people either."

He ignored his food and moved around the counter, slipping in beside me and turning me to face him. Then he wrapped his arms around me and tugged me in close. I sank into his embrace, loving the warmth and comfort he brought me. The feeling of security. The man was good and kind, someone I was so happy to have in my life. And mine. Whether I was ready to admit it or not, he was mine.

"I'm not going to push you," he said, keeping his voice soft and quiet. Not demanding or harsh in the least. "Just know I'm ready for whatever label you choose to put on us. So long as there *is* an us."

I choked out a laugh, hugging him tighter. "Okay. I'll let you know when I'm ready for a label upgrade."

"Good. Just...let me know if the whole seeing other people thing changes, too."

"It won't," I whispered, putting as much faith into my words as I had. Not feeling a single bit of static along my skin. Not a lie.

"Then we're good." Ander pulled away, dropping a kiss to my forehead before walking back around the counter. "Now, eat something. You look hungry."

"How does someone look hungry?"

He waved in my direction. "Like that. And try eating more than just a cookie."

I picked up my burger, making a show of lining it up to take a bite. "Fine. But only since you made me such a cute, little burger."

"I know your weak spots."

We had a fun snack at the counter, both of us chatting and laughing and enjoying our time together. The burger hit the spot, and the company reminded me of why the man in the kitchen was one of my favorites. He had a way of making me feel special and cared for, even if he did get a little grumpy now and again.

We were about to start cleaning up when my stomach twisted and the world went hot. I gasped, pain and heat radiating through my body.

Ander didn't miss my reaction. "What's happening?"

I shook my head and waved my napkin in front of my face. "It's a thousand degrees in here."

He stared at me, brow furrowed. "It's not, though. Are you okay?"

"I don't think so."

He hurried around the counter and pressed a hand to my cheek. "You are a little warm. This seems a lot like an allergic reaction."

"I'm not allergic to anything. Maybe it's food poisoning."

"I literally just ate the exact same things you did. If it was, I'd be sick too."

I knew that. I did; I just didn't want to believe it. "Yeah, that makes sense."

Ander stroked from my cheekbone down to my neck, holding on to me as if to keep me from moving. "I think it's time you go see a doctor."

I huffed a laugh. "Does Reverie Springs even have a doctor?"

My stomach dropped as my memories kicked in, dread twisting inside me. I knew we had a doctor—I had met him at the hardware store. In typical small-town fashion, he had a history with someone I considered a friend. I didn't want to admit it, didn't want to give the man any business, but I had a feeling I would have to.

Ander only confirmed my fears. "Yeah, we do. You're not going to like who he is, though."

"Mary's ex."

"Yup. His name's Don. That's the town doc."

Well, shoot.

Chapter Eleven

My hand felt small and safe inside Ander's much larger one as we sat next to each other at the doctor's office. I hadn't thought it was possible, but Dr. Don had clinic-style hours all day, so we'd been able to go straight there to be seen. Like an urgent care, but small-town style.

"Brylie. I've got one more form for you to fill out."

Ander rose and crossed the room as I smiled at Heather Turlington, Joan "hater-of-unleashed-dogs" Turlington's daughter. Because of course she worked the front desk at the local doctor's office and had been the first face I'd seen when we had walked in. No anonymity in Reverie Springs, that was for sure.

"Here," Ander murmured as he sat back down beside me. "Looks simple enough. Or do you need me to do it?"

I took the clipboard from him and grabbed the pen he offered. "I can do this."

"You sure? You don't look so good."

"Gee, thanks. Just what every woman wants to hear."

He set his hand on my thigh and leaned closer, invading my

visual field until he became the only thing I could see. "You're beautiful as always, but I can tell you don't feel well."

I sighed. The man had a point. I didn't feel well, not at all. I wasn't throwing up or practically unconscious, but I would have much rather been in my bed.

"I *don't* feel well, but I can fill this out. Thank you for offering to help and for sitting here with me. You don't have to stay."

He sat back, huffing as he crossed his arms over his chest. "As if I'd leave you here alone."

Mood...set. The man wasn't leaving.

I filled out the form, noting my very limited medical history. The only surgery I'd ever had was a tonsillectomy at age six, and I had no known allergies. I was about as medically boring as one could get, which made the paperwork go quickly. Once finished, I rose to my feet—waving off Ander when he moved as if to make the trek to the desk for me—and headed over to Heather.

"All done," I said, giving her a smile.

"Thanks, hon. I know—all this paperwork. It's kind of ridiculous but also very necessary." She glanced over my sheet before tucking it into a plastic board thingy next to her monitor. "You don't have much here in terms of medical history. You might want to have your old doctor send over your records, just in case there's something in their notes. You did say you've had this issue before, right?"

She turned to type my information in, her fingers practically flying over the keyboard. The speed of the keys clicking distracted me, and I ended up staring for far too long. Long enough that Heather finally glanced my way and said my name again when I hadn't answered.

"Oh, yeah. Sorry," I said with a shake of my head, still

amazed at how fast she could type. "A few years back. The doctors tested for all sorts of stuff but couldn't figure it out."

She nodded, still typing. "Definitely get those records. Dr. Don will likely want to see what exactly they tested and the results. They can send them to us electronically."

Once finished, she removed the paper from her stand and tucked it into a folder on her desk. One that had my name on the front. "Done. So now we just wait for the doctor."

"Thanks." I paused, suddenly too tired to put one foot in front of the other, needing a distraction from Heather's gaze as I took a moment to regain my balance and strength. "So... doctor's office, huh? I can't imagine how difficult your job has to be."

"Most days, it's just tedious—fill out this form, call this pharmacy, track down these test results. It's no dream job, that's for sure, but I needed a paycheck and am doing my best to break out of here."

Before I could ask her what she wanted to do, the door to the office burst open, and Aunt Gwendolyn came rushing in with her magical, floating skirts billowing around her. Her very colorful skirts. The woman only wore a single layer of gray today. Interesting.

And a good distraction as she looked about terrified.

"Going with color today?" I asked, smiling and nodding at the fabric covering her legs.

Aunt Gwendolyn froze, likely caught off guard by my question, before huffing in irritation. "Of all the things to be concerned about. What are you doing standing over there? Let's get you off your feet."

With that, Aunt Gwendolyn wrapped an arm around my waist and walked me back to Ander, who took over my care and got me settled into my chair. I sat between the two and waited, the time passing and draining what little energy I had. My stomach continued to hurt as I listened to them chat amicably, which only made me even more tired. I wanted so much to return to the manor, go to sleep, and let the sickness pass.

What seemed like hours later but had likely been only a few minutes, the internal door opened and a pretty young woman in scrubs appeared. "Brylie?"

"Looks like it's my turn." I rose to my feet slowly, hanging on to Ander's hand to keep my balance, before trudging her way. I made it all the way to the door before a wave of pure fear overwhelmed me. "Aunt Gwendolyn?"

I didn't need to say more. The woman rose and rushed to my side, hanging on to me and helping me keep my balance. "I've got you. You'll be fine."

She walked with me to an examination room in the back, taking a seat once the lady who'd brought us back closed the door behind her.

"So," I said, trying to keep from letting my nerves get the best of me. "How do you feel about Dr. Don?"

A ridiculous name and one that made me think of some old actor from a television show my dad had watched. By the way Aunt Gwendolyn scrunched her face, she didn't think highly of the man.

"He's a fine doctor, but I don't like how he treated Mary during their marriage. I keep my opinion about that to myself, though—we don't have many options for medical care around here."

So she didn't like him, which made sense. Ander's waitress Mary was a lovely woman and a good friend to both of us. I guess I would not be liking Dr. Don either once I heard the whole story of their breakup.

Though her opinion made me wonder. "Do you hex him?"

"Oh, yes—of course. Every month."

I chuckled, both amazed and not at all surprised. Aunt Gwendolyn was not a woman to cross.

A knock sounded at the door then it opened, Dr. Don walking through with a too-bright smile on his face.

"Ah, Miss Brylie. Good to see you again, though perhaps not under the best circumstances. Hello, Gwendolyn."

"Dr. Don." Aunt Gwendolyn's use of his name came out hard and sharp, surprisingly cutting for just two words.

The doctor didn't acknowledge her tone. Instead, he looked down at his tablet, scrolling and nodding before finally glancing up at me. "So, we're not feeling well today."

I bit back a retort about we versus you. Sass would not be helpful. "Right. It's the third time I've been sick like this in the last week or so."

He washed his hands at the little sink in the corner then approached, reaching under my chin to feel around my neck. "Your file says you get really hot, then sick to your stomach. What else?"

"Uh…I don't—"

"Tired," Aunt Gwendolyn said. "She gets so tired. She slept for two days the first time it really hit her."

"Yeah, I'm overtired now, in fact. I just want to go home and crawl into my bed, which isn't like me."

He grabbed my arm, holding it up and looking it over before reaching for the next one. "Any hives? Rash? Any sorts of unusual skin reactions?"

"No. Just stomach issues, feeling overheated, and the tiredness. I thought it was food poisoning, but Ander disagrees because, well, he makes most of my food."

"He would know how to safely handle food." He looked

over his screen. "What about auditory hallucinations? Sounds that you hear, but no one else does."

"My cussing," Aunt Gwendolyn said.

My brow pulled tight as I frowned.

"When we were at the restaurant with Mary Saturday. You said I cussed at the table when I didn't."

"Oh, right. Is that what you mean?"

Dr. Don nodded without looking up, tapping on his screen. "That's exactly what I mean. Most people hear slams or cries, but I think random cussing fits in the category."

"Guess that knocks out Ander's allergy theory."

"Not at all," Dr. Don said. "Surprisingly, people with a sensitive food or environmental allergic reaction often have auditory hallucinations."

"So, Ander might be right? He thinks this is some sort of allergy, but I had an allergy test in California last time I felt like this, and they didn't find anything."

Dr. Don grunted and stepped back, taking a seat on a little rolling stool before pinning me with a very direct gaze. "Ander is a smart man. It does sound like some sort of allergic reaction to me. Your previous doctor likely did a standard allergen test, which may not have addressed your diet or environment."

"So, what do I do?"

"First, you get me a copy of that allergy test. I want to see exactly what they tested you for so we don't waste your time. Then, I want to chat with Ander—if you're okay with it— about your diet, so I can try to pinpoint more specific allergens to test. Once we have all of that, I'd like to run another allergy test on you." He rolled back, grabbing his tablet and typing out notes. "I can send you to a specialist if you like, but the closest one is almost two hours away. I'm perfectly comfortable handling the test if you're okay with my doing it."

I glanced at Aunt Gwendolyn, suddenly unsure. She nodded once. She knew Dr. Don way better than I did, so I took that as a positive sign.

"I'm okay with you doing the testing."

"Great. I saw Ander out in the waiting room—mind if I call him in here so we can address your current diet?"

"Not at all."

Dr. Don left the room, presumably in search of Ander. I kept my eyes on my feet as they dangled from the chair-bed thing that seemed to be used in every doctor's office ever. It only took a minute until another knock sounded, and Dr. Don walked in with Ander on his heels. My chef caught my eye, looking concerned but visibly calming once I smiled at him.

"Hey," I said, nodding toward Aunt Gwendolyn. "The family section's over there."

He huffed and smiled but headed toward the old lady. Dr. Don settled in on his rolling stool in the corner, taking up far less space than Ander. Something I couldn't help but notice.

"Okay, then," Dr. Don said as he brought his tablet to life. "I understand Brylie mostly eats your food, Ander."

"Yeah. I cook a few meals a day for her and try to keep her kitchen stocked. That's how I knew it couldn't be food poisoning. I'm cautious at both my restaurant and at home."

"I figured as much. So, any changes in her diet lately? Anything that stands out to you."

"She eats a lot of mushrooms on her burgers, and I've got a new supplier out of Thornton. I've been trying out gluten-free baked goods as dessert options to appeal to more guests, and Brylie's been having some of those."

"They're delicious." I shrugged, unable not to. "They really are."

Ander smiled. "Thanks. Uh, so the rest—nothing that I

can think of. No excessive use of the big eight allergens, no major changes. Like I said, mushrooms, baked goods, and—oh." He snapped his fingers and looked right at me. "You've been drinking a lot of tea lately."

"That's my fault," Aunt Gwendolyn said, suddenly looking guilty. "I like tea and have gotten Brylie into it. It's mostly herbal—dried flowers and herbs—and maybe some green tea added in to give us a little caffeine in the afternoon."

Dr. Don nodded. "So mushrooms, which could be bothering her, depending on growing methods. Tea, which could have been affected by pesticides or fungus during the growing of the plants. And gluten-free bakery items. Those tend to have a number of ingredients added that we don't usually eat in an American diet to mimic flour. All three are possibilities for what's making her sick." He set his tablet down and gave me a smile. "So here's my suggestion—get your medical records to me right away. I'll order the supplies I need for the allergy test once I see what has already been tested. Meanwhile, how about we cut out the baked goods and any tea that isn't commercially prepared. Just in case. The mushrooms—"

"I'll get an order in of the ones I used to buy, just for her. And I'll cancel my gluten-free bakery orders so we don't risk anything."

Dr. Don nodded at Ander. "Perfect. Don't worry, Brylie. We'll get this figured out for you."

"I hope so."

We left soon after, Aunt Gwendolyn carrying the notes for the appointment and Ander holding my hand as we walked toward the parking lot. My steps were slow, my gait what could only be called trudging. Every inch of me ached, my limbs heavy and uncoordinated. Tired from the experience and almost defeated, even though there was hope on the horizon. I needed a nap.

"Let's stop at the shops," Ander said once we reached his truck. "I want to make you some chicken soup when we get you home, and I need to grab a few things from the restaurant."

"Perfect," Aunt Gwendolyn said as she slipped into the back seat with Ander's help. "I have a few boxed teas at the hardware store. We'll bring some home so you always have safe tea around."

I knew their care and support was something to be thankful for, but I just wanted to go home.

Ander manhandled me into the truck, waiting for me to buckle my seat belt before closing the door behind me. He jogged around the front then slipped into the driver's seat just as I slouched against the window and closed my eyes. Unable to hold my head up anymore.

"That's all fine," I said. "But I'm really tired. Can we make it a quick stop?"

Aunt Gwendolyn leaned forward and patted my shoulder. "Of course, dear. It will only take me a moment to run inside, and then I can help Ander grab his things"

"I also should only need a minute or two," Ander said as he started the truck. "You won't even have to get out of the truck, Brylie."

Which sounded perfect to me. But fate, as usual, didn't like to be tested. We rolled up into the alley behind the building that housed both businesses, and Ander hissed a curse. I glanced at him then followed his gaze to the wall outside my store. Right next to the large roll-up door we opened to receive freight was a blob. No other way to describe it—a bright-red blob as if someone had grabbed a can of spray paint and released it all on that one spot. The red dripped all the way to the ground, even painting the concrete.

"It looks like blood," Aunt Gwendolyn said, opening her door and slipping out as soon as Ander had the truck in park.

"Too bright. That's paint." Ander hurried around to my side just as I opened the door, offering his hand to help me out. "You sure you want to deal with this now?"

"I should at least take a look."

And look, I did. But even up close, it was just a blob of color on an otherwise nondescript wall.

"Why on earth would someone just...unleash paint like this?" I touched the wall, purposely finding the thickest drip of paint to touch. "This is dry. It's been here for hours at least."

"Where do you think they got the paint?" Aunt Gwendolyn asked.

Ander grabbed my key and unlocked the door to the store. "Probably from right in here."

"No one's bought spray paint lately," I said, following him inside.

"But the deputy found this door unlocked, remember?"

I did. I remembered, and suddenly I lamented the fact that I hadn't been feeling well enough to keep an appropriate eye on my business. I hurried to the paint department, turning into the aisle with the spray paint and looking over the display.

"Okay, they used a bright red, which could be one of many." I bounced around the racking, checking each row, each color, counting cans. "Paint comes six in a box, and I had to order all new when I opened. I've maybe sold ten cans total, mostly green and orange. I've got three colors I don't remember selling that are down to two cans. Red, blue, and yellow."

"Someone took just enough so you wouldn't notice at first. That's sort of brilliant," Ander said.

I huffed. "And irritating."

"Yeah."

"So I should just expect two more blobs—yellow and blue?"

"Primary colors," Aunt Gwendolyn said. "Perhaps the thief is a teacher of little ones."

I blinked, staring at her. "You think a preschool teacher stole my paint then blobbed me?"

She shrugged. "I've heard of stranger things, Brylie dear."

"Of course you have." I rubbed my forehead, suddenly too tired to think. "There's nothing I can do now. I'll talk to Deputy Carmichael next time I see him and let him know about the vandalism. I'll have to clean it up later this week."

"I'll help," Ander said. "Miss Gwen, how about you grab that tea? Then you two can take a rest in the truck while I get the stuff for dinner."

"Of course." Aunt Gwendolyn hurried off, returning in what seemed like less than a minute with two boxes of tea in her hands. She followed as Ander led me outside, making sure the door was locked and secure before trailing behind us on the way to the truck. Ander got us settled then ran into the restaurant, coming out carrying a large pot filled with what looked like vegetables and supplies just a few minutes later. In no time, we were back on the road, Ander driving us to the manor as I rested my head against the window.

The next thing I knew, the rumble of the engine cut off and Ander picked me up, carrying me inside. I tried to speak, to find the words to tell him I could walk, but I had no energy left. I instead cuddled into his chest and let him play the hero to my damsel in distress just this once.

Ander settled me on the couch in the family room, even covering me with a blanket I kept over the back, before moving into the kitchen. Elmer jumped up with me, adding weight and warmth to my fabric cocoon. I could hear the low murmur of Ander and Aunt Gwendolyn chatting but couldn't understand the words. The house warmed as they moved around, though. The feminine energy wrapping itself around me tighter than the blanket was. I wanted to care about the store, to try to figure out who would have vandalized it. Who would have found it necessary over the past week to come for both my business and Ander's. I wanted to care, but exhaustion sat heavy on my shoulders and demanded I let my brain be quiet. There would be no discussions, no thought or plan. There would only be rest.

Chapter Twelve

Tuesday meant getting back to work, which was quite the feat, considering I still felt a bit under the weather. No bother, though. I drank my tea—boxed, commercially made instead of the dirty leaf water Aunt Gwendolyn had been making me—ate a light breakfast of tomatoes and toast and headed out bright and early. Leaf bags and rakes. Helping the town clean up the remnants of the fall leaf drop needed to be my focus.

I also had to call my old doctor to get my records sent to Dr. Don. I wasn't looking forward to it because dealing with healthcare stuff had never been my favorite, but the idea of a new allergy test almost excited me. Or maybe the word I should have used was relieved. It relieved me because no one thought I was being poisoned, a concern I had refused to entertain but that had been sneaking around through my brain. An allergy was making me sick. I could deal with an allergy.

Being poisoned would have been so much worse.

Aunt Gwendolyn had hitched a ride into town with me, so it wasn't a surprise when she came strolling into the store from the stockroom. What was a surprise was the way she frowned after eyeing my chest.

"What?" I glanced down, suddenly uncomfortable. "Did I spill on myself?"

"Where are your stones?"

It took me several seconds to put what stones and my chest had to do with one another. "Oh, those. Right. I must have left them at home."

She sighed and pulled out a little baggie from inside her purse. "Good thing I brought extra. Tuck these in your bra. Right now. You need extra protection."

How rocks in my bra were going to protect me, I still didn't know, but I was not about to argue with her about it. I tucked the stones into the fabric, doing my best to tuck them under or along the chest strap to make them as invisible as possible to customers. Someone needed to patent a bra with pockets for our rocks. I bet they would make a fortune.

"There," I finally said once I had the stones in comfortable positions. "Happy now?"

"Not in the slightest. I realize you don't understand the magic of crystals and why these are so important to your health, but I need you to take this seriously. I'm trying to help you."

I had not paid for a guilt trip, but I'd definitely just been taken on one. I sighed and gave my aunt a hug, whispering, "I know. It seems weird to me, but I'm sure I'll understand better once we have the time for you to teach me about it."

"Soon enough." She patted my back and pulled away. "Incoming. I have no energy for this today."

I didn't even have time to turn around before the bell over the front door chimed, and in walked Deputy Carmichael. Aunt Gwendolyn took off, slipping into a plumbing aisle before heading for the back of the store. Abandoning me to deal with the deputy alone.

The deputy, who had obviously spotted me. His face twisted from a sneer to a smile as he hurried my way, his reflective sunglasses blocking my view of his eyes.

"Miss Brylie. I hope everything is going okay this morning." He stepped a bit into my personal space, looking down at me with a smile that didn't fit his face. "I heard you've been sick. Feeling better?"

Ah, yes. Small-town life, where everyone knows your business. Someone likely saw me at the doctor's office, which meant the entire town knew I'd been sick. So annoying.

"I'm good, thanks. What can I help you with today? Need a rake for all the leaves that seem to never stop falling?"

He huffed as if that was somehow funny. "No thanks. I have a landscaper I pay to keep my yard clean. Never have time, what with working so many hours for the sheriff's department."

My wrist itched. Not like a small "maybe it's a loose hair that has traveled down my arm" sort of itch, but a "there is something huge crawling over my skin" type. The man was lying, though about what, I had no idea. Why would having a landscaper deserve a lie?

"Well, if your landscaper needs any supplies, you send him my way."

"I will. Now, really, I heard you were sick. Is everything okay?"

"Oh sure, yeah. I'm fine. Just seem to have some sort of food allergy."

"Have you had allergies before?"

"No, but apparently they can pop up out of nowhere." I strolled away from the plumbing department in case Aunt

Gwendolyn happened to be lurking—she obviously hadn't wanted to deal with the deputy—which led us toward the paint department. "Oh, hey. I noticed someone has stolen some of my spray paint. I'm going to apologize in advance should anyone be dumb enough to start vandalizing the town."

"Stolen spray paint? Is that what happened out back—someone tagged your building?"

So he'd seen the blob. Likely why he'd just happened to pop in. "That's my assumption. We'll get that cleaned up as soon as we can, and like I said, I'm sorry if anyone does more damage. They must have taken it that day you found our back door unlocked."

"Not your fault. You can't stop all the criminals. I'll file a report and look into the problem for you."

My wrist itched again, even more this time. A sensation of a swarm of baby insects crawling down my arm instead of one big one, which was both no worse and yet far worse at the same time.

Before I could distract myself from the sensation—and visual—of bugs crawling all over me, the deputy sighed and took a step toward the door.

"I should really get back to work. These streets aren't going to patrol themselves."

So darn itchy. "Working hard or hardly working?"

He laughed and wagged a finger at me as if I were a child. "Don't go telling the sheriff on me now. I might have to stop coming in here if you do."

A girl could dream, not that I was about to say that part out loud. "Trust me—I avoid the sheriff at all costs."

"That's not what I heard."

I followed his retreat, confusion boiling up inside me with every step. "What are you talking about?"

He shrugged, still heading for the door. "I heard you and the sheriff worked together to solve your break-in case."

I froze in place, unable to move. Unable to speak for a good ten seconds. The deputy eventually must have realized I no longer followed him because he stopped and turned to face me, looking confused.

"Brylie?"

"Who told you that?"

"The sheriff did."

I huffed, wanting to throw something through my own windows all of a sudden. Remembering how I'd asked for help and been brushed off. How the sheriff had claimed there couldn't be a break-in happening at the manor. How only Ander and Aunt Gwendolyn had been there to help me through that terrifying and rage-inducing event. The sheriff hadn't worked with me—if anything, he'd worked against me.

I hadn't been so angry in months. "Don't believe everything you hear, especially from that man."

Deputy Carmichael stared through his mirrored lenses as if my words didn't make sense, but he was at least smart enough not to challenge me on it. "I'll take that under advisement, Miss Brylie."

With that, he walked out of the store, leaving me beyond mad. Whatever the sheriff might have been, an aid during one of the scariest moments of my life was not it. I huffed and grumbled through the morning, finally calling it quits around lunchtime. I'd had no customers and couldn't get my mood under control. I'd also broken four boxes of lightbulbs and knocked over a display of canned air. It was time to go home.

Aunt Gwendolyn rode with me, sitting silently in the passenger seat as if doing her best to avoid interacting with me. I couldn't blame her. Elmer slept in the back, oblivious.

Once home, I headed straight for the kitchen, but being there didn't calm my rage. Didn't soothe me the way I needed it to. The tick of the clock over the pantry sounded too loud, and the hum of the refrigerator downright grated on my last nerve. I couldn't deal with all the noise. And the heat! It had to be ninety-five degrees in that space. Too hot to move and yet I couldn't hold still. I paced and grumbled and stewed in my anger until a crash sounded from behind me.

I spun and looked, not seeing anything out of place through the opening to the conservatory but knowing the noise had come from in there. Had Aunt Gwendolyn gotten past me somehow? I'd assumed she'd gone upstairs as she'd disappeared the second we'd arrived, but maybe... No, not maybe. No way. I wiped the sweat from my brow and tiptoed into the conservatory, looking around for intruders. Finding it empty. Empty and cool and so very calming in its silence. A small pot that had sat on the workbench lay tipped over on the floor, a little dirt spread around it.

"So you're the culprit. How'd you fall, little one?" I picked up the pot and resettled the little green life inside it. I had no idea what Aunt Gwendolyn had planted, but it looked cute and needed help. That would be my job.

I spent about an hour in the conservatory, sitting on the floor with a few plants around me. Just taking the time to settle my nerves and release my anger. Letting the humidity and lack of noise soothe me. The conservatory wasn't silent—the wind outside caressed the windows on a regular basis, and the old wooden trim around them creaked slightly when it did—but the small sounds of life didn't irritate me. They relaxed me. The air also grew cooler out there, the heat dissipating and leaving me feeling refreshed and comfortable. I had obviously needed to be in the little growing space.

Aunt Gwendolyn peeked her head in at some point, giving me a smile. "All calmed down now?"

"How did you know?"

She walked in, her skirts blowing around her. "The house finally cooled off. I figured your anger had to have burned itself out."

"The house was hot...because of me?"

Aunt Gwendolyn nodded, taking a seat beside me and grabbing a pot with a large fern-like plant in it to fiddle with. "Of course, dear. She reflects your emotions. It took me a bit to zero in on the slight rise in temperature, but now that I've figured it out, I can sense it too. This old house used to do the same thing to Rose."

Oh, my heart. All the times I had sat in the kitchen and felt the room burning. All the times I had gotten irrationally angry about something Ander had done or the noise around me. All the times I had made the house mad with my own anger. And the old girl had done the same for Aunt Gwendolyn's love.

What a memory to have to relive.

"I'm sorry," I said, stretching to grab her hands. "I didn't mean to get so mad that the house...did that."

She gave me a watery smile and squeezed my fingers. "It was honestly a nice reminder of the love we always felt in these walls. I hope you get to experience the same."

"I already do." I smiled at her surprised expression then nodded toward the plant she held. "Come on, old lady. Let's work on your little apothecary here."

So we did. We started with the fern-like plant—cleaning up dead leaves and adding some soil amendments before watering her—then moving to some of the smaller plants on the workbench, like the one that had fallen.

We had just cleaned off the cabinet to give it a good

washing when my phone rang. I pulled it from my pocket, smiling once I saw it was Ander calling.

I answered with a quiet, "Hey."

"You need to get back to town. There's been more vandalism at the store. It's bad."

Smile, gone. Calm, shattered.

I'd never driven so fast. Aunt Gwendolyn sat in the back this time, Elmer riding shotgun as I sped down the highway to downtown Reverie Springs. Everything looked okay at first—tall trees, brick storefronts, a few too many cars and people, but nothing out of order. At least not until I turned to park, and the "out of order" hit us square in the face.

"Oh, his window."

I turned my head at Aunt Gwendolyn's statement, tearing my eyes away from the hardware store. Ander's front window was gone. Just...gone. Broken, I had to assume. The man himself stood on the sidewalk, talking to the sheriff and looking livid. I could understand that, but it wasn't just the window that had been damaged. My store had taken a hit as well. But my damage had been done with spray paint.

"I don't want you to worry about a thing, Aunt Gwendolyn."

She gave me a funny look as we stepped out of the car. "Why would I worry?"

She hasn't seen it yet. I nodded toward the hardware store, biting my lip and waiting. Knowing she wouldn't be too happy. In bright-blue letters that had to be five feet tall and covering my front window, the word WITCH had been painted in capital letters. We stood and stared at it for a long moment, a swirl of rage building over my normally calm great-aunt. Finally, she huffed.

"That T is slanted. Someone needs to work on their

penmanship." And with that, she snapped for Elmer, and the two walked across the street, heading straight for Ander and the sheriff. I stood and stared for a long moment, knowing the woman was far more hurt than her little statement had given me access to. Knowing this sort of hate had likely been a part of her life for a very long time, just not so open and loud.

Whoever had done this had just screamed her personal business to the city. Mine, too.

I crossed the street and met up with Ander and Aunt Gwendolyn as the sheriff walked off. He never even turned to look at me, never gave me any sort of indication that he knew I had arrived, even though my building had also taken a hit. Irritating but expected. Ander, though, caught my eye the second my feet hit the sidewalk, looking furious.

"The useless sheriff isn't going to do anything to help us figure out who did this. I can already tell."

I hurried the rest of the way to him and wrapped my arms around his waist, pulling Aunt Gwendolyn in as well. The three of us forming a unit. A team without the support we needed to stop being harassed.

Just like when the manor had been broken in to.

"We'll have to figure out who's doing all this. Figure it out and make sure they pay for it."

Ander kissed the top of my head then stepped back, running a hand through his messy hair. "I just can't believe it. How did someone have this much time? The paint on your window would have taken a bit, and this crash had to have sounded like an explosion. How did no one see anything?"

I rubbed his arm, catching the eyes of my heartbroken aunt. How, indeed.

"Ready to do some more sleuthing?" I asked, looking

pointedly at Aunt Gwendolyn. She'd been a huge help last time
—looked like we would need her again.

The woman's expression shifted from sad to determined.
She reached into her purse and pulled out a notebook, pen in
hand. "I've got the book. Let's figure out some suspects."

Chapter Thirteen

The lights from the sheriff vehicles lit up Main Street, bouncing off the brick buildings and giving an almost eerie glow to the sidewalk. The shadows from the trees appeared darker than usual, more ominous and threatening, with their branch claws hovering overhead as they waited for the chance to attack an unsuspecting victim. As if those strips of shade made by the branches would somehow come to life and snatch you right off the ground if you walked through them. As if they were scratching at the building fronts, just waiting to creep inside. The broken window on the restaurant sure did give them an entrance.

Ander paced along the front of his business, looking furious and ready to attack. Or ready to defend. I stood just outside of the light, fading into the shadows closest to my store with Aunt Gwendolyn beside me. We'd locked Elmer in the van to sleep since the poor beast could barely hold his head up. He wasn't built for late nights or commotion. Neither was I, to be honest, but between the damage done to the two businesses and the way Ander looked about ready to explode, I needed to be here.

"This won't go well," Aunt Gwendolyn said out of the blue. I turned to look at her then followed her gaze, spotting the sheriff as he approached a very harried-looking Ander. Yeah, this wouldn't go well at all if the sheriff behaved in his usual fashion. Time to act.

"I've got him." I swept across the concrete, rushing without running to get to Ander's side. Crossing the hole where the restaurant's window had been just a few hours before. Someone had thrown something through the glass. My window had been vandalized as well, but only with paint. I could fix that on my own—cleaner, elbow grease, and a solid power washing to the building would likely do the trick. But Ander's restaurant? That wasn't getting fixed quickly or without significant cost. And irritation if the sheriff's interest was piqued.

"You've got a mess here, Ander," the sheriff said just as I reached the man in question. Without thought, I grabbed Ander's hand and squeezed it, letting him know I was there. That I would stand with him through this. He squeezed me back just as strong but never turned to look at me, keeping his focus on the sheriff.

"I would call this more than just a mess."

The sheriff nodded and pulled a notebook from his pocket, tugging a pen from the coil at the top and flipping it open to what I had to assume was a blank page. "So, give me the story again. Where were you when this happened?"

Ander sighed, squeezing my hand once more. "As I said, I was inside the restaurant cleaning up for the night when I heard the crash. There was nothing that I noticed before that— no sound of people talking, no disturbance—and no, I did not have my radio blaring. The vent fan was on, so that could disguise some noises. But otherwise, the restaurant was quiet."

"You work without music? And why are you here so late? This isn't your normal schedule."

"I was finishing up. I was already done for the night and turned off the radio because I had planned to leave on time, but I noticed some mushrooms I had meant to sauté. I wanted to finish those before I left for the night. Once I had them done, I started to clean up what little mess I'd made, so yeah—the radio had already been off, and I was running late getting out of here. That's when the person threw that chair through the window."

Mushrooms. Likely for me. He had been in the restaurant when the perpetrator threw something through the window because of me. He could have been hurt. I gripped his hand harder.

The sheriff just nodded and kept writing notes. "And you didn't see anyone when you came out from the kitchen?"

"No one. Not a car or a pedestrian. I even ran outside to look up and down the street, which is when I noticed the vandalism at the hardware store."

That earned a grunt from the sheriff, though he didn't bother looking in my direction. "You got insurance on this place?"

"Yeah." Ander sighed, his expression growing tighter. More stressed. "I'll have to call my agent in the morning to see how to handle this since I technically rent from myself."

That caught the sheriff's attention. "How's that?"

"It's the way my businesses are set up. One business owns the building and rents it to the restaurant, which is a separate entity. It keeps my financials a little clearer and protects me should one or the other ever be involved in litigation."

The sheriff didn't seem convinced of...whatever he needed to be convinced of. "This is the third incident of vandalism to your restaurant this month."

He didn't ask a question, just left that statement hanging. I frowned, thinking it over. The window was number three. There had also been the damaged chair—someone had intentionally broken his wrought-iron chair. But the third, I couldn't place. What had...

"Bees," Aunt Gwendolyn whispered as she walked up behind me. "Window, chair, and bees."

I swear, that woman could read my mind. And she was right—window, chair, and bees. Which meant this was also my third time dealing with vandalism—window, blob, bees. Fourth if you counted the heart someone had drawn by the door. And I'd had paint stolen, so maybe five events for me. That was a lot. Too many.

Ander hadn't moved or spoken. The sheriff finally looked up and frowned.

"You got anything to say to that?"

"What...the number three? Yeah, you counted right for me. This is the third event at my place in the last few weeks."

"Seems to be a pattern."

"I agree."

"Any idea why you're being targeted?"

"Not a one."

"Got any enemies?"

Ander laughed, pulling his hand from mine to run it through his hair. "Only my sister, but this isn't her style."

I stared up at him, the mention of his sister catching my attention. He rarely talked about the woman, but I knew he had a difficult relationship with her. If any. His calling her an enemy was new.

The sheriff looked up from his notebook. "Any chance she—"

"She lives in Tennessee, and, like I said, this isn't her style. It's not possible."

"Okay," the sheriff said with a sigh. He closed his notebook and pocketed it before looking over the front of the restaurant once more. "So then we look local. Though it could have been someone driving through town."

I couldn't hold my tongue for that one. "Three times for him and at least that many for me in just a few weeks? I doubt the driving-through-town scenario."

The sheriff finally gifted me with his attention, looking me up and down with an ever-deepening frown. The energy of his suspicion hitting me square in the solar plexus. "You do seem to attract trouble, Miss Scott."

Hot. My entire body grew almost unbearably hot. I took a step forward without thought and raised my hand as if to... I didn't know. Point at him? Wag a finger in his direction? Didn't matter my intentions because Aunt Gwendolyn chose that moment to bump her body into mine and send me almost crashing into Ander.

"That should make you happy, Clarence. That trouble gives you something to do, or were you looking forward to another fall of sitting in your deer blind in your uniform instead of actually, I don't know, policing?"

The man looked ready to spit nails. "You don't... You can't... I'm Sheriff when I'm working!"

"Then do some work, Clarence." Aunt Gwendolyn stressed the man's given name, standing tall in his shadow and not allowing him to intimidate her. The sheriff did not look happy, and he kept his ire directed at Aunt Gwendolyn. He also kept his words to himself. Likely didn't want to be hexed again. The woman had a bit of a reputation for spraying stinky stuff at people she didn't like—best to stay on her good side.

"Fine," the sheriff eventually said, closing his little notebook with a snap and tucking it away once more. "But we'll be talking about your lack of respect for the law, Gwendolyn."

Aunt Gwendolyn chuckled. "I don't have a lack of respect for the law. I have a lack of respect for lazy law enforcement officers."

"Okay, then." Ander huffed a laugh, patting me on the back and coughing in what seemed to be an attempt to hide his initial response even as he moved to separate the two. "Let me know if you need anything else, Sheriff. For now, I'd like to get this building secured."

It took the sheriff a good five seconds to stop staring at Aunt Gwendolyn, to pull back his anger and embarrassment enough to turn away from her. Finally, he gave Ander a brisk head nod and said, "I'll be in touch."

With that, he walked away, returning to his vehicle and turning off the lights that had kept the restaurant glowing. The building went dark, the sidewalk plunging into deeper shadows that hid all aspects of the crime that had occurred. The sheriff had left us to deal with the mess completely on our own. Shadows that ebbed and flowed in the night breeze and whispered as the drying leaves met one another while they danced on the air. Shadows that cut us off from the rest of the townspeople, that left us alone and almost hidden. That isolated us. I couldn't say the sheriff's behavior surprised me, but it did annoy. If that man would just do his job...

"You shouldn't have egged him on, Miss Gwen," Ander said, his face hidden from me in the dark but his voice calm and not at all angry. "He's just going to make things worse."

"Perhaps. But I couldn't stand to see him disrespect you and Brylie that way. The man grates on my last nerve when he acts all holier-than-thou just because someone was dumb enough to give him a badge."

Ander coughed another laugh. "Miss Gwen—"

"I know, I know. Be nice. Blah, blah, blah. I'm going to check on Elmer. Maybe he can help me figure out how to ignore that old coot." Aunt Gwendolyn patted my arm and headed across the street to the van. Leaving Ander and me alone in the dark. The energy around us settled into something warm and comfortable but with an edge. A residual anger—not at each other, but at the situation we found ourselves in.

I grabbed Ander's hand and leaned against his side, staring into the darkness before me. "This isn't random acts of vandalism, is it?"

"Nope."

"We need to figure out who's doing this because the sheriff isn't going to help us."

"Yup."

I smacked his arm, sighing as he chuckled under his breath. "You're going to have to give me more than one-word answers at some point."

Ander tugged me closer and kissed the top of my head before turning us toward my building. Both of us relaxing into the hold of the other, enjoying the quiet moment of the two of us connecting even if we weren't really alone and it was under some pretty yucky circumstances.

Finally, he gave me more than a single word.

"Witch Hardware. I sort of like the sound of that."

I laughed—couldn't help it. "In Reverie Springs? Wouldn't that get a bunch of people up in arms? It would be worse than Elmer going leashless."

"I think the locals are pretty used to Miss Gwen at this point."

Perhaps. Though, that spray paint said otherwise. They hadn't painted WITCH on the store as a way of celebrating the witchcraft in our family; they'd done it as a warning to others. They had used the word as an accusation. As an insult or a warning. They had used it as if it was something to be feared. And I wasn't about to tolerate that.

"Come on," I said, tugging Ander toward the store. "Let's find some supplies and board up your window. We can deal with suspects and motives in the morning."

Chapter Fourteen

The next morning, we met at the restaurant. Ander had closed it for the day to give himself time to deal with insurance and cleanup, but he'd brought Mary in to help him and cooked breakfast for us.

"This really is too much," I said as he settled us at a large, round table in the back.

"I needed to work." Ander hurried off, coming back with a plate of bacon and biscuits to go with the already-filled platters of eggs and sausages. What looked like an entire loaf of bread sat on the table as well, toasted to perfection. He had worked, all right.

Mary gave me a subtle smile as she poured the coffee for us. "Miss Gwen, would you like coffee or tea?"

"Coffee, dear. I feel like I'm going to need it."

I couldn't help but stare as she picked up the mug Mary handed her and took a sip. "That's something I don't see often."

She winked at me. "You also don't see Ander's beautiful restaurant closed and boarded up as if it went through some sort of storm. But here we are." She took a sip, looking down into the mug as she pulled it away from her lips, frowning. "By the end of this conversation, there may be Bailey's in here *with* the coffee."

Ander dropped a hand on her shoulder as he finally returned to the table and moved to sit beside her. "I can make that happen, Miss Gwen. Just give me a sign."

I sipped my coffee and kept my eyes on Ander as the other women made themselves plates and settled in to eat. He looked absolutely wrecked—far beyond exhausted, well past angry. The man looked as if this vandalism had thrown his entire world into chaos and he didn't know how to quiet it down. He didn't eat, didn't reach for coffee or tea or anything. He simply sat in silence and stewed. My grumpy chef had departed, leaving me with a man shattered and filled with rage. My heart broke for him.

I rose to my feet—doing my best not to affect a snoring Elmer—and made my way to Ander's side of the table, my steps short and slow, my intentions clear in the way I stared at him. He held my gaze, that stormy energy brewing between us, offering me a small smile when I approached his seat. He even offered me his hand once I made it to his side, ever the gentleman. I grabbed his, squeezing his fingers with mine, and moved to settle onto his lap. Wrapping myself around him and giving him my warmth in an attempt to calm the storm within.

He nuzzled into my neck and breathed deeply, sighing. "Thanks."

"Any time," I said as I ran a hand through his hair, the stormy energy pouring off him calming slightly. "You look worn out."

"I feel worn out, but there's just...so much to do."

"I know. But you can't run yourself into the ground." I pulled back to give him a smile. "Who would feed me?"

He laughed. Big and bold and full of life. He laughed until the other women quieted and turned our way, watching the big man lose control enough to bring smiles to their own faces. Until he almost seemed to run out of the energy to continue laughing. Until I was certain he would get through this just fine.

"Okay. No more snuggling." I patted his arm and rose to my feet, returning to my own seat. "We've got big work to do."

"Right," Ander said with a sigh as he settled deeper into his seat, our grumpy chef returned. "This has gotten out of hand."

I pulled a notebook out of my bag and grabbed a pen, ready to make notes. "So, in regard to the restaurant, we've got someone throwing things through windows, breaking metal chairs, and dumping honey all over a dumpster—"

"Which is a weird one." Mary frowned. "Was that aimed at the restaurant or the hardware store?"

"No idea, but I'll connect the two. Hardware store-specific, we've got breaking in through the back door and stealing spray paint."

"Don't forget the marker," Aunt Gwendolyn said.

My brain skipped, my memory completely failing. "Huh?"

"You said someone stole your sign marker two Sundays ago. They wrote on the window, remember?"

"Oh, right. The marker." I tapped my pen on the notebook, staring at the list of transgressions with absolutely no idea how to tie them all together. Finally, I sighed in defeat. "What on earth does all of that have to do with one another?"

Mary stretched to look at my list, sitting back with an almost embarrassed expression on her face. "Someone doesn't like how busy this corner's getting?"

"Wouldn't be unheard of for a local to get cranky about progress." Ander pushed back from the table, shifting down in his seat to almost recline so he could stare at the ceiling. "Though, why the focus on the restaurant? I've been here for years at this point. And to be honest, the hardware store had been there for even longer before Miss Rose's passing. The only quiet time was that handful of years between Rose's and Brylie's leadership. Otherwise, this corner has always had both businesses running."

"So maybe we look for suspects first and motives second." Aunt Gwendolyn pulled out her notebook. "I've begun to compile a list."

Ander looked over the list with interest. "Your list has only one person on it. The sheriff?"

"Always a possibility," I said with a nod. "Maybe Thomas Lee."

"Again?" Aunt Gwendolyn asked. "What did he do this time?"

"He was in the store alone a while back. I kept running into him, and he had time to steal the spray paint."

Aunt Gwendolyn didn't look convinced. "I'll add him, but I think that one's a stretch."

"Joan Turlington," I offered once she finished writing. "She's always angry at me, but she also got into it with Ander because he lets me bring my dog in here."

"Don't forget the deputy," Ander said. His dark eyes met mine, and he shrugged. "The man seems way too interested in you and the store. Could be for nefarious reasons."

"Nefarious?"

"I said what I said." A knock sounded on the door, and Ander hissed under his breath. "That's likely my insurance agent. I need to deal with this."

The three of us watched him cross the room and open the door. The man who walked in and shook Ander's hand stood a good six inches shorter than the chef, his dark hair, glasses, and collared shirt giving me the impression that he was exactly as expected—an insurance agent. Likely even a dad if the New Balance sneakers he wore were any indication. An insignificant sort of man. And yet, somehow, I got the worst vibe from him.

Aunt Gwendolyn's scowl seemed to match my opinion.

"What?" I asked her, keeping my voice down. "Do we not like him?"

"I don't know him, but he gives me a bad feeling."

"Who...the insurance guy?" Mary asked, following our gazes and whispering right along with us. "That's Nick Timmons. He's from Thornton. He grows mushrooms for Ander."

My heart sank. Was Nick Timmons the old mushroom guy or the new one? Because Ander had changed suppliers, then changed again because of my possible allergies. I had no idea if this man had won or lost business, but by the static he sent out into the universe when dealing with Ander, I had a feeling he had been a losing supplier.

"Is he... Did Ander stop buying from him recently?"

Mary frowned. "I think so."

Oh no.

Aunt Gwendolyn shrugged, reaching for her coffee. "He could be Santa Claus from North Pole, Maine, and grow snozberries in the snow for all I care—I still get a bad feeling about him."

She spoke the truth. The man practically reeked of bad vibes.

All three of us watched as Ander led Nick outside, presumably to look over the damage done to the building during the vandalism. Our planning moment had passed, our attention stolen, and I really needed a nap after the night before. I wasn't going to get one because I needed to work in the store, but I wanted one. And that meant my attention span was naught.

"I think it's time to close this down. We've got a decent start—we just need to pay attention and keep our ears open."

Mary grinned. "That's my job. I hear all the juicy gossip because people forget I exist and this is a public space."

"Very true." I rose to my feet and stretched. "I'm heading over to the store to get some work done. What are you two up to today?"

"I need to run over to Hilton to pick up Louise's dance shoes."

"Oh, would you mind some company? That nice candle store is on that strip, and I need a few new things. I was going to ask Brylie to take me next week—"

"I would love the company, Miss Gwen." Mary rose and held the chair as Aunt Gwendolyn followed suit. "I'm just going to clean this table up so Ander doesn't have to, then we can head out. Thanks so much for inviting me, Brylie."

"Any time. Let us know if you hear anything." I waited for her to disappear into the kitchen before moving closer to Aunt Gwendolyn. "You really don't like the insurance guy?"

"Not a lick. And you don't either."

Not a question, a statement. I shrugged, worrying my lip with my teeth for a moment. "He makes me cold. Does that make sense? Like, Mary is warm and open and pleasant. This guy is just...cold. And harsh like static, but not like lying static. Just...annoying static. Even though he smiles and stuff, he rubs me the wrong way."

"That's your intuition telling you to watch him. So, watch him."

Aunt Gwendolyn and I helped Mary clean the table and even stored some of the leftover food since Ander was busy outside before they headed out. Once she and Mary had left for the day, I snuck out the back to keep Ander from being distracted and opened the hardware store. Elmer followed along behind me as normal, his expression droopier than usual. It took me until I set a bowl full of kibble down to understand why—Ander hadn't fed him. The poor dog had been just as spoiled over the past few months as I had, but while I'd been fed well, the dog had not.

"He didn't mean to forget you, buddy. He's got a lot on his plate."

Elmer huffed, ignoring his food bowl to retreat to his bed under the counter. I was going to have to cook for the dog, it seemed.

The day ended up being relatively quiet—a few small sales and an order for a generator that made my week—so I spent most of my time cleaning, straightening, and ordering product. At least until Ander's least favorite customer came strolling inside not long before close.

"Miss Brylie. So good to see you." Deputy Carmichael and his mirrored glasses headed my way, shooting me a smile as he moseyed down the main aisle toward where I had been setting twinkle lights on an endcap. "Christmas decorations already?"

"I like to get them out early since people may want to use this nice weather to get their outside decorating done." I took a deep breath, bracing myself to deal with the man before turning his way and pasting a smile on my face. "How can I help you today, Deputy?"

"Just happened to be in town, wanted to see how you're doing after last night."

My wrist itched, a definite sign of a lie, though about what, I had no idea. What a bad way to start off a conversation.

"I'm fine," I said, growing more uncomfortable by the second. "More worried about Ander and the restaurant than a little paint on my window."

He huffed. "Seems like more than just a little paint."

Because of the word it spelled, if I had to guess. Because of the calling out of my family's history. I may not have known about our witchy roots for long, but I wasn't going to deny them. Perhaps the rocks in my bra fed my sense of right and wrong in that moment, but my composure snapped. I didn't have the time, the energy, or the patience to deal with someone else's ignorance.

"Still doesn't matter. Call me a witch all you want—someone wants to come here and try to burn *me* at the stake? They'd better be prepared because I'm not going to sit back and let them decide my fate. I've got more chemicals in this store than I know what to do with, so they'd better mind their own business before they're the ones who burn."

The man had the audacity to smirk. "You're not scared at all, are you?"

I set the last box of lights on the shelf and turned, pulling a box cutter from my pocket to break down the box the lights had come in. "Not even a little bit."

I sliced open the box, keeping my eyes on those mirrored lenses. Practically ripping that box in two as he watched. His energy shifted, his confidence wavering.

"Good. That's good." He looked past me toward the back of the store, straightening his stance and shifting his energy to something deeper, darker. Meaner. "Just be careful.

Wouldn't want to see your business accused of insurance fraud."

That took me completely by surprise and threw my own confidence out the window. "What are you talking about? I'm not filing an insurance claim."

"No, but your neighbor is."

Before I could question that statement and why Ander filing a valid insurance claim could be seen as fraud, Heather Turlington—of the leash-law-loving Turlingtons—walked into the store carrying a small basket and looking at me as if someone had died.

"Oh, Brylie. I was hoping you'd be here. Good afternoon, Deputy." She nodded at Deputy Carmichael before pushing the basket at me. "Here. I made you some cookies. I heard about the damage, but I couldn't believe it until I saw it. It's so bad."

Except it wasn't, so her concern seemed misplaced. "I... Yeah, it's really not that bad."

"Oh, but it is. It so is." She finally managed to shove the basket into my hands. Each individually wrapped cookie practically gleaming in the paper straw. "Like I said, I brought cookies. I had planned to drop them off to Ander at the restaurant, but he isn't there, so I figured you're the next best thing." Her face fell, likely her wording hitting her. "Oh, not like that. I just meant I had hoped he would share them with you, so giving them to you is as good as giving them to him. I'm so sorry. And Deputy Carmichael, I would have brought you some since you missed cl—"

"It's no problem, Heather. I know where to find you if I need a treat."

The tone he used filled me with a sense of cringe, but I couldn't focus on that. Instead, my thoughts had gotten caught up in the fact that she'd said Ander wasn't at the restaurant. Where the man could have gone, I had no idea—I'd assumed he'd be next door all day, dealing with cleanup. Though I guess he didn't have to tell me if he needed to be elsewhere. I wasn't his keeper, and yet it seemed odd that he would have left without checking in on us. Just as it was odd he hadn't cooked breakfast for Elmer.

Ugh, selfishness did not make me feel good. "They look amazing," I said, trying hard to stay focused on the two people in my store. "Was there anything else you needed before I shut down for the night? I don't have anything as tempting as cookies, but I can definitely offer you some leaf bags for the road."

"Oh no," Heather said with a laugh. "I'm good. Thomas is handling all that for me this year. I should get going, though. I didn't mean to keep you here late."

"Can I walk you out?" Deputy Carmichael asked, looking right at Heather. "I was going to head out anyway."

"Oh, sure." Heather gave me a weak smile. "Enjoy the cookies, and again—so sorry for my wording. It's been a long day."

I nodded. "For all of us."

"Yeah. I bet." She turned and headed for the door with the deputy following behind her. He didn't say goodbye—not that I needed him to—and she didn't turn around. The entire interaction had felt oddly off, as did the fact that Ander had left without letting me know.

"C'mon, Elmer," I said as I passed the checkout on my way to lock the door. "Let's get home so I can cook you dinner."

Chapter Fifteen

T hree days. Three days passed as time was wont to do. I worked, Elmer snored, Aunt Gwendolyn hovered, while checking my bra for rocks, and the town went about its business. Everything totally normal, and yet I had never felt so lost and out of sorts.

"Brylie, dear," Aunt Gwendolyn called from inside the store.

I leaned to look in the front door. "I'm out front."

The woman appeared from within the shadows, bursting through in a deep red muumuu with a gold and orange pattern throughout. The fabric looked shiny and soft—like a silk or maybe a thin satin—and the entire outfit screamed color. The only sign of her mourning clothes was a dark gray scarf tying up her hair.

"You look lovely today," I said, giving her a smile. "What's the occasion?"

"Red is the color of my enemy's blood and imbues me with power." Her smile turned downright threatening. "It's brewing day."

I stood frozen for a long moment, trying to make sense of her words. I knew what they meant, but I had not been prepared, I had not readied myself for another brewing day. I doubted the town was ready.

"Brewing day?" I thought over my financials, my heart thumping hard at the thought of all the time off I'd taken recently and how slow sales had been. "Like...hexing brew? Today? Here?"

She laughed. "Oh no, dear. I'll go back to the manor and brew out there. Unless you need me to stick—"

"Nope." I waved my hands and shook my head, knowing I was making a fool of myself but unable not to. "You can brew out there. I'm all good here."

The sly smile she shot me told me she knew why I wanted her at the manor, but she didn't push it. Instead, she looked up and down the front of the building.

"You've done a great job on this. I can't even see where they painted 'witch.'"

I followed her gaze along the front of the building, nodding my agreement as my panic level at being subjected to her hexing brew stench dissipated. "Luckily, they only painted on the windows. If it had been the brick, this would have taken me so much longer."

"And how's Ander doing with the repairs at his restaurant?"

My stomach sank, that lost feeling growing within me. "I don't know—I haven't talked to or seen him since Wednesday."

Aunt Gwendolyn froze, staring at me with an odd, almost confused expression on her face. As if she couldn't understand the words I had just strung together. I didn't understand them either, so I was no help.

"I was going to make some tea," I said, hoping to kick the uncomfortable energy between us away. "Would you like some?"

"Of course," she said, her smile softening. "I'm sure he's just really busy with the restaurant."

I nodded but didn't answer her because Ander was always busy with the restaurant, but he had never disappeared on me for three days. Not for *one* day. I hadn't even received a text from him since that morning at the restaurant. Who was so busy they couldn't text a "hey, sorry—really busy"? Apparently Ander Mendoza, that was who.

"I'll handle the tea," Aunt Gwendolyn said as she disappeared into the back of the store. I stopped at the front counter, checking on Elmer. The dog had his body in his bed and his head hanging over the side, his ears lying across the floor like two black blankets of fur. And he was snoring, as expected.

"At least you're predictable."

"Who's predictable?"

I turned, a smile immediately coming to my face as Mary walked in. "Well, hi there, stranger. What brings you here today?"

"I'm in need, and the only person I could think of who might be able to help me is you."

We hugged hello, and I led her toward the back. "Come, then. Aunt Gwendolyn is making some tea. You can join us."

She blanched. "I don't want to intrude."

Aunt Gwendolyn appeared at that moment, carrying a tray with a teapot, three cups, and a plate of cookies. "You could never intrude, dear. Come—drink with us."

"Three cups," I said, eyeing the old woman with suspicion. "Did you know she was stopping by?"

Aunt Gwendolyn set the tray on the table in my storeroom. "No, but my intuition told me we needed three, so I listened. A good thing, too—tea with Mary sounds delightful."

"Oh, well, thank you." Mary took a seat as Aunt Gwendolyn handed her a cup filled almost to the rim. "This is really nice—like a fancy high tea sort of thing."

"Much less fancy than that, but a nice break for a cup of tea in the afternoon is a treat." Aunt Gwendolyn took her seat, using tongs to place two sugar cubes in her cup. "What brings you in, Mary? Looking to do a project at the house?"

"Sort of." She frowned into her cup, stirring in a sugar cube. "I think—"

"Clockwise, dear."

Mary looked up, likely surprised to have been interrupted by Aunt Gwendolyn. "I'm sorry?"

"Clockwise. Sugar attracts sweetness into your life, so you'll want to stir it clockwise. If you stir counterclockwise, you're asking the universe to banish the sweetness from your life."

"Really?" Mary looked down at her cup. "I thought it was just tea."

I huffed a laugh. "Nothing is just anything to a witch."

"Very true." Aunt Gwendolyn winked at me. "So let's do this right. Everyone stir clockwise—" she paused until Mary and I both moved our spoons in the correct direction, "—and let's take a moment to think of all the good we want to come into our lives. Health, wealth, relationships, good friends, good food...all the way down to that pretty red purse I've been eyeing for months. Whatever would make your heart happy, give it a moment of your time."

I tried to focus on higher sales or more customers, but the only thing my mind could picture was Ander. The missing chef.

"Good," Aunt Gwendolyn said. "Now, let's set those spoons down and thank the universe for her attention."

She set her spoon on her plate and lifted her cup, whispering something I couldn't quite hear before taking a sip. I met Mary's eyes and shrugged, performing the same ritual Aunt Gwendolyn had done, and saying a simple thanks before drinking. I had no idea if that was enough to welcome all the good from the universe, but I figured it was at least a start.

"Thank you, Miss Gwen," Mary said once she had taken her first sip. "That was a lovely moment. And this tea is delicious."

Aunt Gwendolyn nodded. "It's boxed, but I can't let Brylie drink my home brews just yet. She's fighting off some sort of reaction to unknown allergens."

"Right...how's that going?"

I shrugged, reaching for one of Aunt Gwendolyn's cookies. "I'm eating simply for the moment. Once I get back to the doctor for the test, hopefully we can identify what's making me so sick."

"Ugh, I'm so sorry. That can't be fun."

"It's not, but at least I have treats." I held up the cookie before taking a small bite, giving myself time to chew and swallow before continuing. "You were going to tell us why you stopped in today before we had our magic tea-stirring."

"Right." She scrunched her face for a moment, looking half mad and half scared at the same time. "I was hoping you sold one of those video doorbell things."

"Got a problem?" I took another bite of the cookie, already

knowing it wouldn't be the last of the day. I really needed to get my sweet tooth under control.

"Maybe. Someone came knocking on my door last night. Late last night."

I sat up straighter, suddenly really concerned for her and Louise. "How late?"

"After midnight. And before you ask, I don't know who it was. I was too afraid to answer the door."

"Smart woman," Aunt Gwendolyn said. "Best to stay inside."

I nodded. "Totally. That had to be terrifying."

"It was, which is why I was thinking about the doorbell."

"For the same price as just the big-brand doorbell, I can get you an entire alarm system with multiple cameras, all working off an app on your phone. I'd have to order it, though."

She looked down at her cup, fidgeting with the handle. "How long will it take?"

"I'll have it all on Tuesday. I'll even come over and help you install it."

That got her attention. Her head jerked up, her eyes meeting mine. "Really?"

"Of course. We must take care of each other."

"I'll come this afternoon," Aunt Gwendolyn said, setting her purse on the table and digging into it with gusto. "I'll set some wards for you. Or you and Louise can come stay at the manor until Brylie has your alarm working. We have the room."

"Oh yes," I said. "We do. If you feel unsafe—"

"I appreciate the offer, but I'm sure we'll be okay." She eyed Aunt Gwendolyn with something close to fear. "What are you looking for in there, Miss Gwen?"

Aunt Gwendolyn huffed but must have found her quarry

because she raised her hand, set her purse on the floor, and smiled. "Stones. Put them in your bra, dear. They'll protect you."

Mary shot me a worried glance.

I could only shrug. "There's no sense in fighting. I've got a handful in mine already."

"Okay," Mary said, reaching for the rocks Aunt Gwendolyn held out to her. "Th-thank you for these."

"It's no problem."

I hid my grin behind my teacup, knowing there was no sense in trying to argue the effectiveness of rocks in your bra with Aunt Gwendolyn. Best to just stick them in there and make her happy.

Mary's phone pinged, and a frown appeared when she tapped into whatever the message was. "Oh shoot."

"What's wrong?"

"There's a delay with the window guy." She shook her head, tapped a response, then set her phone back down. "I had been hoping this would go smoothly for Ander, what with him not wanting to open the restaurant again until the window is fixed. He's going to pay me sort of an unemployment so I don't go broke, but I would much rather be working."

Her words punched me square in the chest. Ander hadn't talked to me in days, so the fact that he wasn't opening the restaurant until the window had been repaired was news to me. It appeared to be news to Aunt Gwendolyn, too.

"That seems like a hard decision, keeping the restaurant closed. I wonder why he's choosing that path." She stared right at me, questioning. As if I knew.

Thankfully, before I had to try to explain that Ander wasn't telling me anything, the bell over the front door chimed.

"Customer. Let me go see what's happening." I hurried

from the back room, needing a little breathing space. Needing to get away from questioning eyes. I had no idea why Ander had cut me off, but he obviously had. And that hurt.

"Miss Brylie." Thomas stood on the welcome mat with his hat in his hands. "I was hoping I would find you here."

"What can I do for you today, Thomas?"

"I'm looking for a couple of things, but..." He fidgeted with his hat, looking uncomfortable and way younger than his age. "Well, I need to finish my harvest to go to the farmers market tomorrow and make some money, but I can't because I don't have the right tools. I'm running out of daylight, ma'am."

Because it was already midday. I may not have grown up around farmers, but I knew hard times. I understood trying to figure out how to gain access to the $200 tool that would bring you thousands of dollars of work when your pockets were empty. And I had learned early what being a good neighbor meant.

"You grab what you need. I'll make note of it, and you can come pay me next week. Sound good?"

His smile could have lit the entire store. "Yes, Miss Brylie. I can even drop off the money Monday morning at your house if you—"

"There's no need for that. Just pop in next week. It's fine." The room suddenly felt very warm, the heat causing my head to hurt and my stomach to turn. I needed Thomas to shop quickly. "So yeah, go ahead and grab what you need."

"I'll be right back."

I laid my head down on the checkout counter as he disappeared into the garden department, the heat and the nausea making me want to pant to try to fight it off. I just needed to write up Thomas's purchase. Once done, I could escape into the back again. I could call for Aunt Gwendolyn, I could—

I suddenly itched. Not a little, not in one spot—my entire body seemed to burst into hives in a split second. This was bad.

"Aunt Gwendolyn," I called, moving to sit on the stool behind the register. "Aunt Gwendolyn!"

The woman in question appeared at the same time as Thomas, both hurrying toward the register.

"You all right, Miss Brylie?"

I looked at Aunt Gwendolyn, something in my face obviously giving me away.

"Oh, Thomas. Let me ring that up for you."

I shook my head, fighting hard to keep my stomach contents where they belonged. "Just write it down. No payment today."

Aunt Gwendolyn nodded and reached for a pen, scribbling SKU numbers and making notes of the items as quickly as she could. Thomas kept watching me, looking concerned, but I fought hard to keep a small smile on my face. Customers didn't need to know about my health concerns.

"Thanks again, Miss Brylie," Thomas said as he finally headed toward the door. I followed behind him, knowing I needed to lock up. That I needed to shut the store down before I made a fool of myself.

"Have a good market this weekend."

But as Thomas reached the door, something caught my eye. A blue something and lots of it. The man had bright-blue paint droplets up the back of his pants at the ankle. Blue like what was used to paint the word "witch" on my window. I could barely move, could hardly breathe. All I could do was stare at that blue paint as it disappeared on the other side of the door.

"Brylie? Sweetie—"

"It's him." I fell to my knees, unable to hold myself up. "Thomas painted the window."

And then I threw up all over my welcome mat.

Chapter Sixteen

I never had been someone who lounged in bed. My dad owning a small business meant I had worked by his side from the time I grew tall enough to see over the counters to the day he died. But this sickness—this allergic reaction, if Dr. Don was correct—tended to knock me out and make me into someone who took to their bed and stayed there. Which was exactly what I'd done the second Aunt Gwendolyn and I had made it home from the store.

Twenty-four hours after crawling into it, I finally crawled out of it.

Elmer wasn't in my room, which meant Aunt Gwendolyn had to be home. I crept down the stairs, my socks slipping on the wood floors. The pictures in the hallway of Rose's ancestors looked less judgmental than usual, almost seeming to want to disappear into the wallpaper around them. Perhaps they could empathize with being ill. Or maybe I just didn't have the energy to give attention to the old paintings.

I had just reached the doorway into the kitchen when Elmer huffed a bark from within and came running, his paws clicking and his long ears flying behind him. I couldn't hold in my laugh—my dog had missed me.

"Me too, bud."

"Brylie?" Aunt Gwendolyn appeared from the conservatory, smiling my way. "Oh, you're up. How are you feeling?"

"Like someone hit me with a truck." True enough statement, considering how achy my body felt and the loud banging in my head. "What's been happening?"

"Oh, nothing. Elmer and I were just starting to think about dinner. Are you hungry?"

My answer should have been a resounding yes since I hadn't eaten anything over the past day, but instead, I shrugged. "I could eat."

Which seemed enough of an answer for Aunt Gwendolyn. She shuffled me into the kitchen and sat me at the counter before heading for the pantry closet.

"Oh, I will never get used to these metal shelves." She dug around inside for a minute before huffing in irritation. "I think we need to run to the grocery store this week."

"Probably." I laid my head on the counter.

"I've got some homemade chicken broth frozen." She held out a box of rice and one of noodles. "What's your pleasure?"

"Rice. Definitely."

"Then we're having chicken and rice." She put the pasta away and closed the door before walking to the refrigerator. "Have you heard from Dr. Don about your allergy test?"

"Not yet. I'll have to call him tomorrow."

"Let's make sure we do that, okay? It would be good to know what it is that's making you so ill."

Before I could respond, Elmer barked and took off toward the front hall. I sat up, listening. Wondering what that dog had heard. Aunt Gwendolyn said nothing and didn't respond to the commotion, which led me to believe she already had an inkling.

"Expecting someone?" I asked. She didn't get a chance to answer before Ander came striding into the kitchen, looking completely frazzled and exhausted.

"Hey." He walked straight to me, wrapping me in a hug and holding me close. "I'm so sorry you're sick again. I know I haven't been around much—the stupid insurance and the restaurant and trying to deal with..." He sighed, hugging me tighter. "I'm just really sorry. Especially about you being sick."

I nodded, almost wanting to cry. Between the exhaustion scraping against my bones and still not feeling well enough to do much of anything, I had slipped to the end of my rope. But Ander made things better. He held me in place and made me feel safe and warm. How could I do anything but forgive him?

"Fine," I said, eventually pulling out of his hold. "You're forgiven...for the moment. I don't have the energy to fight anyway. Now, sit—Aunt Gwendolyn is making chicken and rice soup."

"I can help." One quick squeeze to my hand and Ander was up, rounding the counter to take over the stove. Aunt Gwendolyn laughed and swatted at him, but the man simply guided her to the counter to sit while he cooked.

"Well, at least let me make my niece a cup of tea," she said, opening a cabinet and pulling down a box of what looked like my favorite spearmint blend. "The woman needs her herbs."

"Fine, but that's it," Ander said, tugging the kettle to the front right burner so she could use it. "I'm making you ladies dinner."

The two worked together at the stove, laughing and joking with each other as I watched from the counter. They brought joy to the house, a happiness that resonated past the walls and through the halls. Willow Manor grew warmer and brighter, everything settling into a comfortable sort of glow.

At least until Ander started complaining.

"You have no onion," he said, staring into the refrigerator. "Or celery."

"We haven't had much time to grocery shop." I nodded toward Aunt Gwendolyn. "That's why we're making the soup. Aunt Gwendolyn already made the stock with all the good veggies, so we just need that and the rice."

"You can't have soup without mirepoix to start it. That's just...not cooking."

I stretched my neck, trying to extinguish the burn growing there, taking a deep breath to control the heat building within me. Or was it the house responding in anger? Because suddenly, the kitchen felt overheated and uncomfortable.

I took another deep breath. "Making food here is—"

"Impossible," Ander said with a huff. "Making real food here is impossible."

Interrupting me was impolite. Complaining about our lack of whatever food he felt was necessary to complete his perfect meal added to that sense of disregard and rudeness. But what really threw me over the edge and ignited my temper was when he slammed my refrigerator door closed. Not shut, not allowed to close. He pushed it so it slammed hard enough for the ceramic cookie jar sitting on top to rattle. That was...too much.

Aunt Gwendolyn either saw or felt my rage, because she tried to step in with a firm, "Brylie."

But I was too far gone. I slammed my fist on the counter, making Elmer bark and drawing every bit of attention from the others in the room.

"Ander Mendoza." I wiped the sweat from my brow,

breathing hard and giving in to the heat. Diving deep into the flames. "If you are going to sit here and complain about my kitchen, you can go back to your own. We don't need you here."

Aunt Gwendolyn stared at me, standing frozen in the silence that fell. Ander didn't move either. Both watched me as if I might explode, as if I was the wrong who was in the wrong. Even the house sat silent, her energy on a precipice. Everyone waiting on me to make the first move.

I chose to retreat.

"Sorry," I said as I slid off the stool. "I'm just going to..."

Before I could cry in frustration, I hurried into the conservatory. Into the space of plants and life and peace. Aunt Gwendolyn followed me.

"Brylie. Honey."

"I'm okay." I sighed and shook my head, trying hard to find my center. "Mostly."

"That certainly didn't seem okay."

I looked up at the ceiling, staring through glass at the dark sky above. My eyes adjusting and finally finding stars and planets and all manner of space light shining bright against the inky blackness. Reminding me of how small I was in terms of the universe. Of how little all the stress and the tiredness and the anger mattered. At least in the grand scheme of things. At that moment...they mattered.

"I just don't feel well," I finally said. "And I don't like it."

"Maybe you should go back to bed."

"No. I should go apologize to Ander and hope he'll forgive my cruelty."

"Oh, honey. That man will forgive much more than a random outburst. Though this sickness is getting worse. It's time to do something."

158   MILLIE THORNE

"Like what?"

"We're going to see Dr. Don tomorrow. I don't care if he's gotten all his supplies or not. This is too much for your body, so if he doesn't have the stuff, we will find out who does and get you there."

Relief washed over me, calming the fire. Cooling me down from the inside out. I wanted to cry but not in sadness or frustration. In relief. I needed someone else to help me, needed someone to take the reins and drive so that I could stop being in control of everything. Aunt Gwendolyn had just done that without my having to ask.

"Okay."

"Yes, okay." She wrapped her arms around me, holding me close. "It'll be okay."

I sniffled and nodded, relishing in her softness. In her warmth and the comfort she gave me so freely. I sank into her feminine energy and simply existed in between her heartbeats.

Eventually, though, a noise from the kitchen caught my attention, and my good mood sank a little.

"I have to apologize to him," I whispered.

"Yeah, you do. Are you ready yet, or do you need a few more minutes?"

No one wanted to have to confront someone they had wronged, to look them in the face and admit their own shortcomings. To offer their confession and ask for amends. But waiting wouldn't change what I had done or said, and Ander deserved to be released from any confusion he might be under because of my behavior.

"No waiting." I pulled away, sniffling again but giving her a weak smile. "Just...don't let me throw up all over my feet again."

"I'll do my best."

With a pat on the back, Aunt Gwendolyn walked into the kitchen. I stood and took a deep breath, looking up at the night sky one last time. Making a silent request for peace and strength from the universe. And then I, too, walked into the kitchen.

Ander stood to the side of the long counter that divided the sitting area from the working area. He had a towel in his hands and appeared to have been washing dishes. And then there were his eyes. Those dark eyes bored into me, watching every moment. Tracking every movement. The pressure of being the subject of that stare didn't help my nerves, but I was the one who had been wrong. And I needed to fix that.

"Hey," I said as I walked right up into his space. He set the towel down, still only watching me. Not moving much. "I'm sorry about that. I didn't mean—"

He wrapped his arms around me and pulled me into a hug that had me losing control. I cried against his chest as he shushed and rocked me slightly. As he held me up in a moment when I just wanted to fall.

I did not deserve this man.

"Ander—"

"I know you think you should apologize for that outburst, and that's fine—I'll take it and forgive you. But I owe you a bigger one. With all the stuff going on, I pulled away and didn't give you an ounce of my attention. That's not right of me. That's not how I want to treat someone I care about. So I'm sorry I haven't been here to check on you, to make sure you're okay, and to take care of you. I wasn't judging you ladies for not having something in the kitchen—I was judging myself for failing to keep you fed."

I sniffled, chuckling softly. "We're grown women. We can feed ourselves."

"I'm sure of that, but I've been here feeding you both for months. Disappearing for a couple of days without notice and then being upset that you didn't magically know what I would need to make you a meal? That's unreasonable."

"Yeah, it kind of was. But that didn't give me the right to yell at you the way I did."

He tugged me in closer and kissed the top of my head. "We can agree to disagree there because I deserved it. I'm just sorry for my behavior over the last few days, including tonight. I'm not reacting well to the stress of this vandalism thing."

"It'll get better."

"Yeah, for both of us."

He let me go and guided me to my stool at the counter, moving into the working area of the kitchen and ladling a bowl of soup for me. Within seconds, I had soup and crackers before me, along with a cup of iced tea.

"Mint," Aunt Gwendolyn said when I grabbed the glass to take a sip. "It'll help keep your stomach settled."

"Thanks. Both of you."

Ander winked my way as he set a bowl and crackers in front of Aunt Gwendolyn. He then ladled one for himself and leaned a hip against the opposite counter, blowing on a spoonful before taking a bite.

"That's some good stock, Miss Gwen," he said, shaking his head and making a growly sort of mmm-hmmm noise.

Aunt Gwendolyn grinned and sat up straighter. "Why, thank you, Ander. It's nice to know I haven't lost my touch in the kitchen."

"Not at all, ma'am. This is a delicious soup. Hits the spot."

I had to agree—Aunt Gwendolyn's stock had a complex flavor profile, likely from all the herbs she tended to cook with.

She liked to bring her magic into the kitchen, and the food benefited from it.

Sadly, I couldn't eat much since my stomach still didn't feel normal. I set my spoon down after a handful of bites and picked up a cracker, breaking off a corner and popping that into my mouth.

"So," I said once I finished my cracker, feeling a little nervous about opening this can of worms but knowing it needed to be talked about. "You said the restaurant stuff was stressful. What's going on there?"

Ander frowned into his bowl, stirring it in a mindless sort of way. Aunt Gwendolyn noticed it at the same time I did apparently.

"Counterclockwise, dear." She smiled when his gaze popped up to meet hers. "If you're talking about anything negative, stir it counterclockwise. To banish that energy."

"Thanks for the tip." He changed the direction of his spoon, following her guidance. "Insurance is a scam. An absolute scam. They're fighting me every step of the way on replacing the window, and it's driving me insane."

"They don't want to cover replacing the window?"

"Oh, they'll replace it—with one that isn't energy efficient or doesn't offer the same UV protection mine did. They want to give me half of what that window cost me and think I should just take it and be thankful. Cheap bastards." He shook his head, taking another spoonful of soup and swallowing it down before continuing. "The front of your building looks good, though. You got all that paint off."

"Not all but most. I have a high-power pressure washer coming—a commercial-type one—to give the whole front a good cleaning. It should be here Tuesday on the truck."

"I can help you clean it Tuesday afternoon."

I shook my head. "Can't. Mary ordered an alarm system through me, and I told her I'd help her install it, so that's my Tuesday afternoon."

He frowned. "Everything okay over there?"

"She said someone came knocking on her door after midnight and made her nervous, so she wants some cameras in case they come back."

"Good call on her part. I'll help you install that. Can't have my favorite employee afraid in her own house."

"Thanks. I'll take the help, for sure. Especially since I'm hoping to have my allergy test tomorrow."

That caught his attention. "Did the doc call?"

"No, but Aunt Gwendolyn has laid down the law." I smiled her way.

"That's right," she said. "We're going to his office tomorrow and having him start something or send us where they can. She's been sick for a whole day again. This needs to end."

"What time are you heading over there?" Ander asked.

"First thing," Aunt Gwendolyn answered. "The office opens at nine on Mondays."

"I'll take you ladies."

"You don't have to do that," I said, shaking my head. "I can drive myself."

He set his bowl down and came around the counter, moving my stool with me still on it so he could stand directly in front of me. Hover over me. Crowd me.

"If my favorite employee deserves my help and attention, so does my favorite girl. I'll take you, and I'll make sure you get home so you can rest. Understood?"

I sighed and tugged him in closer, dropping a soft kiss to

his lips. Scrunching up my nose when his beard tickled my chin. "Understood."

"Good girl." He gave my thigh a little smack then retreated, heading back to his bowl of soup. "So, other than the test tomorrow, what's on the agenda? Want me to start on the trim above the cabinets in here?"

I looked up, knowing the trim needed to be fixed as some of it had been stolen. Gleaves Philander—the man down the road who was good with his wood—had created the custom molding for Rose and thankfully was able to recreate some for me. But the top of the cabinets couldn't hold my attention. The conservatory practically sang to me, calling me back to her. I rose to my feet and followed the siren song, entering that space and letting my bare feet enjoy the feeling of the brick floor. Letting her coolness and sense of life fill me.

"I think I'd like to do something in here," I said, looking over my shoulder.

Ander nodded, not arguing a bit. "Then let's push off finishing the kitchen so we can get this space the way you want it."

Guilt swamped me, bringing her friend doubt along for the ride. "I mean...but we use the kitchen more."

Ander rolled his eyes. "And it's completely functional. If you feel drawn to finish the conservatory, let's finish the conservatory. It'll make you happy, and I must assume Miss Gwen would like that as well."

"Oh, yes. That's a wonderful idea." She rose to her feet and joined me over the threshold, grabbing my hand and standing with me in the moonlight. The house seemed to hum its approval, the energy around us turning warm and soft. Comfortable. Willow Manor liked the idea.

"Then we start working in here tomorrow," I said, squeezing Aunt Gwendolyn's hand.

"Feels like it's a good time to do that, yes. The plants will thank us, plus, it'll give us a chance to work on your witchcraft."

And for once, I didn't balk at that. I didn't pull away or question her practice. Rocks in the bra, stirring food in certain directions, and now, plant magic.

Let someone paint the word witch on my building. I was one. And next time someone tried to make me feel intimidated by calling out that fact, I might just hex them.

Exactly like Aunt Gwendolyn would.

Chapter Seventeen

Monday morning dawned bright and sunny, bringing with it a massive side of anxiety.

"It'll be fine," Aunt Gwendolyn said as she patted my hand. "The doctor will figure things out."

"And if he can't?"

"Then we'll find another one."

I had no idea where she got her confidence from, but I leaned in to it. If Dr. Don couldn't help me, we'd find someone who could. There had to be someone. Right?

"Good morning, Miss Gwen. Brylie." Heather Turlington smiled from behind the reception desk as we walked in. "I was going to call you this morning, Brylie."

"You were?"

"Yes. The doctor has received all your allergy test supplies and wanted me to get you on the schedule."

I stared at Aunt Gwendolyn, wide-eyed. Had she somehow manifested this?

"Is that what you're here for?" Heather asked, obviously

unsure why we were standing in front of her while silently staring at each other. Oops.

"Yes," I said finally. "Sorry—it's been a rough weekend for me. We were coming to see the doctor because I spent another couple of days sick."

"You poor dear. That's not fun." She tapped on the keyboard and watched her screen, sucking on her teeth as she read the monitor. "Ander mentioned you were ill when I ran into him this morning, so I started digging for your supplies the second I walked in the door."

That made me frown. Where would Heather have seen Ander? The sun had barely risen, and the restaurant was closed. He'd dropped us off, but she would have already been at work. There was no way—

"Dr. Don's got time this morning if you do." Heather smiled up at me, which stopped my brain from spinning out of control. For the moment.

"We've got time," Aunt Gwendolyn said, filling in the silence when I didn't. "Let's get this done."

Ten minutes later, I lay on a table in the doctor's exam room with a gown slid over my arms and open in the back. Aunt Gwendolyn sat by my side with the doctor's assistant prepping me for the test. I still had an inkling that something was going on, that Ander running into Heather so early when it couldn't have been at the restaurant needed to be addressed, but I was too stressed and scared about the test to focus on it.

"It'll be fine," Aunt Gwendolyn said, keeping her voice soft. "You should try to relax."

As if it were that easy. Try to relax and *bam*...relaxed. That wasn't going to happen. Still, I nodded, squeezing her hand harder. Trying to settle my stomach and calm myself. An impossible task, especially when a knock sounded and the door opened.

"Good morning, Brylie. Miss Gwen. I hear you had a bit of a rough weekend." Dr. Don settled on the rolling stool and slid up beside me, giving me his megawatt smile.

I did not have it in me to smile back. "I was pretty sick. I need to know why."

"Understood." Dr. Don tapped on his tablet then handed it to his assistant. "I had another conversation with Ander the other day about your diet, so I've got a solid selection of allergen samples. Fingers crossed we zero in on the culprit first round."

My neck stiffened, my body growing warmer. Once again, Ander's name being brought up had increased my anxiety. This time didn't make sense, though. I had known Ander and the doctor were going to go over my diet. They had talked at my last appointment, and I'd given my permission. Having a second discussion—when I wasn't there to witness it— shouldn't have upset me. But it did. It truly did.

"We're going to start on your left shoulder. Let me know if anything hurts too much or if you start to feel hot, itchy, or uncomfortable. Okay, Brylie?"

"Got it." I nestled into the pillow under my head and stared at Aunt Gwendolyn. She smiled down at me, singing softly and keeping a solid hold on my hand. Anchoring me as the doctor began doing something along my back that burned and scratched. I closed my eyes and sank into the pain, focusing on the fact that the burn would lead to answers. That I might never have to spend another day in bed with what felt like an alien trying to bust out of my stomach once this test was done. We just had to get through the uncomfortable part.

"I heard about what happened on Main Street last week,"

the doctor said at one point, his voice calm and quieter than usual as he worked. "It's a shame the restaurant has to be closed, but you seemed to get the paint off the front of your business lickety-split. I was out of town, and it was gone by the time I returned."

My wrist suddenly started to itch. I couldn't think about anything but that sensation, couldn't stop my brain from tearing apart the cause. Could it be the allergy test? Or was Dr. Don lying to me? And about what? Seeing the damage? Not seeing it? Maybe he—

"You say you were out of town," Aunt Gwendolyn said, obviously taking over the conversation. "Where had you gone?"

"To the shore. I like to spend a few days on the beach now and again to recharge."

The itch moved up my arm, rolling over my nerves and settling in across my shoulders. He was lying. I had no doubt. At least not until Aunt Gwendolyn hissed.

"Oh no." She gripped my hand tighter. "Doc—"

"I see it." His cool hands landed on my back as the tension in the room notched up more than I would have expected.

"What's happening?" I asked, shifting slightly as my upper back seemed to catch fire. "Why am I burning?"

"We've figured out one culprit, for sure." Dr. Don leaned down. "I may need to give you an antihistamine if this gets much worse, but I think it'll settle down in a bit."

"What is it?"

"Something you've probably never heard of." He sat up, his hands returning to my back. "Brylie, I want you to focus on your breathing for me. If you start feeling congested or like it's getting hard to breathe, tell me right away, okay?"

"Should I be worried?"

"No. I don't think we're going to get to that point, but that was a fast and powerful reaction. I want to check a couple more things before we call it a day, though. Miss Gwen—"

"I've got her." Aunt Gwendolyn gripped my hand in both of hers, smiling down at me. "I won't let anything happen to you."

And that, I believed. I could have begun itching from head to toe in that moment, and I would have never even considered my aunt was lying to me. The woman had me in her hands—literally—and she wouldn't let go so long as I needed her.

"Thanks."

I gave myself over to Aunt Gwendolyn, focusing on the feel of her hand tightly holding mine. Letting the sound of her voice as she returned to singing lull me into a quiet, calm state. I was almost asleep when Dr. Don finally rolled away and leaned down to catch my gaze.

"All finished," he said. "How are you feeling?"

"Fine." I moved my shoulders, frowning as an intense burn lit up my skin. "Okay, maybe not fine."

"Breathing okay?"

"That's perfectly fine."

"Good." He grabbed his tablet and started tapping on the screen. "I'll step out for a moment so you can get dressed, then we can talk about what I've seen."

With that, he rose to his feet and left the room. Aunt Gwendolyn handed me my clothes. I dressed myself as quickly as I could, thankful I'd chosen to wear a comfortable bralette to the appointment. The skin on my back would not have been happy being squeezed by anything with more substance. The soft flannel I'd pulled from my closet soothed, though. A definite plus.

"How are you feeling?" Aunt Gwendolyn asked once I had dressed and probably looked ready to deal with Dr. Don again.

"Not too bad. Though, that wasn't the most comfortable test in the world."

"I imagine not. When the one—"

Dr. Don chose that moment to knock and open the door, peeking in with a smile. "Ready for me?"

"Of course." I sat up straighter, readying myself for the news. Reaching for Aunt Gwendolyn's hand. "So...how did it go?"

The doctor settled onto his rolling stool and tapped on his tablet before looking my way. "You have a pretty severe allergy to tiger nuts."

I had really been looking forward to an aha moment. To him saying something that resonated with me and made me immediately realize what to change. That was not what I got.

"What's a tiger nut? I don't even eat nuts regularly."

"It's really not a nut—it's a tuber, like a potato. It comes more from the Eastern Hemisphere but has grown in popularity here because it has good vitamin content and other benefits for people looking to eat a nutrient-rich diet."

"I..." I looked at Aunt Gwendolyn, even more confused. "I don't think I eat them."

"People who are gluten free grind them into a flour to substitute for wheat."

Lightbulbs—lots of them—practically exploded in my brain. "Ander has been buying desserts from different bakeries, trying out all kinds of gluten-free things."

Dr. Don looked up, frowning. "Yes, he has. You also reacted to coconut, though not as strongly. That's another flour often used in gluten-free baking."

"Guess we go back to gluten," Aunt Gwendolyn said. She

didn't stop there, though. "I've also used coconut in some of my teas."

I glanced over, my stomach dropping at the sadness on her face. I immediately reached for her hand and gave her a smile.

"You didn't know. *We* didn't know. You're not to blame for this."

She patted my hand. "Still. You've been so sick. If I added to that—"

"My guess is it's way more the tiger nut than the coconut." Dr. Don shot me a wink when I looked his way, as if he knew how much of a guilt spiral Aunt Gwendolyn had been heading for. "Coconut is much more common in the American diet. She would have suffered from these attacks a lot more frequently had that been the culprit."

Aunt Gwendolyn nodded. "Yes, perhaps."

"No perhaps," I said. "Though, let's cut out the coconut in the teas for now."

"Good call." Dr. Don rose to his feet. "And let's get you an EpiPen to carry, just in case."

"You think her allergy is that severe?" Aunt Gwendolyn asked, also rising to her feet.

Dr. Don nodded. "Absolutely. The more she's exposed to tiger nut, the worse her response can get. I was worried today." He looked my way. "I sent a prescription to the pharmacy over in Scottsborough. It's a bit of a hike, but that's the closest one we've got that will likely have one for you today."

"Thank you, Doctor. Really."

"It's no problem. I just want to see you healthy and thriving." He closed the cover on his tablet and nodded once, still smiling as I scratched at my wrist. "If you're ready, I'll see you out."

Ready was an understatement. I hopped off the table and

headed into the hallway with Aunt Gwendolyn behind me. Dr. Don followed us, opening the door into the waiting area and giving us a quiet goodbye. Heather Turlington caught my eye as I crossed the waiting area, so I gave her a smile and a wave but didn't stop. The doctor had come up behind her to point to something on her screen. I didn't want to interrupt their work.

We had just stepped outside when a familiar voice called my name. I turned to find Ander jogging across the street in my direction, looking downright grumpy.

"Hey," he said when he stood before me. "I'm so sorry I'm late. This insurance guy..." He sighed and ran a hand over his beard. "Doesn't matter. How did it go? What did he find out?"

"Tiger nuts," I said with a shrug. "I have to get an EpiPen because the reaction I had to them was pretty strong."

"And coconut," Aunt Gwendolyn added. "She can't have that either."

Ander frowned. "I don't use tiger nuts for anything. Coconut, sure, but not often. I'll have to check the pantries to see if there's anything hidden."

"He said people use tiger nuts in gluten-free baking. You think maybe the treats you've been getting—"

"I stopped buying the gluten-free ones a while ago. My guess is it's in something else, but I'll make sure my current baker doesn't use either of those in anything. We don't want you sick." He gave me a quick side hug. "So, now what?"

"Home. I have to drive out to Scottsborough at some point to pick up my prescription, but I'm not up for it right now."

"I can go for you this afternoon. Let's get you home so you can rest a bit."

With that, the three of us piled into our two cars and headed for the manor. Aunt Gwendolyn kept up a running conversation, but I could tell she wasn't quite herself. I had a feeling neither of us would be entirely back to normal until our kitchen had been cleared of the items that had been making me sick.

When we arrived home, we headed straight to the kitchen as I had assumed we would. I let Elmer outside and then settled on the floor with him when he came back in, needing his weight and snuggles. I hated leaving him alone, but even I hadn't felt comfortable taking him into a doctor's office.

Aunt Gwendolyn beelined it for the tea cabinet. "Ander, dear. Do you think tiger nuts have another name? Like a plant name?"

Ander came in at that exact moment, giving me a quick once-over as if checking on me. "It's a sedge plant. Look for nutsedge or chufa."

"Perfect."

Aunt Gwendolyn emptied the tea cabinet and began looking over every box, reading every label intently. Ander headed to the pantry, grabbing each box and bag. Reading labels as if his job depended on it. I sat on the floor with Elmer, growing warmer and more uncomfortable. Especially as I stared at the metal shelves he had practically demanded. They just didn't look right in there, and it annoyed me more with each passing day. Either that, or the tiger nut the doctor had used for my allergy test was working its way through my system and making me cranky. Could have gone either way, really.

Thinking of the doctor reminded me of Heather, which took my thoughts in another direction.

"Heather Turlington mentioned she saw you this morning," I said, staring at Ander.

He nodded and glanced my way before pulling another box out of the pantry. "I had asked her last week for a list of the ingredients in her gluten-free flour. I hadn't pushed her because I'd stopped buying the treats she makes on the side, but she called last night and asked me to meet her so she could give me her recipe."

"Did you give the information to Dr. Don?"

"Of course."

The kitchen grew warmer, the heat hanging heavy in the air. "You could have just given that information to me, you know."

"Seemed faster to go direct." He pulled out a bag of something, grunting when he read the label and moving to set it on the counter. That gave me a full view of the pantry, of the metal shelves. Of the section of my house that didn't fit with the rest. The heat grew bolder, my skin burning with it. I couldn't stand to be in the room anymore.

I slid out from under Elmer and rose to my feet, slipping into the conservatory. Needing the cool, life-filled space to soothe the burn in my soul. To calm me.

Aunt Gwendolyn appeared at the entrance, looking worried. "Are you okay?"

"Yeah." But I wasn't, and I didn't know why. So I kicked off my house shoes and stood barefoot on the brick, grounding myself. Breathing in the air that was much wetter and more filled with life than anywhere else in the house. And I allowed the quiet of the conservatory to fill me with a calmer energy.

"We should fix up this room."

Aunt Gwendolyn paused. "I thought we already decided to—"

"We did. I'm just... I'm tired of dealing with the kitchen. This room needs us." I ran a finger along a dirty shelf, breathing deeper as I took in the space. As I truly settled into the feel of life the conservatory provided me. "Now. We can work on it now. Let's grab some supplies and start cleaning."

But Aunt Gwendolyn was nothing if not intuitive. "You've had a rough morning. Are you sure you feel up to it?"

Not at all, but the need sat deep. It ate at me. And the idea of watching Ander deal with all the stuff on those metal shelves only made me unhappy. "Yup."

"Okay, then. I'll get the broom."

Chapter Eighteen

We spent all day and night in the conservatory—cleaning, organizing, redecorating. Aunt Gwendolyn had even painted some of her jar lids red to indicate those herbal mixes contained coconut. An easy visual deterrent for me should I decide I wanted one of her homemade teas. We hadn't finished by any stretch, but focusing on that little, living space had improved my mood. As had making sure everything in there was exactly as I wanted it—no shiny metal when I felt the room deserved wood.

But on Tuesday, I had to go back to work. The people of Reverie Springs needed their flush valves and wire nuts. And apparently, I was the woman to sell those items to them. And sell them, I did. All day long.

"I'll neaten up the back," Aunt Gwendolyn said before heading toward the storeroom, likely since we would be closing soon. She and Elmer had spent the entire day at the store with me. Not unusual for the dog, slightly more unusual for the old lady. I appreciated her attention, though. And having her in the store had brought in some interesting clientele. Seemed

Aunt Gwendolyn didn't just brew hexes but also had a reputation for love spells, made money bowls, and had a talent for divination by means of throwing bones. And the ladies of the county knew it.

Either they had been hiding before or Aunt Gwendolyn had been keeping her little side hustle a secret from me. Something I would have to get to the bottom of at a later date because the store had been too busy to question her. And even though we would be closing in a matter of minutes, it stayed busy.

"Evening, Brylie." Deputy Carmichael strolled in, uniform crisp and clean, unnecessary sunglasses perched on his nose like always. "Heard you've been sick. Weird allergies, huh?"

His words stunned me, setting me back on my heels like nothing else could have. "You heard...from whom?"

"Just around," he said with a shrug. "No trouble over here, I assume. No criminals terrorizing you?"

"Not today, Deputy." I sighed, trying hard to refocus on him. Still wondering who would have been talking about my health to anyone, let alone the deputy. "Are you looking for something?"

He crossed his arms, shooting me a smile as his biceps bulged under his brown uniform. "Just thought I'd pop in to chat. I've been worried since you discovered the missing spray paint."

Worried, schmorried. I had no faith that the man cared about the theft from my store. In fact, he might have been the one to take the paint, a stretch even for an unspoken thought, but possible. I was still pretty sure the culprit had been Thomas, but I couldn't be sure. I had to figure out a way to prove it.

As if summoned, the man himself walked into the store looking tired and harried. "Evening, Miss Brylie. Deputy."

"What can I do for you, Thomas?"

"I just need to get some lime. It's time to bump up the soil for my pumpkins before the big fall rush at the farmers market."

"Oh, sure. I've got that in the garden center. Do you need help or—"

"No, ma'am. I can grab it." He nodded to the deputy as he walked past. "She's the most helpful woman in Reverie Springs."

"I'm sure of it." Deputy Carmichael watched Thomas walk away, his smile falling. "You might want to watch yourself around him."

My blood pounded, my body going into high-alert mode immediately. What did he know? And was it the same stuff I knew? "Why's that?"

"I've heard he's a little down on his luck. He may look to you and this store as an easy target."

"I'm no one's easy anything." I grabbed a broom and swept out from behind the counter, my brain working through everything I knew about Thomas. Had he hit rough times? Likely—he'd asked me to front him for some equipment he'd needed, but he'd also paid me back immediately as he'd promised. He'd shown up in pants stained with the paint that had been the same color as what had been stolen and used to deface my building, but those work pants looked to be older than me. That paint could have been from a past project. He was also my neighbor, a farmer, and had access to the chemicals that had almost killed Elmer earlier in the year.

I leaned in to the idea that he was the one attacking the

store and restaurant, even if it didn't make a ton of sense to me quite yet.

"Found it," Thomas said as he came around a corner with a dark green bag in his hands. "I knew I could count on you to have what I needed."

I shot him a smile, moving around Deputy Carmichael to stand before my register. "I'm glad I could help. I'm going to need some of those pumpkins to decorate the porch and storefront. I love fall."

"Hopefully whoever is responsible for stealing from you and painting your window will be caught by then." Deputy Carmichael stared hard at Thomas, the air growing thick with tension. "You know someone is vandalizing our community, right?"

Thomas kept his eyes on the deputy, but his hand shook as he handed me a bill from his wallet. "I heard. It's a darn shame. Though the hardware store looks good—no permanent damage."

"Just needed a little elbow grease to clean it up," I said, handing him his change. "It's the restaurant that took the biggest hit. Poor Ander still can't open the place."

Deputy Carmichael snorted. "Play stupid games, win stupid prizes."

My neck grew warm, my skin growing a bit too tight. "What's that supposed to mean?"

Aunt Gwendolyn suddenly appeared at my side, looking worried. "What's happening up here?"

"Nothing to worry about," I said, focusing on the uncomfortable energy I sensed. Choosing not to ignore it. "Deputy Carmichael just made an implication about Ander somehow being involved in the damage to the restaurant, and I'd like to know more about what he's claiming."

The deputy put up his hands as if in surrender and took a step back, though his smirk never faltered. "I'm just someone who knows criminals."

Aunt Gwendolyn stalked after him, looking ready to spit fire. "Ander Mendoza is not a criminal."

"Yeah," I said. "What on earth would even make you think something like that?"

"I'm just saying—money makes people do a lot worse than break a window. And he's about to get one heck of an insurance payout."

"Poppycock," Aunt Gwendolyn said. "Ander would never."

"Exactly. He would never." I crossed my arms, my anger burning through my veins like fire. The nerve of the guy.

The deputy shook his head. "You really take after your witchy aunt, don't you?"

Before I could even wrap my head around that particular statement—insult? compliment?—a huge commotion sounded from the alley behind us. I was already running toward the back of the store when Mary raced in from the front.

"Call 9-1-1. The restaurant is on fire."

Aunt Gwendolyn gasped but grabbed the phone, dialing as I dove for the fire extinguisher near the storeroom doors. I ran outside with Thomas, the deputy, and Mary—all heading next door to Ander's beloved restaurant. But it didn't seem to be the building that was on fire—it looked to be the dumpster. The same one that had been doused in honey and covered in bees.

I pulled the pin on my extinguisher and began spraying next to Ander, both of us working to reduce the flames. It didn't take long for us to get the fire under control, and there didn't appear to be too much damage, though the scorch marks on the brick would likely stick around for a long time. Still, it could have been way worse.

"What on earth is happening?" Aunt Gwendolyn asked as she hurried outside and headed straight for Deputy Carmichael. "How many times can someone attack this business before you figure out who's doing it?"

The deputy didn't say a word to her, just unclipped his radio while keeping his eyes on Ander. "You can cancel that team response. Dumpster fire is out. Repeat, dumpster fire is out."

"Ten-four, Deputy. We'll send over a single engine to verify and clean up if necessary."

"Roger that. I'll make sure we've got access tomorrow for any sort of investigation needed." He reclipped his radio to his shirt before stepping in our direction. "Brylie, you're closed tomorrow."

That struck me as not necessary. "Why?"

"So our fire investigators can come take a look at this area." His frown deepened as he turned toward Ander. "What happened this time?"

Ander looked ready to spit nails. "I was inside cooking—"

"I thought the restaurant was closed."

"It is. I was working on a few new dishes and had brought Mary in to help me clean and do a small tasting. I was waiting for the hardware store to close to bring Brylie and Miss Gwen over. But before we could do that, I smelled smoke coming from out here, so I sent Mary to get help and make sure she was out of the way because I didn't know where the fire had started."

The deputy made a note, not looking up. "So what's the

cause of the fire—you throwing hot grease away or something?"

Ander's face grew red, the energy around him buzzing at a level I had never seen before. "Throwing... Are you accusing me of starting this?"

Deputy Carmichael shrugged. "Some people like to cut corners and end up slicing off more than they can chew."

That accusation obviously hit Ander the wrong way. He stalked forward, arm up and finger pointed. "Now you wait one—"

"He was in the kitchen," Mary said, edging in front of an obviously pissed-off Ander as if to hold him back. "I was in the restaurant with him the entire time. He never would have had a chance to set that fire."

I couldn't let any of that slide, though. "He's not the kind of person to set that fire."

Ander looked my way, something warm in his dark eyes, but the anger returned as he refocused on the deputy. "I didn't start this fire."

But Deputy Carmichael didn't seem convinced. "How much insurance do you have on this building?"

"That's not your concern."

"It is since this attempted arson investigation will likely fall on me to run."

"When your department decides to actually investigate any of the vandalism happening to my restaurant and her hardware store, then I'll answer that question. Until then, how about you focus on the fact that someone set this dumpster on fire instead of how you can screw me over?"

The men continued to argue back and forth, the tension rising, but Aunt Gwendolyn walked out of the hardware store with Elmer at that moment, and I felt drawn to them. Specifically, my great-aunt.

I hurried over to her. "What's wrong?"

"Thomas and the deputy were in the store when the fire started." She pulled a piece of paper from her pocket, the list of names from the other night when we had been spitballing who could be vandalizing our businesses. "They were both on the list, and they were both in the store."

"Maybe they set the fire then came inside."

"Maybe, but it doesn't seem logical to stick around, does it?"

Criminals didn't always work in logical ways, but she had a point. She also had some decent intuition, which meant I needed to follow her lead. "So then, it's likely Joan."

"Out of the suspects we identified, yes." She shook her head, frowning. "I just don't feel like this—alleys and dumpsters—is her style."

"Is there such a thing as a crime style?"

"Oh, yes." Mary appeared beside me, obviously having heard us chatting. "Most serial criminals have trademarks or calling cards. Specifically murderers, but I have to imagine people trying to mess with Reverie Springs businesses, too." I stared, unable not to, until she finally shrugged. "I like true crime shows."

Aunt Gwendolyn nodded. "I can see that. So we're coming to your house after this?"

Mary blanched. "I don't expect you to after this. I know it's stressful—"

"Stressful is not feeling safe in your home." I patted her arm and gave her a smile, catching the deputy walking away and Ander slipping into the back door of the restaurant. Without saying goodbye. Odd, but I had other things to worry about. Specifically, Mary and her home. "Your alarm system arrived on the truck today, and we're coming to install it. Seriously, it'll take less than half an hour to set you up. I've done them a few times."

Thankfully, she looked relieved. "Okay. Thanks. I'll owe you big for it."

"You will owe us nothing." A fire truck appeared at the other end of the alley, rolling slowly toward us. "Guess the professionals are here to handle this mess."

"Let me just tell Ander I'm leaving," Mary said before rushing toward the restaurant. She returned within a minute, carrying a brown paper grocery bag folded over at the top. "Ander asked me to give you this. Said it's a safe meal for you."

I took the bag, feeling almost guilty about it. "I should go and thank him."

"He's super grumpy right now. I don't know if you want to deal with that."

"I am not a fan of grumpy Ander," I said, fighting against the increasing weight of guilt and expectations. "He seems grumpy a lot lately."

Mary shrugged. "It's the stress. He's working so hard to be able to reopen the restaurant, but the insurance is dragging their feet and making him jump over all these ridiculous hurdles. The man is barely sleeping."

Guilt overload, for sure. "I had no idea he was having such a hard time."

Mary bit her lip, looking super uncomfortable, before finally sighing. "Not to be rude, but you would know if you spent some solid time with him. I know that you've been sick, but he's struggling, and he needs you."

Drowning. That was how it felt to hear those words from someone I knew cared about both of us. As if the pressure of our relationship had cut off all my oxygen and left me unable to breathe. Not at all how I wanted to feel.

"There's been a lot going on," I said, my voice just as weak as my words. Thankfully, Aunt Gwendolyn and her intuition caught on and redirected the conversation.

"Brylie, you don't need to make excuses. You both have a lot of bad right now—it's a virtual storm of negative energy. You'll come back together and support each other when you're on solid ground once more. Now, go lock up, and then the three of us can take care of Mary's house. I brought some cedar to burn away any negative energy."

I wasn't about to tell Aunt Gwendolyn no. But I also couldn't leave without relieving at least a little guilt, so once I had the front door locked, I stopped at the counter to send Ander a quick text.

Thanks for dinner. We're heading to Mary's to install her alarm. Lunch tomorrow?

His response came before I could even reach the back room.

Too long. I'll be at your house for breakfast. Sorry I can't help you tonight.

I turned off the lights and made my way to the back door, where Aunt Gwendolyn and Mary were waiting for me. Just as I shut the door behind me—pausing to make sure the lock had latched—my text alert went off again. Ander had sent me one last message.

Stay safe for me.

Chapter Nineteen

I woke up sweating, the house feeling way too hot and stifling. Even kicking off the quilt I slept under didn't help. The air itself seemed to be the problem, which made no sense. Fall in Reverie Springs had been cool—the days filled with sunshine and breezes, and the temperature had been what I would have described as ideal. Some people had even taken to turning their heat on at night to stave off the coldest hours. Not me; I liked a cooler sleeping area. This heat, this temperature? This was not ideal. Though, by the brightness streaming through the windows, I had overslept.

A low growl from the floor had me turning over and looking down to find Elmer staring back at me. He didn't look happy. His tail remained flat against the floor, his body stiff, and his big, dark eyes locked on mine.

"I can't read your mind, sir."

He barked, and I nearly jumped off the bed. The beast rarely barked and usually only for good reasons. Suffocating in air thick with some sort of late fall heat wave at a time when my store should have been open already seemed like a good enough reason.

"Okay, boy. I'm up." I grabbed my phone as we headed out of the room, swiping it to life on the stairs. A text from Ander sat in my notifications, so I tapped to open it.

Stopped by, but you weren't up yet. Glad you're resting—see you later today.

"Oh, shoot. I missed him." I hurried Elmer outside, choosing to step out the front door instead of the back simply to save time. A basket of pastries sat on the welcome mat, a large black ribbon tied to the top. "He brought treats."

Elmer sniffed the basket, circling it with his nose pressed to the cellophane keeping everything covered.

"They're not for you," I said, shooing him off the porch so I could pick up the basket. Ander had outdone himself with this one. A bunch of delicious-looking treats sat inside, and I couldn't wait to have one with my morning cup of tea.

But when Elmer and I returned to the kitchen, something other than pastry caught my attention. The pantry door sat open, the metal shelves inside visible and still oddly annoying. More than annoying, really. I hated them. They may have been sturdy and totally functional as Ander proclaimed, but they were ugly. And Rose's home deserved not to be ugly.

"Come on, Elmer. Let's grab a few supplies." First came a measuring tape to measure the width and depth of the shelves and height of the lip at the front. Then we moved to the unattached garage Rose had built so Aunt Gwendolyn could brew her stinky potions. I found exactly what I needed there— flat boards of the correct depth and some smaller pieces to use as trim. A quick run through the table saw and some nails popped in with my nail gun, and we were headed back inside with my prototype.

"This had better work." I emptied everything off one shelf and wrangled the wood over the metal. It took some serious pivoting, and I cursed under my breath more than once, but finally, it popped into place. I took a step back, admiring my work. "What do you think, boy?"

Elmer didn't answer, but I didn't need him to. The wood shelf covering all that metal looked amazing and was the perfect solution so both Ander and I could be happy with the pantry. Style finally met function. Even the house seemed to like the shelf—it practically hummed with good energy, the harsh heat from earlier having shifted into a warmth that felt right. Felt comforting and safe.

"Happy house, happy Brylie."

I snapped a picture of the incomplete pantry upgrade then made myself a cup of congratulatory tea. Once settled in at the counter, I carefully selected what looked like a raspberry Danish from the basket. I had eaten more than half when I finally picked up my phone and tapped to open my messaging app, selecting Ander's and my conversation.

Want to see what I've been up to?

I followed that up with a picture of the pantry and another message.

You and me in one spot, looking pretty.

He responded almost immediately.

That hasn't happened much lately. I should probably ask you out on a date so we can make this about more than pantry shelves.

I grinned at the screen, my heart thumping.

How about we start with a late dinner tonight? I'll cook for you after the restaurant closes.

You're on.

I took one more bite of the pastry and finished my tea,

typing out another message before I began cleaning up after myself.

And thanks for dropping off the basket of pastries. That was a wonderful gift to wake up to.

My phone rang seconds later, Ander's contact info popping up on the screen.

I answered it with a smile on my face, putting the call on speakerphone mode so I could work a little while chatting. "Hey, I thought—"

"What basket?"

The world froze, a sudden tightness in my chest making it hard to breathe. "What do you mean, what basket? The one you left on the porch."

"Brylie, I didn't leave you a basket of pastries. Did you open it yet?"

I spun slowly, my muscles going stiff as I focused on the basket with the cellophane removed. As I noticed the last bite of the raspberry Danish sitting on a napkin on the counter.

"I already ate one." Four words. I only spoke four words before my lungs seemed to seize and my entire body began to burn up. "Ander..."

"Where's your EpiPen?"

I couldn't answer him. The entire room had begun to spin, and the need to rip off my skin so I could escape the burning itch coming from it had overtaken me. But I knew he had my best interests at heart, so I forced myself to move. Elmer began barking, adding to the cacophony of sounds running through my head. The deep, obnoxious noise he made taking more of my energy to ignore than I would have liked. I shuffled toward my purse, where I had stuck my EpiPen, moving cautiously across the wood floor. I could hear Ander yelling something over the phone, but I couldn't understand the words. Couldn't make out what he wanted to tell me. The phone fell to the floor as I reached the chair where my purse hung, my arms too weak and heavy to hold on to it a moment longer.

"Brylie?" Aunt Gwendolyn's sweet voice cut through all the heat and the pain and the confusion. It carried over the barking and the rushing of blood in my ears as my heart beat in a pattern that seemed too fast and too hard. I looked up to see her standing in the doorway, her light blue dress nearly touching the floor and hair in one thick braid hanging over her shoulder. She looked like an angel, and I felt like death.

"Oh, Brylie. No." She rushed over and picked up the phone, reaching for me in the same moment as she brought the phone up toward her face. "No, I've got her."

Four words. Again with four words that sent my world spinning on a different axis. I would have to ask her the importance of the number four. I could never remember and we hadn't touched on numerology too much, but four seemed important in that moment.

Aunt Gwendolyn yanked my purse off the chair and dumped it out, sending all sorts of things flying across the floor. Thankfully, my EpiPen wasn't one of them. She grabbed it and dropped the phone, scanning the instructions on the side before pulling on the device. Once ready, she placed one hand on my knee and pushed down, holding the pen up and over my thigh.

"Just breathe, Brylie."

I did as I had been told, fighting to take a deep breath as her hand dropped. As if stabbing something violently, she punched down with the pen onto my thigh. A prick and a burning sensation followed, the whispered prayers of my great-aunt joining the tumultuous sounds around me. Aunt Gwendolyn laid me on the kitchen floor, staring down at me. Looking absolutely terrified. I wanted to tell her it would be okay, that I would be fine, but I couldn't. One, because breathing still took more effort than it should have. And two because I had no idea if that was the truth. I certainly didn't feel fine.

Slowly, though, fine began to return to me. Exhaustion sat heavy on my ribs and made me lie down on the floor, but breathing became easier and my heart settled into a rhythm much more normal than an Olympic sprinter. Eventually, I was even able to smile up at my great-aunt, who had been sitting beside me, rubbing her hands over my rib cage and muttering words I was unable to understand.

"Are you casting a spell on me?"

She stopped muttering, looking down at me with more fear in her eyes than I had ever expected to see. "You do that again, and I'll spell your mouth closed."

I huffed, too tired to laugh. The sound of my name in a male voice interrupted us. I stretched for my phone, now under a chair at the edge of my reach, and tugged it toward me. Ander had remained on the other line.

"I'm okay," I said into it. The sound of an engine roaring came through loud and clear, his voice barely breaking over the rumble.

"Someone tried to poison you. Do not touch that basket until I get there."

I glanced at Aunt Gwendolyn before whispering, "Okay."

She took my phone and ended the call, using a chair to help push herself to her feet. "Let's get you someplace more comfortable."

Aunt Gwendolyn helped me up, then led me to the family

room. She settled me onto the couch with a pillow under my head and a blanket placed over me. I snuggled into the warmth, still too tired. Slightly chilled too. Elmer followed me, huffing his irritation as he lay directly in front of me. Setting up a wall of Basset hound between me and anyone who might try to do me harm.

"I'm okay, boy," I said as I patted his head. "There's no danger in here."

Aunt Gwendolyn snorted. "Depends on what you mean by danger."

The front door opened, the sound of heavy footfalls hurrying toward us setting all three of us on edge. Elmer even stood up and barked. But it was Ander who came racing down the hall and into the family room, looking frazzled and filled with rage and worry. He caught my eye and headed straight for me, dropping to his knees in front of me with Elmer by his side.

"Are you okay?"

"I am." I ran my fingers through his hair, so very grateful to see him. "I thought the basket was from you."

"I know, and I'm sorry that it wasn't."

"It's okay." I nodded to Aunt Gwendolyn, who took the hint and shuffled into the kitchen. Staying close but giving us a little privacy. Once she had disappeared toward the stove, I sighed. "I've missed spending time with you."

"Me too." He frowned. "But with you. Not with me."

"I know what you mean."

"Good, because that sounded weird to me." He leaned closer, breathing me in before murmuring, "We've both been really busy."

"That's not an excuse." I rolled forward, settling in so I

could hold his hand. Needing a connection with him. "What's happening with the restaurant? With the insurance?"

Ander shook his head. "You could have died. Now's not the time—"

"It's the perfect time. We're both here."

He shook his head again, hanging on to my hand like a lifeline. Staring at me with the dark eyes that had never faltered. Never shied away. The man had been a constant in my life since I'd met him.

"Tell me," I said.

Finally, Ander sighed. "The window is expensive because I had UV glass in it—saves energy and keeps out the afternoon sun, you know? So, on paper, it looks like I'm getting all this money, but they can't replace the window as is. They have to rebuild part of the wall, and that's not covered by the insurance because it wasn't caused by the chair through the glass. I don't want to open the restaurant until the window's fixed, but I can't replace the window without repairing the brick, and I can't afford to repair the brick without opening the restaurant or cashing in some investments."

"That sounds stressful."

"It has been. But it's nothing compared to you and your health." He brought a hand to my face and moved a lock of hair, tucking it behind my ear. "How are you feeling?"

"Guilty."

"Why guilty?"

"Because I was beginning to think maybe Deputy Carmichael was right and you were trying to somehow game your insurance."

Thankfully, Ander laughed. "I'm not that smart."

"You are. And I should have never even questioned your

intentions like that. You're a good man, and I should have trusted in you."

"And I should have talked to you more. I've just been so stuck in this place in my head with the restaurant and worrying about you that I went silent. You can't trust someone who doesn't communicate."

"Let's do better."

"Definitely." He leaned forward for a small kiss, sighing as he pressed his forehead to mine. "I was so afraid."

"Me too."

We sat that way for several minutes, both of us seeming to enjoy the connection—both physical and emotional. It wasn't until Aunt Gwendolyn called my name that we broke apart.

"Oh, Brylie. I love what you did with the pantry. Are you going to do the same with the rest of the shelves?"

Ander raised an eyebrow. "You feeling up to showing me your handiwork?"

I smiled and threw off the blanket. "Absolutely."

He helped me up then held my arm as we walked into the kitchen. Aunt Gwendolyn stood before the pantry, cup of tea in hand. Smiling as I came around the corner.

"Feeling better?" she asked, her voice tight but happy. Almost back to normal.

"Absolutely." I nodded toward the open door. "See? Your shelves are still there, strong and sturdy. They're just...prettier now."

Ander looked over my shelf cover and nodded. "Good mix of both of us right there."

"Exactly."

He turned, a smile on his face, looking as if he was going to say more, but then something over my shoulder caught his attention, and his expression changed into one of pure anger. "Is that the basket?"

"Yeah."

He strode to the counter, peering inside. I stood with Aunt Gwendolyn and watched, waiting. Finally, he pounded a fist on the counter and cussed under his breath.

"That's Heather Turlington's stuff."

All the air seemed to disappear from the room. "What?"

He cussed again, pacing the length of the counter. "I hired her to make gluten-free treats to try at the restaurant, remember? I tried out a few other people too, but those are hers—I recognize that napkin in the bottom from when she brought me samples to try."

"You think there're tiger nuts in there?"

"With the way you reacted? Absolutely and lots of them, but she didn't have that on her list of ingredients. I checked with her."

"That doesn't make sense. Why did Dr. Don test me for a tiger nut allergy if they weren't in anything I was eating?"

"I told him to."

"You did what?"

"I told him to. Because I knew people used tiger nut flour in gluten-free baking, so I added it to my list for you just in case. We don't eat much tiger nut in this country—I was worried there was something in a mix that you were ingesting and he wouldn't test for it."

Every time he'd been involved with speaking to Dr. Don around me, I'd gotten irritated or annoyed. I hadn't liked him stepping in. This time, all I could feel was grateful.

"Thank you for taking care of me."

He stopped pacing, staring at me with a heated look that

held far more emotion than I could have ever imagined. "Always."

My heart fluttered, though not from an allergy or the epinephrine. This flutter had been brought to me purely by the charm of one Ander Mendoza.

I bit back a grin and nodded toward the basket, needing to focus. "So what do we do about her?"

"We verify she's knowingly giving you tiger nuts. And then we figure out why she's trying to kill you."

Chapter Twenty

Turned out investigating Heather Turlington wasn't nearly as hard as one might have expected. All it took was one phone call from Ander. Well, a phone call with the possibility of a business deal attached. Ander told her he needed to inspect her kitchen space before he could hire her bakery business as the sweets supplier for the restaurant. Heather had jumped at the opportunity, as had I.

My inclusion had not gone over well with Ander, though.

"Quit pouting," I said. "You'll be right there with me. I'm not in danger."

Ander kept his eyes on the road and a frown on his face. "She knew you had an extreme tiger nut allergy and still dropped off a basket full of treats made with tiger nut flour. You're clearly in danger."

"I won't eat anything."

He gripped the wheel tighter as he turned into a driveway and pulled to a stop. "Don't even touch anything."

I nodded. "Okay."

"Promise me."

"I promise."

With a sigh, he reached across the seat and tugged me closer, resting his forehead against mine. "Ten minutes, and we're out of here."

"Okay."

With that, he sighed and hopped out of the truck, hurrying around the front to open my door and help me down. Gripping my hand tight, he led me to the front porch of a little, Cape Cod-style house with flowers lining the steps and a happy, lavender-painted front door.

"Cute house," I whispered.

He grunted as he knocked. "Cute house...for a murderer."

"Attempted, at best."

The door opened, and Heather stood bathed in the golden light of her entryway with a huge smile on her face. "Well, hi there. I wasn't expecting to see you, Brylie, but I'm so glad you're here. Come in, come in."

I stepped inside, trying hard to keep from both shaking in fear and punching her in the face. "Ander and I have a dinner date planned, so he invited me along to save a little time. I hope you don't mind."

"Not at all. It's good to see you, Ander."

"Heather," Ander replied, his voice clipped and tight. I elbowed him in the ribs as subtly as possible, and he coughed. "Thank you for making yourself available to me. I know Friday nights aren't usually work time."

Heather laughed. "My baking is a side business, so I'm always working late hours on it. I was actually just working on a few bread doughs so I can bake them in the morning. Come on back."

She led the way through a living room and hall, ending in the kitchen with a huge smile on her face. "I used to bake everything in here, but I took your advice and set up a commercial kitchen out back. It's real nice."

Heather kept walking, taking us into another sort of living room—probably her family or recreation room. I tugged on Ander's arm to get his attention.

"You told her she needed a commercial kitchen?"

He leaned close but never took his eyes off our host. "I did. And I'm right about that—commercial kitchens have less food poisoning and cross contamination coming out of them."

I would have replied with something, but all words left my brain as I caught sight of a picture on a bookshelf. There was nothing provocative about it—just Heather standing close to a man about the same age as her, both smiling at whoever had taken the shot. Nothing worthy of all the attention I gave it. If you didn't know the man.

"You're dating Thomas?" I asked, unable not to.

Heather turned, still smiling, though with a little anxiety in the tightness of her lips. "Oh, yes. We've been together a few months now. He's very kind."

I nodded, unable to tear my eyes away from the picture for a good five seconds. The puzzle pieces of him and her—especially with what I knew about her mother—not fitting together. "You make a lovely couple."

"Thanks. We try to keep things quiet around town, which is probably why you didn't know. My mom doesn't really agree with me dating him, but he's so caring and sweet. Well, you should know! He's your neighbor."

I nodded, still trying to force those puzzle pieces together. "He is, and he's always been very polite and respectful."

"See? He's a good man." With that, she turned and headed for a door leading out of her house.

Ander sighed. "Nothing should surprise me at this point, but that did."

"And she never lied. They've been together for months, and her mom doesn't like him." I held up my arm. "Not a single itch."

"Odd pairing, that one."

I understood what he meant—the farmer who had to rent his fields because he can't afford to buy his own and the daughter of the town menace. But others in Reverie Springs might not have seen Joan Turlington as a menace; they may have seen her as a member of the town council, the reader for story hour every Thursday morning at the library, and the committee chair for the annual holiday gathering in town. I had seen the worst of her, mostly because I had taken over two spaces that had belonged to her dead sister. Didn't make her right, but it did make me want to give her compassion.

But then I remembered how she harassed me about Elmer not wearing a leash, and how she spoke to Aunt Gwendolyn. And now she didn't like Thomas for her daughter, likely because he didn't have enough money or possessions to be deemed worthy. Compassion gone. Joan was still a menace in my mind.

We followed Heather out of her house and into a small pull barn that looked decidedly not new. Inside, though, gleamed under bright fluorescent lighting. Stainless steel everything sat in a U-shape on one side of the space, while the other looked to be some sort of dry storage area. It all looked very...professional.

"So this is my setup," Heather started, sounding nervous as she carefully avoided Ander's gaze. "I work here in this section and store everything over here. I have a regular refrigerator for now—I want a commercial model, but they're expensive. I need to make more money with the business for that step. But this does the job. I also have two standard ovens and a small, commercial one just for cookies. Right now, I'm making more regular treats than allergy-friendly, but I can have dedicated spaces for any allergy requests. I keep a few sets of spoons and cookie scoops set aside for each of the eight main allergens. Just in case."

"You did all this?" I asked, calculating the cost of such a space. The woman had really invested in this baking business. "Who are you baking for?"

She shrugged, her cheeks darkening. "No one, really. I wanted to work with Ander or another restaurant—I just think that would be the best way to get my goodies out there. But for now, it's just me and a Facebook page, taking on one client at a time. And my baking group—I host classes on Monday nights. Half the town has shown up at one point or another."

Ander squeezed my hand, catching my attention. He never turned my way, though. Instead, he began questioning Heather on her food safety procedures. He kept his grip on my hand as he asked and she answered, never releasing me from his side. I let my hand stay neutral, not squeezing back, as I listened. Not once did the woman lie. I never itched in the slightest, a good sign that she was telling him exactly how she handled her business.

"And what about your gluten-free flour mix? What's your recipe?"

Heather squinted a bit, obviously struggling to keep the smile on her face. "That's a company secret."

"Ingredients need to be on any packaging for individual treats and listed for the restaurant owner in case someone has an allergy or intolerance."

Heather never wavered. "I had labels made for some

cookies I was contracted to make because the customer wanted everything individually wrapped and sealed." She pulled a box from under a work space covered in just about every cooking utensil known to man and pulled a roll of soft lavender-and-green labels from it. "I may be new, but I read the rules. You told me to operate as a commercial kitchen, and I am. You can see the ingredients for anything I make, but the recipes aren't available to anyone outside my team."

Ander took the roll of labels from her and looked them over, one eyebrow raised. "That's fair. And these are accurate? Every ingredient in your—" he read from the label itself "—'gluten-free monster cookie' is listed here?"

"Yes. Every single one."

He glanced at the label again. I did the same, noting each ingredient. No tiger nut flour. No tiger nut anything.

"They sound amazing," I said, giving Heather a smile.

She let out a breath, relaxing a little. "Thanks. I started making them for kids parties, but they're more popular with adults."

Ander grunted. "There're pretzels in here. You make those or buy them?"

And so it went. Ander questioned her about how she handled her kitchen, and I stood there wondering how on earth tiger nut flour had gotten into the treats I'd been given if it wasn't something she cooked with. Eventually, I got bored and let go of Ander's hand, heading over to the pantry-like shelves at the back of the room. Heather had wood shelves a lot like what I had wanted in my pantry. What I'd accomplished once I'd covered the metal ones with scrap wood. Heather's were just wood, though, and they bowed in the center, likely from all the weight on them. Having that metal structure underneath in my own pantry suddenly seemed like an even better idea.

Sagging shelves notwithstanding, the pantry looked like some sort of Pinterest project—everything labeled and neat, with like-sized containers standing together as sentinels on the shelves. Nothing seemed out of place; nothing stood out. And not a single bin said tiger nut.

"We have to go," Ander said, appearing at my side without warning. He grabbed my hand and pulled, the tension pouring off him making my throat tighten.

"What's wrong?"

Heather followed us out, yelling something about following us over. I still had no idea why we were in such a hurry or where we were going, but I had a feeling asking more questions would only irritate Ander. He seemed like a man on a mission.

Once we were both inside the truck, he started the engine and threw the vehicle into gear, roaring out of Heather's driveway and speeding down the road toward town. Still silent.

I finally had to say something. "Ander—"

"What?"

"Where are we going?"

"My house." He made a turn so fast and sharp that I squeezed and grabbed hold of the handle above my head.

"But why are we in such a rush?"

He hit the gas after the turn, speeding down the straightaway through the dark. "Because my house is on fire."

Chapter Twenty-One

The chaos surrounding Ander's house made my heart pound like nothing else. Fire trucks, the sheriff's car, and what looked like fifteen or twenty different neighbors' vehicles lined the driveway and spilled out onto the street. Ander had to park almost in a ditch to get even relatively close to the house.

"Why are there so many people here?" I asked as soon as he helped me down from the truck.

He held my hand and ran us across the street, heading right into the melee. "It's a volunteer fire department. Sometimes, when the call goes out, people who aren't volunteers show up."

And show up, people had. They ran around the house, taking orders from an older lady in a hard hat with a bullhorn. Tugging hoses around and spraying water wherever the lead woman told them to. Ander and I stood back, watching in horror as dark smoke poured through a hole in the roof. This was bad. This was very, very bad.

It only got worse when the sheriff came strolling over, looking fresh as a daisy. No firefighting for him apparently.

"Ander," the sheriff said, glancing at the man in question then returning his gaze to watch the firefighters at work. "Seems like you've been busy lately."

Ander's energy practically exploded, his anger making itself known in the air around us. "What's that supposed to mean?"

"It just means you've had a lot of discussions with your insurance people in the past few weeks, and you're about to have another one. Seems rather convenient."

I could feel Ander's temper rise. I tried to hang on to his hand, to give him some sort of support, but his anger got the better of him. He dropped my hand and stepped up to the sheriff, moving right into the other man's face.

"You think it's somehow convenient that I've just lost everything I own?"

The sheriff looked away, his expression contrite. As it should have been—Ander's house burned not a hundred feet away, and the sheriff wanted to imply insurance fraud? Before anyone had even seen or looked into what might have started the fire? Ridiculous.

My phone rang right as the sheriff began slinking away. I pulled it out of my bag, saw Aunt Gwendolyn's info on the screen, and tapped to answer.

"It's not a good time," I said, not needing a greeting.

Aunt Gwendolyn didn't miss a beat. "I heard. Are you okay? Is he?"

I flicked a glance at Ander then went back to staring at the house. "As much as he can be, considering."

"I can't believe someone set his house on fire. This is too much, Brylie. It's just too much. I'm going to hex them into next month when we figure out who it is."

"Before you start brewing a hex for the arsonist, can you do me a favor?" I held Ander's gaze as he looked my way, knowing he should hear what I was about to say.

"Of course, dear."

"Can you please make up the guest room for me? Ander's coming to stay at Willow Manor."

Ander's frown deepened and his brow furrowed, but he didn't argue. Instead, he reached out to grab my hand, giving me a squeeze.

"Elmer and I will get right on that. Tell Ander I wish I could be there to support him, but I don't have a car."

"And you can't drive."

"Well, I mean, I could in an emergency. I drove you once. And this seems like an emergency."

"When was the last time you drove regularly?"

"Before Rose and I moved in together."

"So, like...fifty years."

"A little more."

"Yeah, there's no need for you to have a car at this point. Even for emergencies."

She sighed. "You're probably right. But I can make up a mean guest room."

"Get to it, then," I said before ending the call. "She's sorry she can't be here to support you."

"Nothing to support." Ander ran a hand through his hair and over his beard, groaning in a way that sounded like a growl. "I feel like I should be doing something."

I leaned into his side, knowing nothing I had to say would matter in that moment. He could only watch as his world burned.

About twenty minutes after we arrived—as the firefighters continued spraying water on the building—Deputy

Carmichael came strolling onto the property. He headed straight for Ander and me, sunglasses firmly in place. At night.

"Looks like I'm missing all the fun," he said once he stepped beside me. His energy felt off, something harsh and static dragging against my skin as he spoke. "I was already on a run out on Route 12 when the call came in. It doesn't look good, does it?"

I scratched at my wrist, the itchiness coming on strong and quick. "Route 12. Isn't that out by Thomas Lee's place?"

Deputy Carmichael turned my way, his sunglasses offering me a picture of what I looked like in the moment. And what I looked like was a woman holding tight to the man at her side. The man who was not the deputy.

"Couldn't tell you. I was out responding to a possible wild animal sighting."

The burning itch moved into the palm of my hand. The man had just lied again, though why, I had no idea. Who cared if he knew where Thomas lived? How was just knowing the street a person resided on lie-worthy? The ridiculousness of the lies threw me off, made me feel off-balance and out of sync with the world around me. I couldn't think through a reason someone would feel like protecting that sort of information.

Suddenly, the roof caved completely in, and the firefighters began yelling to one another and running around the building. Ander looked ready to rush inside, so I held his hand tighter. Both of us watching in horror as his home became tinder.

"Is that Miss Gwen?" Deputy Carmichael asked, leaning closer so I could hear him over the noise. I turned to look down the driveway and spotted her rushing toward us.

"Looks like she found a ride."

"You know," the deputy started, "if you ever need a ride, you can call me."

I recoiled, leaning harder into Ander and hoping my face said something close to *Ew, no.* "That won't be necessary. Like, ever."

"Oh, Ander. This is so horrible." Aunt Gwendolyn wrapped her arms around Ander and held him tight, forcing him to curl over her so he could hug her back. "I'm so sorry for this. I've got the guest room all ready for you, though. Willow Manor will welcome you home."

Ander glanced my way before nodding. "Thanks. I really appreciate the kindness."

"Of course, dear. You're family. It's what we do for family." Aunt Gwendolyn frowned, looking around the driveway before sighing. "Ander, can you please drag Elmer away from that car?" She shook her head and looked my way. "He's been sniffing anything and everything all day. It's like he's on the hunt, but I can't figure out for what."

My dog came strolling over, looking awfully grumpy. "What's going on with you?"

He huffed and sat on my feet, watching the people rush around Ander's house. I knew that stance, though. The way he didn't plop, how he kept his back against me and moved only his head. Elmer was on guard duty. Against what, I had no idea. Though considering the literal fire before me, I had a feeling the dog was on the right track.

"I didn't know he was a fireman," Aunt Gwendolyn said, stealing my attention. I followed her gaze, finally landing on Thomas, who looked right at home in his firefighter's slicker and helmet as he took an ax to a small tree at the corner of Ander's home.

"When did he get here?"

Ander grunted. "Thomas? I saw him when we pulled up."

"Huh. I guess I missed him." I yawned, unable not to, and leaned into Ander. "Will the entire town show up here?"

"Probably."

And he wasn't kidding. As hours passed, more and more Reverie Springs residents showed up. Some brought food and drink for the firefighters, some came to ask Ander if he needed anything, and some came to be lookie-loos and watch the show. Joan Turlington fell into the latter group.

"I wish she'd leave," I said, sitting in a borrowed bag chair one of the ladies from town had dropped off for us. "It's almost creepy how she's staring at Thomas."

"At least she's stopped glowering at Ander," Aunt Gwendolyn said, sipping on the tea one of Ander's neighbors had brought. "That felt excessive."

I nodded, taking in Ander's journey as he walked in front of his house. He had gotten up to talk to the sheriff and county fire investigator and hadn't looked happy. Not that I expected him to—all that was left of his house were a few partial walls and a whole lot of ash—but I had hoped the fire investigator would keep the sheriff honest and doing his job. I had a feeling that wouldn't be the story Ander had to tell.

"Brylie."

I turned to find Heather Turlington approaching. She wore a concerned expression, a thick gray cardigan, and carried a basket of something that made my stomach turn.

"Hi. What are you doing here?" I glanced over her shoulder, nearly flinching as I saw Joan standing behind her.

Heather didn't seem to notice my distraction. "I just wanted to drop off some breads and treats for you. I heard Ander will be staying with you, and I thought these might take a little strain off. You know...that way, you don't have to think about what to eat as much."

Aunt Gwendolyn grabbed the basket before Heather could hand it to me, smiling at the woman. "That's so very thoughtful, Heather. I'll take care of these for Ander and Brylie."

Heather seemed stunned but kept a smile on her face. I kept my eyes on Joan, who looked positively livid. "Thank you, Heather. I really appreciate the gesture."

"Of course." She glanced over her shoulder, obviously looking to where Thomas stood with the other firefighters. "If there's anything else you need..."

"You've done enough," Joan said, forcing herself into the conversation and stealing all the attention of the group. "Now, let's go before the smoke ruins our clothes. We don't want to stink."

Something in the way she said the word stink riled me up, and the look she shot Aunt Gwendolyn only added to the feeling that the woman had spewed an insult. I had no intention of letting her get away with such a thing.

"Smoke is very cleansing, actually. Gets rid of all the bad vibes and negative energy around you." I smiled up at Heather. "You might want to do a smoke cleanse on the regular...considering."

Heather glanced at her mother, eyes wide and face pale. Joan looked ready to spit nails, which suited me just fine. I sat a little deeper, reaching down to pet Elmer who sat beside me. Decidedly not leashed.

Joan took a step toward me, raising her finger to point like some sort of villain from an old movie. "You're going to get—"

"What?" Ander said, interrupting and stepping in front of me. "What's she going to get, Joan?"

Heather tugged on her mom's arm, both women backing

up. "Nothing. It's late, and my mom's tired, is all. I just wanted to bring some treats for y'all."

Ander whipped his head around, glancing from me to Aunt Gwendolyn. She had a solid hold on the basket of baked goods and met his eyes with her own green stare. She even gave him a head nod as if to say *I've got this.*

I reached for Ander's hand and smiled up at Heather. "Thank you so much for the basket of goodies and have a safe drive home."

Heather nodded, still pulling her mother away. "If there's anything I can do, just call me. Ander has my number."

With that, the women turned and walked away, Heather obviously speaking to her mother in a way that screamed she wasn't happy. I watched them go to make sure they didn't turn around and come bother us again. Finally relaxing once they disappeared past the trees lining the driveway.

"Well, that was fun." I tugged Ander closer, looking up at him. "What happened with the inspector?"

"He can't tell too much right now, but he thinks the fire started in the kitchen. His team is coming to secure the scene, and then he'll be back tomorrow to do a full walk-through."

"Secure the scene? That sounds like a criminal investigation."

"It is."

My stomach dropped. "They think someone set your house on fire?"

"The sheriff thinks I set my house on fire."

"But you were with me."

He smiled down at me. "I know. And I told him that. Doesn't mean he's not going to try to make my life harder about this."

"Not happening," Aunt Gwendolyn said, rising to her feet.

"I'll go talk to that cretin. You know he was held back in kindergarten for a lack of social skills. Maybe he needs to revisit the lessons they taught him there."

"While I appreciate the offer, Miss Gwen, I would much rather just get out of here."

"You can leave?" I asked.

"Yeah. There's nothing left to do. I can come back tomorrow and see if there's anything to salvage, but my doubt is high."

I looked past him at the shell of the structure left, at the smoke still rising from the depths, at the ash everywhere. Yeah, I had no hope he would be able to salvage anything either.

"Let's go home, then," Aunt Gwendolyn said, hoisting the basket Heather had brought. "I'm just going to give this to the sheriff."

"What if there's something worse than tiger nuts in there?" I asked.

Aunt Gwendolyn just smiled. "That's why it's going to the sheriff and not the firefighters. I'll be right back."

Ander pulled me into a hug as we watched her go, sighing into my hair. "I'm sorry to invade your space like this."

"You're not invading anything."

"I'll figure something out soon. Once I can find a place to stay—"

"You're staying with us." I rose onto the balls of my feet to kiss his cheek. "We'll get through this. Together."

He stared down at me, those dark eyes almost black in the shadows. "You sure you want me around that much?"

That was the easiest question to answer. "Absolutely."

Chapter Twenty-Two

Saturday mornings at the hardware store were usually quiet and slow, with everyone too busy sleeping off Friday night or spending time with their kids on various sport fields to need much in the way of leaf bags and electrical tape. Not so the morning after Ander's house burned down. Within half an hour of being open, almost the entire town had walked through my doors. Heather and Thomas had walked in to see how I was doing and buy some duct tape as they lamented the fire and Ander losing his home. Deputy Carmichael came too, mirrored sunglasses in place but smirk missing. He had seemed more concerned with where Ander might be—back at the manor—and what he might be doing—dealing with insurance companies—than anything to do with hardware, so it didn't take me long to shoo him on his way. And Dr. Don. He popped in to see how I had been feeling and to ask about Ander's blood pressure, not that I knew much about that. He'd also asked about Mary, a conversation I danced around as if I'd been on pointe shoes for most of my life. No way was I giving him a drop of that information.

I had already reached my limit of lookie-loos popping and dropping and strolling in to "check on me" when the bell over the door rang for the thousandth time. I sighed and turned, ready to paste on my working smile and do my best to be nice, but thankfully, I didn't need to.

"I'm so glad it's you."

Aunt Gwendolyn practically sparkled as she strolled inside, her pink-and-teal caftan defying gravity as usual and her dark gray shoes still grounding her in her mourning period. "Good morning, my dear. I have come to make you tea and see how you're doing."

"Tea sounds amazing." I gave her a quick hug then led the way to the back. "How did you get here? And where's Elmer?"

"Ander drove me over, and he took Elmer with him for the day. An insurance person is coming to finalize the payment for the restaurant window, and then another is coming to look at the house."

"On a Saturday?"

"Apparently a house fire moves you up in the queue for the adjusters." She filled the electric kettle with water and pulled a bag of various types of tea from her purse. "Pick a flavor, Brylie. I brought all your favorites."

I peeked inside the plastic, zeroing in on one particular label. "Ooh, green tea with ginger. That sounds perfect."

Aunt Gwendolyn frowned. "Are you feeling okay?"

"Yeah, fine. In fact, I'm hungry. Let me run and grab a little something from my office."

"Commercially prepared only," she called, as if I didn't already know to stick to things with clear labeling. I'd been sick enough lately—there would be no more homemade treats for me unless Ander made them.

But as I walked into my office, my heart stuttered and my

stomach knotted. On my desk sat a gift basket filled with pastries and cookies, all individually wrapped in cellophane. All labeled with commercial-looking stickers. The pink-and-orange branding didn't look familiar, and the logo with the two brooms wasn't anything I had seen before. I approached carefully, almost afraid something would jump out of the basket and attack me. Undeniably afraid that someone had somehow broken in to the back of my store and—

"Brylie?" Aunt Gwendolyn appeared beside me, concern in her voice. "What are those?"

"Treats." I gingerly picked one wrapped cookie from the basket, turning it over. A food label had been stuck to the back, listing ingredients and nutrition info. There was even a certified gluten-free stamp on the bottom.

"Where did they come from?"

"I have absolutely no idea." I flipped the cookie back over, showing her the front. "Two Witches Bakery. Ever heard of them?"

"Never." Aunt Gwendolyn took the cookie, examining it the same way I just had. "That's Ander's address."

I snatched the cookie from her. "What?"

But she didn't need to answer. Right there in the small print near the bottom sat the company information. "How... Ander didn't mention starting a business."

"How do we know that he did?"

"It's his address."

"Well, it's not like someone trying to kill you would use their own." She tugged her phone from her bag, tapping the screen before holding it out. A ringing sounded from the speaker, and then Ander's voice came through.

"Everything okay, Miss Gwen?"

"Perhaps. Ander, dear—did you by chance start a bakery and drop off products in Brylie's office?"

Silence. Lots of silence. When he finally spoke, he sounded far angrier than confused. "No, ma'am. I most certainly did not. Is she okay?"

"I'm fine," I said, directing my voice toward the device. "Just a little freaked out that there's a basket of baked goods in my office with a company name that hits a bit close to home. Oh, and your address is on the back."

Ander cursed under his breath. "Let me cancel this—"

"No," Aunt Gwendolyn and I said at once. I glanced at her, pinching my face a bit so she would hopefully understand that I wanted to be the one to keep speaking. "I'm fine. We're both fine over here. You need to deal with the insurance people."

"Are you sure?"

"Yes. Of course. If anything else happens, we'll pack up and go home."

He sighed, his voice tight as he replied, "Fine. But keep me updated until I can get there."

"Understood. Good luck." With that, I ended the call, and Aunt Gwendolyn placed her phone back in her bag. "So, it's not Ander's company—"

"But it has his address on the back."

"And the name is surely a nod to us."

She nodded. "Most certainly. So how did they get in here?"

I groaned. "It could have been anyone. Half the town stopped by today, mostly to gossip about the fire at Ander's house."

"Nosy neighbors," she said with a tsk. "Anyone here long enough for them to... What? Break in to the back door?"

My stomach dropped, and I immediately exploded into

motion. I ran all the way to the man door at the back, checking the lock and the latch.

"It's fine," I said, pushing the door open to make sure the lock had engaged. "It's locked and secured just fine."

"So no one broke in. Were you so busy someone could have walked in with the basket?"

"No way." I pulled the door closed, making sure it latched and the lock engaged. "I wasn't so busy as to not notice someone carrying something like that. In fact, I never left the checkout—no one needed help in the aisles, so anyone coming in would have had to walk past me."

"So then, how did they—"

I groaned, Absolutely frustrated and feeling so very stupid. "There had to have been two of them."

Aunt Gwendolyn frowned and cocked her head. "What? Why do you say that?"

"Two of them." I waved at the door. "One came inside, while the other walked around to the alley with the basket. The one in the store snuck inside the back room and opened the door from here."

"That's a lot of effort."

"As is baking a bunch of different treats, designing a front and back label to make them look legit, and individually wrapping them."

"Very true." She sighed, looking up toward the ceiling. "Who would go to such trouble?"

I led the way back to the back room, my mind already spinning. "Joan and Corbin."

"Were they in the store this morning?"

I blanched. "No."

"Then I doubt it. We haven't seen them together in weeks, and we don't really know why they spend time together."

"To try to kill me?"

"I doubt that, too."

"Fine." I sat and grabbed my teacup, staring into it for a moment. "Thomas and Heather."

"They make the most sense."

"But they almost seem too obvious, you know? Baked goods... Anyone wanting to frame Heather would choose baked goods to do it."

"Very true. And Thomas has been a trusted friend for years. What could he possibly gain by being involved in such a thing?"

"I have no idea." I sat back, still holding my cup of tea, staring at the woman who had brought so much to my life. Suddenly terrified. "What if the cookies aren't meant for me?"

"What do you mean?"

"Two witches. Two. Me and you."

"But I don't have any sort of food allergies."

"Maybe there's something more than just tiger nut flour in those cookies."

Aunt Gwendolyn appeared horrified. "But I haven't been sick."

"Well, that's true." I sighed, frustration making my head hurt. "So maybe it is focused on me."

"And whoever it is seems to know you have a food allergy and is exploiting that."

"True. So, who knows?"

"Dr. Don."

I scrunched my face. "He's kind of a jerk and Mary has issues with him as Louise's father, but he's sort of a nonentity, you know? I just can't see him doing...anything this devious."

"Very true. He's a bit of a lumpy but not really scary." She sighed, stirring her tea—counterclockwise, banishing something—and then nodded. "The sheriff."

I whipped my head in her direction. "He knows?"

"I did mention it during a chat one time."

"You chat with him?"

The shrug she gave had her braid sliding over her shoulder. "It was more of a hex, but there were words exchanged."

I blinked. And blinked again. "You hexed the sheriff."

"He did deserve it, dear. He's been very difficult for Ander to deal with."

I had no argument for that. "True. But he doesn't seem like a baker, and he was one of the few who didn't come to the store today. He could have been the one coming in through the back, but who is he friends enough with to do such a thing?"

"No one. Horrible social skills, that one." Aunt Gwendolyn huffed, rising to her feet to begin aggressively cleaning up the mess from our little tea break. "Two witches, food that could kill you, and attacking Ander's business and home. How are all of these things connected?"

"I have no idea. Who would want to attack Ander?"

"Anyone who wanted to open a restaurant?"

"Is there anyone?"

"Not that I know of." She glanced my way, seeming almost sheepish. "It could be someone who wants to date you."

I coughed a laugh. "What?"

"You're a strong, independent woman," she said, shrugging once again as if that should have been well-known information. "Weakening you makes you easier to catch."

"You're talking about me like I'm some sort of prey."

"And getting Ander out of the picture means you'd be all alone."

I froze, pieces falling into place. "And if I thought Ander was the one making me sick..."

"Two Witches Bakery."

"His address on the back." I shook my head, still not quite seeing it. "It's too easy."

"It's basic. Blatantly obvious and easy to prove those wouldn't be from Ander. Who would think you'd fall for that?"

The words rattled in my head, bringing pictures with them. Memories and feelings and doubt. Thoughts that didn't fit and yet somehow did. A picture forming where none should have been.

"We need to talk to the sheriff," I said, moving toward the front door while my head spun with possibilities. "And do you know any of the firefighters who were at Ander's yesterday?"

Ten minutes and a quick walk down Main Street to the only mechanic shop in town, Aunt Gwendolyn and I stood before a big, bearded, barrel-chested man of about my age who apparently went by the name Josh.

"I wanted to thank you for all you and the firefighters did to try to save Ander's house," Aunt Gwendolyn said, pushing the basket of Two Witches treats into his dirty hands. Never let it be said the woman wasn't up for an opportunistic bribe when called upon.

"Thank you, Miss Gwen." Josh took the basket and nodded, looking slightly uncomfortable. "It's just part of my job."

"I thought the firefighters were all volunteer," I said, unsure if the word job had been intentional or not.

Aunt Gwendolyn's smile grew. "All but Josh here. He manages the team and handles their training, so he gets paid through the city. His mom, Viola, handled the job for decades before she retired, though she still shows up at the fires and helps out. Isn't that right, Josh?"

"Yes, ma'am. Mom was at Ander's, in fact. Kept me from dealing with the new bodies so I could take the more experienced team into the back to battle." He nodded my way. "I've been meaning to pop into your store and introduce myself, but things have been real busy over here. It's nice to meet you."

"Nice to meet you as well. Guess I know where to bring my van if it needs service."

"You drive the minivan, right?"

"Right."

"You need an alignment. Your rear end is looking off-kilter." He nodded toward the rack, where a brown truck rested suspended in the air. "Bring it by next week, and I'll take care of it for you. Wouldn't want you driving through your first snow with that sort of issue."

I blinked. I hadn't even really thought about snow in terms of driving. I'd never lived in a place that got cold enough for snow, so I only had a generic sort of "need special shovels, gloves, and salt" hardware store knowledge. Driving? Oh no.

"Josh," Aunt Gwendolyn said, regaining his attention. "That fire yesterday terrified this old woman. It destroyed Ander's house so fast."

I frowned, having never heard the tone she was using or the breathiness of her voice. It seemed like... Was she flirting? Josh couldn't have been much older than I was. The idea of her flirting with him—a man young enough to be her grandchild—seemed odd. Especially with the whole man part.

Josh didn't appear to be picking up on her tactic, though. "Actually, ma'am, it was a slow mover. That fire likely burned for hours before it grew enough to be noticed from the outside."

"Hang on," I said, suddenly way more interested in him than Aunt Gwendolyn's performance. "What do you mean? Like, it had been set and then just...waited?"

Josh nodded. "You ever seen the movie *Backdraft*?"

"Yeah."

"Like that, but much less Hollywood. The fire burned through the house for a long time, but it didn't get hot enough or have enough oxygen to really blow up. It sort of smoldered and waited for its chance. One big gust of oxygen and *bam*... kitchen inferno."

I remembered the movie—the need for oxygen and the almost poetic way the actors described the way the fire held its breath and waited for an opportunity. But in the movie, the opportunity had been doors opening. No one had opened Ander's door. He'd been with me, so...

"What would have been the big gust of oxygen?" I asked, frowning. Overthinking.

"Don't know for sure, but it started in that kitchen." Josh moved across the work floor, waving to a customer who had just pulled up behind the overhead doors. "My guess is Ander's furnace kicked in. The day wasn't cold, but the temperature had dropped a bit as night fell. Once that furnace started blowing air through the house, it was game over. But that's just a guess."

His furnace. He had turned his heat on—he'd mentioned that. I hadn't even thought about the possibility of forced air heat and how it could have affected the fire. Such a simple thing, usually so safe and stable. Until it wasn't.

"I need to get back to work," Josh said, red rag in hand and two guys behind him guiding the car into the bay. "You bring that van in next week, Brylie. I'll get you ready for winter in Reverie Springs."

Ugh. Winter. I tried to smile, but I had a feeling the expression lacked any sort of oomph. "Thanks. I appreciate it."

We said a quick goodbye and got out of his way so he could work, heading back toward the store at a slower clip than usual. My brain kept spinning, my thoughts chaotic and swirly. Too many faces to pinpoint one, too many opportunities to set a fire no one would be able to stop.

"What do you think?" Aunt Gwendolyn finally asked, keeping her eyes on the path ahead and giving nothing away. But I would have bet money her thoughts had gone down the same path mine had. That she had just as many suspects dancing around in her mind. Ones we needed to start eliminating.

"I think we need to know more about where people were yesterday."

Chapter Twenty-Three

If there was one thing a small town was good for, it was gossip. It only took one conversation at the grocery store to find out that Heather and Thomas hung out at a bar just outside of town every Saturday night for line dancing. Bars and line dancing weren't my sort of thing, but nothing could have stopped me from heading over there. I even wrangled Mary into going with me—leaving Little Miss Louise at the manor with Aunt Gwendolyn and Elmer, of course—for moral support.

"No Ander tonight?" Mary asked as we walked across the parking lot toward the door.

I checked my phone one last time before pocketing it. "He's been dealing with insurance agents all day and then had to talk to the fire inspector."

"On a Saturday?"

I shrugged. "Guess so."

"Too bad. A male presence would have been nice."

We walked in, both of us coming to a stop just inside the entrance. The bar had a huge wooden dance floor with what looked like horse stalls around three sides that held booths to sit in. A long, wooden bar took up the entire left side of the non-dance floor space, with tables and chairs filling the right.

"Are those..." I started to ask but couldn't finish. The words wouldn't come to me.

Thankfully, Mary found them. "Saddles. And spurs. On select barstools. Yes, they are."

"Well...giddy up, then." I gave her a stiff smile before leading the way across the floor to an open spot at the bar. "Did you used to hang out here? Like, before Louise?"

Mary hopped onto a barstool—one without a saddle for a seat—next to me and shrugged. "Not really. I've been a few times, but bars weren't really my thing. And Don would have never come to a place like this."

"How is the good doctor?"

"Irritating." She signaled to the bartender, who nodded in a sign of "be right there." "He's the one who came knocking on my door in the middle of the night. He's done it twice since."

"Why?"

"Claims he misses me." She didn't look my way, instead focusing on the bartender, who strolled over with an inquisitive look. "Can I get a gin buck? And she'll have..."

"Whiskey sour, please."

"Be right up." The bartender moved to make the drinks, taking less than a minute before she set the two glasses before us. "Want to start a tab?"

I nodded and handed over my credit card, turning on my stool to watch the line dancers while taking a sip of my drink. I waited for Mary to do the same before circling back around.

"So...he misses you."

"I knew you wouldn't let that one go." Mary smiled and shook her head. "He doesn't. He's just going through some things and is feeling nostalgic. And drinking. He's obviously drinking."

"Have you called the sheriff?" I frowned as Mary's neck seemed to darken. "What?"

"Um, no," she said with a shake of her head. "That hasn't been necessary."

A man showing up to her house in the middle of the night without warning seemed like something to report to law enforcement, so I had to be missing something. "Why not?"

"My neighbor heard the commotion and came over to check on me." She took a sip, keeping her eyes decidedly on the dance floor. "Don hasn't been back since."

Huh. That sounded...far more vague than necessary. "Who's your neighbor?"

"Josh."

My brain did a stutter-step. "Josh... Mechanic Josh? Firefighter Josh? Son of Viola Josh?"

That red moved all the way up her neck and to her cheeks. "Yeah."

"Oh," I said, biting back a smile as the picture finally painted itself into view. "And how is neighbor Josh?"

She coughed, her face nearly bright red. "Fine. Good. Fine. Yeah. He's... Well, he may come up here a little later."

"Mary, Mary, Mary." I shook my head, biting back my grin. "Are you about to go on a date with me as a third wheel?"

She huffed a laugh and ducked her head, smiling my way. "It's not a *date* date. Though, in my defense, I assumed Ander would be coming with you."

"Interesting." I sat back, so very happy for my friend. "He'd better be a gentleman, or Aunt Gwendolyn will hex him."

"He's fully aware of that fact." She nodded, eyes back on the dance floor. "Incoming."

I looked up in time to see Deputy Carmichael sauntering over. An overly dramatic term but there was no other word to describe his walk as he beelined for me. He kept his eyes locked on mine—no sunglasses tonight—as he walked slowly and with purpose. When he finally reached us, he nodded to the waitress, called out a beer brand, and settled into a sort of lean over me.

I had never been more uncomfortable, but I had a job to do. For Ander.

"Hey, Deputy Carmichael," I said, pasting on a smile I hoped shone brighter than it felt. "Fancy meeting you here tonight."

"Call me Greg."

I took a sip of my drink and nodded, his name something I hadn't even thought about. One that simply didn't fit him in my brain. "Greg, then."

Nope. That wouldn't be working for me.

His smile widened, and he leaned a little closer under the guise of reaching for the beer he'd ordered. "I haven't seen you out before. Grown tired of what you have at home?"

I sort of frowned and looked at my drink as thoughts of Ander blew through my mind, assuming that had been his target. But by the way Mary stiffened and the huff she let out, I had a feeling I wasn't mistaken.

"Nothing at home to grow tired of."

Deputy Carmichael moved even closer, his hand finding my shoulder. "Ah, so we're playing that game."

I glanced at Mary, absolutely lost as to the subject of the conversation. She didn't appear to be, though.

"Crazy fire yesterday," Mary said, leaning over me and forcing the deputy to ease back and remove his hand from my shoulder.

"It was a good one. Brought out the county fire department, though." He took a drink of his beer and shook his head. "No one wants that."

"Why not?" I asked.

"They override what we already know. They're going to finish that investigation and find anyone but Ander Mendoza a suspect for the arson." He took another gulp of his beer, pulling his lips back over his teeth afterward and looking out toward the dance floor. "Doesn't matter what the county investigator says—I know he did it."

I wanted to stand up and rant at the man, but at that moment, Josh the mechanic appeared. He placed his hand on the bar behind Mary, settling in nice and close to her. "Brylie. Greg." He glanced down, his stern expression falling into something warmer and softer. "Evening, Mary."

"Hi, Josh." Her neck reddened again, her cheeks already beginning to darken. Oh, she liked him. A lot. And by the way he looked at her, those feelings were reciprocated. How fun.

"Good to see you, Josh," Deputy Carmichael said, reaching over to shake the man's hand. "You're right on time. I was just about to take these women to the dance floor."

Josh glanced down at Mary, raising his eyebrows in a sort of *Want to?* silent question. Mary finished her drink and slid off the barstool, stepping between my knees so she could block out Greg while leaning in close to speak into my ear.

"You have to get the info on where he was and what he knows. Nothing else matters."

With that, she gave me a smile then disappeared into the crowd of people doing some sort of spinny line dance but with partners. I set my drink down, hands sweating since Ander's feelings seemed like they should matter a whole heck of a lot and gave Deputy Carmichael a smile.

"I don't know how to dance like that."

He grabbed my hand and tugged, yanking me off my stool. "I'll teach you."

And with that, he dragged me onto the floor and started teaching me a dance that I found fun and easy to learn. Within a few minutes, Deputy Carmichael had me stepping and spinning and twisting under his arm to some old George Strait song my dad had loved. But when the song turned slow and Deputy Carmichael moved in as if to grab me around the waist, I pushed away.

"Sorry—it's hot. Let's go grab a drink instead."

He nodded stiffly, following me back to my spot at the bar. Mary had remained on the dance floor, slow dancing with mechanic Josh and looking awfully small with his big arms wrapped around her. Small but comfortable. My happiness for her knew no bounds.

"I'll take a diet," I said to the bartender once I had settled onto my seat.

Deputy Carmichael scoffed. "You're not wimping out on me now, little witch. Gimme another beer, and bring us two shots of tequila."

"What? Oh no." I looked at the bartender and shook my head. "I'm not in for that. No tequila for me."

"Can't handle it?" he asked.

"No, I just don't want to drink that much tonight."

"Too bad." He nodded to the bartender and raised his voice to yell, "Two shots!"

The bartender stiffened for a second before shooting me a small nod, then she set about grabbing drinks for people and pouring shots. She finally brought over two small glasses filled with a clear liquid, both with a wedge of lime on the side.

"Here you go, hun." She gave me a wink and walked

away. My hand itched, but I ignored it as my stomach twisted. Deputy Carmichael lifted his shot glass in the air, waiting for me. The pressure of the moment consumed me, had me reaching for the little glass filled with liquid with a shaky hand. But when I brought it close to my nose, all I smelled was lime. I settled into my seat a little better, clinked glasses with the deputy—who made some sort of toast I didn't pay attention to—and tipped the liquid into my mouth. Water. All I tasted was lime-flavored water. The bartender had just pulled a fast one in my favor. I owed her a big tip.

"So," he said before he bit into his lime. He chucked the rind into the shot glass and pushed it back across the bar. "Why are you really here?"

I shrugged, playing with the swizzle stick in my diet soda. "The fire yesterday worried me. I wanted to talk to people about it."

"Finally figuring out your boyfriend's a criminal?"

"Why do you say that?"

Deputy Carmichael began listing things off on his fingertips. "He defaced his own dumpster to force the garbage company to provide a new one. He broke his own business's window to force the insurance company to pay out a ridiculous sum for a simple window. He then burned his own house down, I assume because he figured out how much money was in insurance fraud and wanted an easy check. Criminal."

But the itch from earlier with the bartender had returned, which meant he likely knew something he had just said wasn't true. Thankfully, I knew a couple weren't. And I wasn't afraid to call them out.

"You seem to be pretty set on that," I said. "There're just a few problems with your theories."

He leaned back against the bar, not looking at all concerned. "Hit me."

How I wished I could. "We didn't get a new dumpster after the bee incident—Mike came and pressure washed it after Old Ben came to take the bees. And the night the chair went through Ander's window, my store was also vandalized."

He shrugged. "Maybe he saw his opportunity with the vandalism and took advantage of the situation."

"And the fire? Ander was with me all of Friday afternoon. He wasn't home to start it."

"The fire simmered in the hallway for a long time before it broke out. He could have started it before he came to your house."

The slight itch exploded, making my entire arm burn. Oh, that had to be it. He knew more about the fire than he was letting on and was lying about it instead.

"It simmered? I hadn't heard that." I scratched at my wrist, my own lying making my so-called gift flare. "Though I didn't even know it started in the hallway. Josh said the kitchen."

"Yeah, the kitchen." Deputy Carmichael frowned. "What did I say?"

"The hallway."

He chuckled. "I must be tired—I meant the kitchen. Though it really could have started anywhere."

Itchiness. So much itchiness. "True. The inspector was coming out today so I assume we'll know more after he's done, but Ander hasn't called yet."

Not a lie...that I knew of. I had tucked my phone away, so he could have called already. Though the itching continued. Too many lies for me to avoid the particular nuisance.

The deputy sort of snorted. "If you were my girl, you wouldn't be out at a place like this without me by your side."

I stiffened. Couldn't help myself. My father hadn't raised me to need to be protected. "I'm a grown woman—I can take of myself, and Ander knows that."

"You're bait." He leaned closer, invading my space and making me really uncomfortable. "Every man here watched you walk in. If you gave any of them an ounce of attention, they'd try." He rose to his full height once more. "Ander's a fool."

"Ander's no fool, and they can try all they want. I'm just here to have fun with my friend."

At that moment, Heather and Thomas walked in. They both noticed me and smiled my way, though they seemed tight, their accompanying expressions almost confused. At that moment, I realized just how close Deputy Carmichael had been standing to me. I took a step away from him, nearly bumping into Thomas as he approached.

"Oh, hi," I said, giving both him and Heather, who stood by his side, a smile. "Nice to see you two out."

"Yeah, it's sort of our thing. Line dancing Saturdays." She did a little dance move that looked a lot like a shuffling of her feet. "No Ander tonight?"

"He's still dealing with the fire."

Deputy Carmichael leaned in at that point, nearly hovering over my shoulder and getting way too close again. "Thomas. Heather. Good to see you both."

"Greg." Heather looked from him to me and back again. "I didn't expect to see you two together."

I rolled my eyes and shoved Deputy Carmichael back. "We're not. He's just being clingy."

"You came without Ander," he said. "I'm shooting my shot."

"You have no shot."

"How is Ander?" Heather asked, reaching to touch my elbow. "I can't believe that fire."

"He's okay. Dealing with insurance."

"Defrauding insurance," Deputy Carmichael mumbled before taking a swig of his beer. He sputtered a "What?" when he saw my glare.

"You know what." I shook my head and turned back to Heather and Thomas. "That fire was crazy, though. I can't believe how fast it burned through the house."

Thomas nodded. "Kitchen fires can be rough, but that one was a doozy. There was almost no stopping it."

"A chef with a kitchen fire," Heather said, shaking her head. "That almost defies logic."

"Yeah, well, let's put away this talk of the fire and go burn up the dance floor," Thomas said, grabbing her around the waist. "I need some time with my lady."

The two wandered off, Heather giving me one last wave before disappearing into the crowd of people dancing. Deputy Carmichael leaned over my shoulder once more, whispering into my ear.

"Want to dance?"

I shook my head. "I think I'm going to head to the restroom. I'll be right back."

Without a second glance, I did just that, slinking through the crowd to the back corner, where a dark hallway led to my destination. Once finished, I started the return trip, nearly tripping over my own feet when I saw the man sitting where Mary had been. Ander had arrived, and he looked ridiculously unhappy to be taking up space alongside Deputy Carmichael. At least until he saw me approaching, then those dark eyes locked on me, and a small smile tugged his beard upward. He winked, and I grinned, increasing my pace.

"Hey," he said once I reached him. "You look pretty tonight."

I settled into his embrace, breathing him in. "I'm so glad you're here."

"Wouldn't have missed it." He ran a hand down my back. "You want to dance?"

"You line dance?"

"Not in the least, but I'd try for you."

I shook my head. "It's okay—I'm not a big line dancer. How'd the meeting with the fire inspector go?"

"It went. Let's talk about that later. It's been a long and frustrating day."

"Sure. Of course." I ran my hand down his neck, rubbing his shoulder a bit. "What can I do?"

"Dance with me." He nodded toward the floor. "They're about to change the song up."

At that moment, the music shifted into a slower song, couples moving from dancing side by side to in each other's arms. I grinned and grabbed Ander's hand, tugging him onto the dance floor. Not that I had to tug hard—the man seemed eager to follow me. Once we found some space, he spun me into his arms and pressed his body against mine.

"We should have done this before," I said as we swayed to the music. "I didn't know you can dance."

"I can't. Not really. But the seventh-grade sway is a tool in my arsenal."

"You're very good at it."

"Why, thank you." He danced us in a circle before slowing us down once more. "Everything been okay here tonight?"

"You mean besides Deputy Carmichael calling me bait and implying you set your house on fire?" I rolled my eyes. "Fine. It's been fine. Not a productive night in terms of figuring out who's been vandalizing things or who might have set your house on fire, but I'm glad to see Mary out having fun."

"Her and Josh, huh?"

"Looks like it."

"Good. He's a lot better for her than the doctor ever was."

"You knew her when they were a couple?"

"Yeah, and I never liked the guy. She's a good woman with a huge heart. She deserves someone to spoil her."

"Like you spoil me?"

He looked down at me, his face growing serious. "Exactly,"

A simple answer—no explanation necessary.

We danced a few slow songs, chatted with Mary and Josh, and thankfully avoided Deputy Carmichael for the rest of the night. And when it was over, when we had danced our fill and had decided to leave, Ander wrapped an arm around my shoulder as we walked past Deputy Carmichael.

"Have a great night, Brylie!" the deputy yelled out, raising a glass in my direction. Purposefully staring at Ander as he followed up with, "Thanks for all the dancing."

Ander chuckled and kissed the back of my hand. "Guess I'm the best fisherman of the bunch."

Deputy Carmichael frowned. "Pardon?"

"I'm the one leaving with the bait." He shrugged even as I smacked his shoulder. "Keep trolling, son. You'll catch something eventually."

And with that, we walked out with Josh and Mary behind us.

Chapter Twenty-Four

I spent my Monday morning pacing through the manor with just Elmer to keep me company. He did not pace. He spent the morning sunning himself on the kitchen floor, though I didn't blame him. I would have liked a little extra nap time myself, but my brain wouldn't let me stop thinking about the previous night at the bar.

"What am I missing?" I asked to the empty house, not expecting an answer. I didn't receive one either. Sometimes the manor helped, and sometimes she ignored me. "Thanks, home. Guess I have to figure this one out on my own."

As if on some sort of cue, the doorbell rang. I hurried down the hall to the front door, swinging it wide once I reached it. Thomas stood on the porch with a big basket of what looked like muffins.

Oh no.

"Good morning, Thomas. What's all this about?"

He shrugged. "The blueberry crop has been better than expected this year, so Heather's been making muffins out of them. I figured I would bring some over for you."

"Oh, that's really sweet of you." I took the basket, holding it gingerly as Elmer took the time to give the man a solid sniff. "I was about to make a cup of coffee. Would you like to join me for some?"

"Thank you. That's mighty kind." He stepped inside, wiping his boots on the mat and leaning down to give Elmer a pat on the head before following me through the hall. "Heather said to tell you there is absolutely no allergen to worry about in there. She mentioned that was important."

I laughed and set the basket on the counter. "She didn't tell you what the allergen was?"

"Oh no. She wouldn't. Something about hippos, but also, she doesn't like spreading info about people. Since she works for the doctor and doesn't want people worried about her gossiping about their health stuff."

"That...actually makes a lot of sense." I moved around to the coffeepot and reached for the can of grounds. "Don't tell Aunt Gwendolyn about the coffee. She's been having me drink a lot of tea lately."

"That's not something I've ever gotten used to, I'm afraid."

"I'm growing accustomed to it and do enjoy a cup at night, but sometimes, I just want some coffee." I set up the brewer to do its thing and turned around, smiling. "How goes the fall harvest?"

"It's good. It's really good. Another year or two like this one, and I'll be set up proper for Heather." He ducked his head, suddenly looking almost shy. "Crop farmers don't always have the most stable incomes."

"Maybe not, but Heather doesn't seem like the type to sit back and complain about money. She's a go-getter."

"She is. This bakery business of hers has her working so many hours, but she's determined to make it a success. That's one of the reasons she was so adamant about telling you there were no allergens—she wanted you to be willing to try her stuff without worry."

I nodded, noting that nothing itched. Not even a little bit. The man wasn't lying to me. And to be honest, I hadn't expected him to. For whatever reason, I had a feeling he and Heather weren't as much involved in all the shenanigans as I had once thought. "Well, I appreciate that. I've been struggling a bit lately with finding things that don't make me sick."

"That's really unfortunate." He took two muffins out of the basket, setting each on a napkin. "Here's to finding safer treats for you."

I poured two cups of coffee once the brew finished and handed one to Thomas, picking up the blueberry muffin once done. I tore off a small piece and popped it into my mouth, hoping I was right about Thomas's sincerity. If not, my day off would be a rough one.

"That's delicious," I said once I had finished my bite of muffin and took a sip of my coffee. "Heather really does have a talent."

Thomas nodded. "She does. She's even teaching some baking classes now."

"Oh, right—I remember her mentioning that. Baking class sounds like fun."

"It sure seems to be. She's only teaching a few of the ladies from the women's auxiliary right now, but she's hoping to build education into another arm of her business." He raised his mug and took a sip of his coffee, almost grunting as he pulled it away from his lips. "Oh, and Deputy Carmichael, of course."

"Deputy Carmichael what?"

"He's another student of hers. I tend to forget because he

hasn't been by in a couple of weeks, but he spent a lot of time in her commercial kitchen learning from her."

Because he believed in continued learning. The memory of that particular conversation didn't override my confusion, though. "Deputy Carmichael bakes?"

"He does—said it was a stress reliever of sorts." He took another sip of his coffee. "I'd figured I'd have seen Ander or Miss Gwen by now."

"Aunt Gwendolyn is at breakfast with a friend, and Ander is over at his house, digging through the rubble to see if he can save anything."

Thomas shook his head. "I doubt there will be much. That was one rough fire. Funny how it started in a hallway, of all places."

I froze, staring at him. Noticing the veins in his hands and the deep tan of his skin for the first time. The strength he exuded without trying. Obsessing over his hands as my brain spun. "I thought it started in the kitchen."

"So did the rest of us. Turns out, it started in the hallway. Some sort of weird, drafting thing that smoldered until it got air."

Fragments of memories from conversations with Josh and Ander, with the deputy, spun through my mind. "How did you know that?"

"The inspector came by Ander's house Saturday. He's a good man—honest as all get-out and used to work arson cases in New York. That man has seen it all. He recognized some marker that indicated movement and...something else. I can't really remember, but he called Josh yesterday about it. I happened to be at the firehouse when the call came in. Josh was pretty surprised by the news because it's such a rare thing to see."

"How does a fire like that just start in someone's house?"

"It doesn't. That fire was arson."

My stomach clenched, and the room grew hot. For a moment, I thought perhaps there had been tiger nut flour in the muffins after all, but then I realized even Thomas seemed to be sweating a little.

"It sure is getting hot," he said, setting down his coffee cup. "I should probably get out in that field before the midday sun sends me hiding in the house. Thanks so much for the coffee, Miss Brylie."

"Any time," I said as my thoughts swirled and spun. A starting point in the hallway. Deputy Carmichael had known that, had mentioned it Saturday night. And yet the determination from the inspector had come during that Sunday phone call to Josh. *After* anyone would have known about the change in origination point.

How did that happen?

Elmer and I walked Thomas to the front door, but when I opened it, the porch wasn't empty.

"Deputy Carmichael," Thomas said, looking almost confused. "What brings you out this way?"

Mirrored sunglasses hid his expression, but an energy I didn't like rolled off his body. "Just came to speak with Miss Scott."

A chill flew up my spine at the use of my surname—the man usually called me by my first one. "Is there some sort of problem?"

"Not at all." He smiled, revealing way too many teeth. "I just wanted to have a chat."

I glanced at Thomas, whose expression seemed to match my feelings of concern, before pasting on a weak smile.

"Of course. Come on in. It was good to see you, Thomas. Please tell Heather I said hello."

He nodded, watching as the deputy walked into the house before turning and heading down the stairs. Inside, the foyer had grown hotter than before, the air almost stifling. The house wasn't happy with the deputy being there.

"Sorry for the heat. I'm not really sure what's going on, but it just started warming up in here." I hushed Elmer when he growled, my stomach sinking even further. This was bad. Very, very bad. "So, what can I do for you today?"

He tugged off his sunglasses, his pale blue eyes meeting mine for the very first time and making me freeze in place. "Is Miss Gwen around?"

Red flag. Red flag. "She's out at the moment but should be back any minute now." I used my legs to push Elmer back down the foyer, trying my best to keep him behind me as he continued to growl and huff. "What exactly did you need to talk to me about?"

"I came to ask you out on a date."

The world stutter-stepped, and I would have to imagine my expression appeared less than flattered. "Pardon?"

"A date. You, me, dinner. Maybe a movie. I want to take you out on a date."

My answer came easily. "No."

"Excuse me?"

"I said no." I shrugged, watching as the bathroom door swung open all on its own just behind the man. Willow Manor seemed interested in the interaction happening. "Thank you, but no."

"Is this because of Ander?"

"Not really. I mean, I do prefer to spend my time with him. But this is about me and my decisions. I'm not interested in dating you, whether Ander's in the picture or not. So, no thank you."

He blew a breath out of his nose, beginning to pace the width of the foyer. His energy growing darker. More stormy and violent. More...malevolent. "You'd rather date a criminal than me."

Statement, not question. A creak sounded from behind me, likely coming from the family room. The house growing even hotter as I stood before the man. "I'd rather date someone who took my opinions into consideration and respected my choices. This isn't about one man versus another."

"Of course it is. He doesn't even have a place to live anymore, and you're still choosing him."

"He didn't make bad decisions that caused that—his house burned down."

The deputy lunged forward, his face twisted into an expression I could only call livid. Stopping a mere foot before me. "He made me burn it with his bad decisions."

Elmer howled, the long, low sound turning into a rough bark. As he finished, a door slammed from above me, a definite warning from the house. She needn't have worried; I was absolutely paying attention.

I was also on the move—slipping deeper into the house. "Excuse me?"

"That's it." He lunged and grabbed my arm, tugging me with him as he dragged me toward the kitchen. Chaos ensued as Elmer barked and howled, scrambling to keep up, and doors upstairs began to slam in earnest. "I thought you'd see me as a protector after everything. The graffiti, the fire, the baked goods that made you sick—all of it could have stopped if you would have just paid attention."

He threw open the pantry door, looking inside before

shoving me over the threshold. "Now, I need to make you see how much better things would be if you were with me. Sit in here for a minute."

He kicked Elmer inside with me—my poor baby yelping at the attack—and slammed the door behind us. I immediately leaned over, checking on Elmer before taking stock of my situation. The pantry wasn't large like a walk-in room, but I could turn around and move a bit. I had no weapons, though. No way to call for help either. My phone sat on the kitchen counter where I'd left it while talking to Thomas. We were on our own.

"Okay. Weapon. We need a weapon. A big one." I felt around the shelves, finding the roll of knives and magnetic strip Ander had purchased. The one I had refused to let him install because it wouldn't fit the aesthetic I wanted. The knives were good, but they would bring me too close to the deputy. I needed something longer so I could keep space between us.

"What do we do, Elmer? What do we do?"

He whined and jumped at me, knocking me into the lowest shelf. The wood rattled against the supports. The wood I had just set on top of the metal shelves.

The wood that could be removed.

I emptied a shelf, listening for footsteps and so grateful when I didn't hear any. Once I had the shelf empty, taking off the wood cover required far more wiggling and manipulating space than I would have liked, but I managed to get it free. Eventually.

"Weapon acquired." I thought about grabbing a knife for good measure, but I just knew I had more of a chance of stabbing myself than Deputy Carmichael. I would have to rely on the shelf. "Now we wait."

And wait, we did. For far too many minutes, Elmer and I

stood in the small, hot space, listening for sounds of someone coming closer. I tried the handle—I wasn't dumb enough to assume I was trapped without double-checking—but while the lever moved, the door wouldn't budge. He had us secured for sure.

Eventually, footsteps sounded through the door, growing louder. The time to fight back had arrived.

"When he opens the door, you run," I whispered to Elmer. "Don't you dare wait for me. Okay?"

I received no response, but Elmer stood staring at the door, awake and alert. No snoring coming from him for once. Attack dog mode—activated.

The footsteps stopped just on the other side of the door, and the silence around us grew. I waited—not moving, not even breathing—for my chance to strike back. The second the doorknob jiggled, I raised the wood shelf as high as I could over my shoulder, hoping to make it through the doorway so I could swing it before the deputy stopped me.

Within a second, the handle disengaged, the door popping open about an inch and allowing a bright stream of light inside. The world spun into motion, going from still and silent to fast and chaotic in a heartbeat. I took one last breath then charged forward, yelling as I shoved through the door and swung the wood shelf. Deputy Carmichael appeared absolutely stunned, which likely gave me the extra seconds I needed to swing the wood shelf his way. The flat surface hit the side of his head with a sickening sort of thud, and he stumbled backward. I hit him again for good measure then ran for the front door with Elmer on my heels.

I had almost reached the door when I slipped in a puddle that had not been on the floor when I'd walked Thomas in or out. It didn't slow me down too much, though it did capture my attention for about half a second, as did the fact that the bathroom door was fully closed. Latched. It definitely hadn't been before.

The footsteps coming from the kitchen and tearing down the hall behind me had me ignoring the thoughts of who and how and what, though. I ran instead, throwing open the front door and racing outside. I had just reached the porch stairs when the commotion coming from behind me increased, the deputy cussing as the sounds of someone hitting something hard reached my ears. I turned just in time to see him fall flat on his back, a victim of the water pooled on the floor, apparently.

"Thanks," I whispered, knowing my crazy house had most assuredly had a hand in that moment. But then I looked around and began to panic once more—I had nowhere to go. I didn't have my keys or my phone, the house had the threat inside it, and the only other place to run was into the woods, which seemed like a really bad idea. I'd seen enough horror movies to know a single woman in the woods with a man running behind her wouldn't end well.

I was just about to start running for the road and hope for the best when a guardian angel stepped out of the woods. A guardian angel farmer with a shotgun in his hands.

"Come on, Miss Brylie," Thomas called with a lift of his chin, keeping his eyes locked on the front door of the manor. "I've already called for help. You get on up in my truck and wait for the sheriff."

I turned to do exactly that, but Deputy Carmichael ran out at that point, slowing down when he noticed Thomas. Not stopping, of course. And his expression didn't scream "scared by a man with a gun." Instead, he seemed to almost...smirk.

"You don't want to get involved here, Thomas," he said, looking from me to Thomas and back again. Still not stopping.

Thomas never wavered. "I already am involved."

"Oh, I know you are. You gonna tell her how you and Heather have been slowly poisoning her?"

I took a step back, no longer sure if Thomas was there to help or not. Definitely not heading for his truck any longer.

Thomas just shook his head. "That was an accident. We didn't know our gluten-free flour blend had the bad stuff in it. Once Heather figured it out, we stopped using it." He glanced my way. "I swear, we had no idea. She just wanted you to try her baked goods so you could put a good word in with Ander. I swear."

No itches. Not a single bit of uncomfortable energy running along my skin. The man had not told a lie.

"I believe you," I said, still keeping my distance. "But how does he know that?"

Thomas's jaw ticked. Deputy Carmichael leaned against the porch wall, looking really smug.

"Go ahead, Thomas. Tell her how I know."

"Ain't nothing harmful, Miss Brylie. Heather wanted to get Ander's attention on her business, and she went about it in the wrong way, is all."

"Meaning..."

Deputy Carmichael pushed off the wall, walking slowly across the porch. "You know your farmer here raises bees, right? Or he did before his girlfriend threw his hives into Ander's dumpster."

"That was Heather?"

"Sure was." The deputy's smile grew. "And let me tell you, the little woman has a temper when she's been drinking. Just like her mom."

"You shut up," Thomas said, obviously agitated. "She's not like her mom. And she regretted that."

"Regretted what?"

The deputy took another step toward Thomas. "She threw that chair through the window like a quarterback. I really didn't think it would go through, and then *crash*." He raised his arms, making a sort of fireworks movement with his fingers. "I'd never seen someone look more surprised than that little drunk."

"Stop calling her a drunk!" Thomas yelled as he raised his shotgun a few inches. "She had a rough week, what with losing Ander's business." He glanced my way before refocusing on the deputy. "I swear, Miss Brylie—she's a good woman. She just wasn't raised to know how to deal with stress because... well, you know her momma."

I did. I knew Joan, and I understood how being the child of any sort of addict could affect your emotional growth. I also understood that Ander had been struggling because of her, and that wasn't okay with me.

"All you had to do was tell us. Any of you," I said, making sure to include the deputy. "Ander has been fighting with his insurance all this time, and any one of you could have come forward with that information."

"He told us she'd go to jail," Thomas said with a chin raise toward the deputy. "I couldn't let that happen. But your friend here isn't innocent—Heather may have thrown a chair, but he broke in to your store and stole from you. He vandalized your building."

"Shut up," Deputy Carmichael said, his voice coming out almost like a hiss. "That was to help cover up for your girlfriend."

"Nah. That was because your ego was hurt that you

couldn't get the girl. Ready to start talking about the fire yet, or are you still sticking to the whole 'must have been started by Ander' nonsense?"

I gasped and nearly jumped backward, shock sitting heavy on my mind. These people had messed with Ander's life—his home and his business. They had destroyed things precious to him, and for what? A few hundred dollars a week in baked goods sales and my attention? That didn't sit right with me.

"You burned Ander's house down?" I stepped forward, rage fueling me. Heat and wind growing around me as I stalked toward the man I saw as the biggest threat to Ander. "You destroyed everything he cared about and left him with nothing?"

The deputy shrugged, not showing a single sign of fear. "He's still got you, doesn't he?"

The sheriff turned into the driveway at that moment, no sirens or lights, but driving faster than usual. He jumped out before he even came to a complete stop, gun drawn.

On Deputy Carmichael.

"Put down your weapons, Greg."

The deputy looked my way, anger grating against my skin at his expression, before unbuckling his belt and letting it drop to the ground. Gun, Taser, handcuffs...all lying there for the world to see. All things he could have used against me had he gotten the chance.

I suddenly felt sick to my stomach,

"Come here, buddy," I said, creeping back toward the trees with Elmer. Not wanting him out of my sight. Thomas had set down his shotgun, standing with his hands up as the sheriff crept up to Deputy Carmichael to kick his tool belt away.

Before the sheriff could secure his deputy, the sound of an engine roaring caught my attention. I turned just in time to see

Ander's truck turning into the driveway, the chef passing the sheriff's car and driving straight at me. He jumped out of his truck the second it came to a stop and raced in my direction, grabbing me and pulling me back. Keeping his eyes on the drama unfolding before us.

"Are you okay?"

I nodded, leaning into his touch. "The deputy burned your house down. And Heather threw the chair through the window at the restaurant. And she was the one—"

"Brylie." Ander shook his head, staring down at me as if I had just spoken another language or something. "I...I don't care. Are *you* okay?"

Such a simple question, but the only answer that came to me felt much more complicated than I could explain. Was I *okay*? No, probably not. I'd just been shoved into a closet and chased through my house by a man who both carried and knew how to use a gun. I'd found out how many people had been involved in both making me sick and terrorizing us. I'd run for my life, assuming the person I'd ended up running toward was my savior, only to find out he'd had a hand in all the things that had been happening to and around me.

It would likely be a long time before I could call myself okay, and yet there wasn't anything I could say to explain that.

"I'm fine," I said, my wrist itching at the lie. "Or at least, I will be. Eventually."

"Thank the heavens." Ander tugged me closer, both of us watching as the sheriff took the deputy into custody. Securing his hands behind his back with what looked like plastic zip ties instead of metal handcuffs like I would have expected. Thomas held his place against his truck, still with his hands up. Looking to all the world like a man waiting his turn to get arrested.

The sheriff had to be livid, what with all the paperwork he was going to need to do.

As we watched, two more sheriff vehicles rolled down the driveway, one man and one woman—both in uniform—exiting the vehicles once they'd parked. Both obviously there to support the sheriff, which made me think of Ander and how he'd gotten home so quickly.

"How'd you know to come?" I asked, taking a step back as Elmer settled onto my feet and lay down. Danger over. Attack dog mode—deactivated.

"The county fire investigator mentioned something about the fire being arson, and I got a bad feeling. I tried calling you but got no answer, so I started heading this way. And when I saw the sheriff racing toward the manor, I knew. I just knew something wasn't right."

"The Laveau family intuition rubbing off on you?"

He chuckled, tightening his hold on me. "Perhaps it is."

"Staying in the manor will do that to you." I pulled out of his hold as the sheriff started heading our way, knowing things were likely about to get ugly. "Looks like he might genuinely be doing his job."

"Doubtful." Ander huffed, shifting position to stand more at my side. To step between me and the sheriff. "You ready for this?"

Maybe, maybe not. But there was no way to stop it. The deputy had done some pretty bad things, and he needed to pay the price for that.

"As ready as I'll ever be."

Chapter Twenty-Five

Fall in Reverie Springs finally blew in strong and cold as we rolled into October. The town celebrated every moment, though—from school football games to apple bobbing, pumpkin patches and hayrides to haunted houses—in preparation for Halloween. They even hosted a fall festival, where the empty buildings along Main Street were practically hidden behind tents and tables filled with artists selling pottery and paintings. Where children laughed and sat for face paintings or made silly sand-filled bottles. And where Ander sold street food right out in front of his fully operational restaurant with a gorgeous, UV-blocking window in place. He wouldn't be able to rebuild his home until spring, but his restaurant had been repaired and reopened shortly after Greg Carmichael had pled guilty to arson. Convenient timing if you asked me, but whatever. So long as things could get back to normal.

Or as normal as they could be, considering.

"Hey there," Ander said with a smile from behind his huge

portable flat top grill where some sort of meat on sticks sizzled and smelled amazing. "You having fun?"

I nodded, holding up the caramel apples I'd bought from Heather's booth. I still didn't trust her fully, but she'd apologized to Ander and told the sheriff what she'd done. It looked like neither she nor Thomas would be going to jail, but she'd have to pay a fine and do community service for the vandalism charges. That would have to be enough for Ander and me.

Oh, and he had no intention of ever doing business with her again.

"Heather made these," I said, smiling when he frowned. "Don't pout. I'm sure they're delicious."

"So long as they don't have—"

"Tiger nut flour. I know." I grinned—my silly, overprotective chef—and nodded toward the grill top. "What are you making tonight?"

"Shish kebabs. I've got beef, pork, chicken, and lamb. What's your preference?"

Aunt Gwendolyn appeared beside me, laughing and obviously finishing a chat with some local. "All over your hands. It'll help—I promise."

I rolled my eyes at her antics. "Are you selling salves again?"

She shrugged. "It's not my fault if Dr. Don can't figure out how to help people. Sometimes you just need a little magic." She gave me a wink before turning her attention to the man behind the grill. "Ander, darling—I'm starving. Which do you recommend for a frail old lady?"

"I recommend the lamb, so if you happen to spot a frail old lady, send her my way."

He wasn't wrong—Aunt Gwendolyn was anything but frail. In fact, as she stood beside me in her bright clothing without a drop of gray or black, she seemed stronger than ever. Happier, too.

"Maybe next year we should set up a booth," I said. "I can sell little kits for kids to build birdhouses, and you can sell some of your herbal remedies."

She nodded, her smile growing softer. More melancholy. "Rose and I did that a time or two—it was always fun for me."

"Not for her?"

"She put up with me."

Mary and Josh strolled up, the big man carrying Louise on his shoulders. The three of them looking like the perfect little family.

"Hey there," Mary said, giving Aunt Gwendolyn and me a quick hug hello. "We were thinking about heading over to the stage to watch the music performers. Care to join us?"

Aunt Gwendolyn nodded, taking the food Ander handed her with a smile. "I would love to. I've been looking forward to the shows since they announced the lineup."

I shook my head, not wanting to follow them into the crowded field where the stage had been erected. Still not quite *fine* enough to deal with being exposed to all those people.

"I think I'll stay here and help Ander."

Aunt Gwendolyn squeezed my arm, her smile knowing, her green eyes soft as they met mine. "Whatever you feel is right, dear. Come meet up with us if you end up feeling up to it."

I nodded, watching as the group wandered off. I moved around to the back of Ander's booth, seeking the feeling of protection he always brought with him. Needing to hide out for a bit. Elmer lay on a bed on the sidewalk, snoring away, while Ander practically danced behind the flat top. Needing more than just the view of my favorite chef, I moved in behind him and wrapped my arms around his waist, stealing a hug.

The man froze, one hand coming down to hold my arm in place. "You okay, beautiful?"

"More than okay."

He raised my hand to his mouth, placing a soft kiss on the back. "It's a full moon tonight. You and Miss Gwen getting up to some witchy stuff later?"

I grinned. "Absolutely."

"I'll make the tea. You two always put on a great show."

And that was how I knew he was just about perfect for me. No questions, no tension. Just acceptance. In fact, most of the town seemed to simply adjust to the fact that Aunt Gwendolyn and I were there—rocks in our bras and hexes brewing, salves made for those in need, and love spells available just in case.

I had a home, a family, friends, and a man who cared about me.

And a town that didn't mind when we got a little witchy.

Acknowledgments

A few years back in New York, during a convention for romance writers, I went to dinner with some friends who I had met a decade before through our shared love of Edwards & Bella. During dinner, I tossed out what I had thought was a casual comment, but the women looked at me and said "That needs to be the opening line in a book." Now it is. Thank you to my Twilight friends and family—may you each be blessed with the success you are all striving for.

Lisa knows I adore her, so this is a thanks to her familiar Mully, the handsomest kitty on the planet. May your human forever be worthy of your love and affection.

Thank you to Jacqueline Sweet, who jumped in to assist me in rebranded this series. Her talent is amazing.

Millie Thorne is the not-so-secret pen name of a USA Today bestselling romance author who wanted a little more magic and mystery in her work. She started writing the Brylie Scott Mystery Series after the image of a house crying popped into her head and refused to leave. If Rose Manor had any sort of manners, it would be paying rent after all these years. Millie lives in the Midwest with a family of miscreants and a dog that makes a wonderful doorstop.

For all the latest on Reverie Springs gossip and updates, subscribe to Millie's newsletter.

www.milliethorne.com/news

9 781954 702578